Sarah M. Brownson

At Anchor

A story of our Civil War

Sarah M. Brownson

At Anchor
A story of our Civil War

ISBN/EAN: 9783337409524

Printed in Europe, USA, Canada, Australia, Japan

Cover: Foto ©Andreas Hilbeck / pixelio.de

More available books at **www.hansebooks.com**

A STORY OF OUR CIVIL WAR.

BY

AN AMERICAN.

NEW YORK:
D. APPLETON AND COMPANY,
443 & 445 BROADWAY.
1865.

AT ANCHOR:

A STORY OF OUR CIVIL WAR.

CHAPTER I.

"KATE, you are nearest the door, do ask Bessie which of us is in luck now." So spoke Emma Lewis, as the door-bell ceased its second ringing.

"Wait until she is graciously pleased to inform us," replied my cousin Kate, who was at that moment engaged in tying her slipper, a performance she never hurried. She had a small foot, had Kate, but then she was under size herself.

"No need, Emma," added Mary Allen, laughing. "Of course Kate is the chosen one; who but Gilbert Stuart would have so little consideration for our lazy toilettes as to call before seven?"

"Nonsense!" Kate ejaculated, blushing as in duty bound; whereupon Emma gave me a wicked side-glance, for everybody, except poor silly Kate, knew very well whose eyes lightened Gilbert Stuart's way to my uncle Tom's dear old home.

Bessie, as foretold by the wise Mary, announced him.

"There, Kate! Now, Kate!" cried Emma, pretending to help, but in reality greatly retarding Kate's efforts to dress. "Bless me! not that eternal silk. Why you'll melt the man!"

"Kate has no objection, I suppose," said Mary, with more malice than one would expect from a girl with a "vocation," for Mary was to be a nun, she said.

"I do not see why you all tease me," Kate muttered, pretending to be vexed. "I am sure Mr. Stuart pays just as much attention to Georgie as to me: why don't you tease her?"

"Georgie!" exclaimed the girls, in arch chorus, "who ever heard of such a thing!"

"Do make them stop," pleaded Kate, turning to me; but I said nothing. I was counting, by the beatings of my heart, the few seconds necessary for me to give to them, as proof of indifference to the visitor below; and if Kate wanted to be such a fool as to fancy every gentleman who came to see "the ladies" was especially *her* adorer, let her think so; she would, perhaps, find out the difference some day.

"I believe, as I am dressed, I will go down," I said at last. "Kate will need considerable time yet to make herself satisfactorily bewitching; " and after leisurely lounging out of the room, I flew down the broad staircase, to meet him whose dear, dark eyes once looking into mine, had so flooded my soul with love and faith that I read, fearless in my own truth, in his ever after quiet gaze, in his calm words, in his low-toned voice, unfathomable depths of tenderness, turning silently to me, as the broad river runs noiselessly to the ocean.

Years have passed since then ; grief, anguish, blood, and death, stand between that day and this, and still I see myself, in the spring-time of my youth, before there had been a thorn or even a withered flower in my pathway, or a cloud in my sky—a blooming girl, whose rosy cheeks and clear, dark eyes might for a moment dim the purer beauty of clear cut feat-ures, and broad, full brow : a creature of light, grace, and happiness, flitting past the frowning pictures, dancing down the dark polished stairs, with white jewelled hands gleaming along the grim carvings! Did angels fold their wings and weep, as she glided swiftly through their ranks, down to the little world that was all the world to her—the world of Love ?

Gilbert awaited me just by the door, leaning, with the unconscious grace of a strong man, against my piano, raising his head slowly, as I came nearer, and letting the light come up, not hastily, to his dark, col-orless cheek, to greet me.

There was one song of which he never seemed to grow tired, a weird kind of thing, with a mystic burden of love triumphant only in death; a song little in accordance with his cool temperament, yet his favorite. I rarely waited for him to ask me to sing it, but gave it unasked; now, when after some conversation in the twilight, he requested it, some indefinable impulse made me answer:

"Not until I know wherein lies its charm."

"Beware! Curiosity lost Eve her paradise."

"Thus, too, may I. So be it," I returned, smiling, secure in my paradise, which could not banish me while he lived. "Tell me, have your two mysteries any connection? Has my song any connection with the mysterious miniature you guard so faithfully?"

For once I had seen him, in looking for a note, take from his pocket an oval velvet case, inside of which I had vainly asked to look. Making the remark, I looked fearlessly up to his quiet eyes, wondering why the smiles should grow deeper, losing themselves in sadness, as he continued to gaze upon me.

"*Must* it be so?" he murmured, more of himself than of me, it seemed. And then, without removing from mine his eyes, growing deeper and more tender still, taking one of my hands in his, he placed in the other the velvet case—open.

It contained a girl's portrait. A fair, young face, fairer, fainter colored, lighter lined than mine; a characterless face, with delicate features, and soft, emotionless blue eyes; my cousin Kate's face, with only a shade of resemblance, a misty, shadowy, flitting resemblance. My cousin Kate's face, but her face subdued, refined, poetized, idealized.

She must love him, or no painter could ever so have painted her.

"Who is it?" I asked.

"It is my *fiancée*," he answered.

Into my veins, even to the tips of the fingers resting in his, ran the hot iron that was to harden in my soul. I smiled, said "How you surprise me!" thought the face "lovely," and, by and by, went up stairs again.

"Why do you not go down?" I asked of Kate. "Mr. Stuart will not think this very kind treatment."

Emma looked at me in surprise. "I should not wonder if they were engaged," I said to her, as soon as Kate had rustled her heavy silk out of hearing. "Suppose you and Mary entertain uncle Tom in the library until I change my hair; it is so tight, it hurts me."

Afterward, rising from my knees to cool my head in the night air, before joining uncle Tom, I saw Gilbert standing in the garden with Kate, tearing the sweet June roses from my bushes, and, when tired of playing with them, tossing them, leaf by leaf, into the fountain.

It was "a way he had."

CHAPTER II.

My uncle Tom was an old bachelor, who had loved the ladies so well in his youth that he could never
decide on one to bless his age, to the exclusion of so
many others. Not but that my uncle was young yet,
and, thanks to his whiskers, which were astonishing,
and to his income, which was equally flourishing, he
was still in good demand.

He was a glorious fellow; his hand, his heart, his
house, and his purse were as open as the generous sunshine, and I, his nearest relative, a sisterless, brother-
less orphan, seemed to be the one point on which he
centred all the affections of his ever warm heart.

Love, from my earliest recollection, had been my
breath of life, but a long line of rock-moulded ances-
tors, fighting, generation after generation, with all
forms and shapes of care and wrong, had transmitted
to me, the last of their line, the strength of soul wrung
from the accumulated trials and triumphs of their
struggling lives.

Like them, I was formed of the rugged New England granite, though my uncle's delicate chiselling, and the graceful draping of steady happiness, made me seem as if moulded from less enduring, but more polished material. I do not know that uncle Tom ever suspected the real under the seeming. He caressed me like a baby, he dressed me, he fêted me, as if I had been born only to be borne through the world in a jewelled car, over a pathway of roses. He had but one object in life, as far as I was concerned, and that was that I might equal my "glorious moth-er."

My "glorious mother," who, as Mrs. Glynn had so imprudently told me, died in the dark and cold, on the open field, not half a mile from her husband's door!

Our house in summer had always some visitors; on the summer of which I have spoken it was full to its utmost limits, our party having been augmented on the day before the opening of my story, by the arrival of my only fashionable relative, my aunt Graham, her daughter Florence, lady's maid, and countless trunks; my cousin Hal, "Lady Louise," his fast mare, his sad-dle, buggy, gun, and fishing-tackle; and my uncle Graham, who, however, had only taken a run down to see his wife and train safely landed at her brother's.

My aunt Graham was the only woman whom I was forced to regard as so immensely my superior that during her visits I always looked upon myself as the

1*

plainest, dowdiest, stupidest mortal in existence. She denounced my grandest dresses as "frights," and my way of wearing my hair she regarded as "too shocking for any thing."

Her whole soul was bent on marrying off Florence, who was now in her eighteenth year, and, despite her really good face and slender figure, was *un*engaged. My duties as a well-behaved relative and polite hostess required, in my aunt Graham's eyes, that I should introduce all the eligible young men of our acquaintance to Florence, retiring immediately afterward to the background.

Before my aunt Graham came, she had written to Kate—she would not have dared do so to either my uncle Tom or me—to know who were at "the house," and before she had been two hours in the parlor I saw that she had selected the victim whose sacrifice was to be the result of the summer's campaign.

And in her selection I must say my aunt Graham showed the taste and high ambition which, she often assured me, were indispensable to a really fashionable lady's "making-up." Carlton Aberthnay, on whom fell her choice, was one of our most admired friends. He was a South Carolinian by birth, and more, a real Carolinian, one of the almost mythical First Families of the South, with just enough of New England training to steady the Southern impetuosity with which he was lavishly endowed. Generous and impulsive, brave and courteous, high-toned and chivalric, there was no door or heart that could be long closed to him.

Had Kate said nothing of his well-stocked plantations, of his almost unlimited expectations, my aunt Graham would have read the consciousness of wealth and position in the unassuming ease and graceful modesty which, to less experienced eyes than those of the sharp woman of the world with a daughter to settle, would have been the last sign looked for.

I cannot say that the light I saw in Gilbert Stuart's eyes had blinded me to all the good in other men, so that they passed dimly before me, darkly as in a glass, but I do know that as we all met in the parlor, a day or two after that scene with Gilbert, and one woman-glance of mine shut out that light, other men came out from the background and shone in more distinct colors. And it was then, I think, that as Carlton Aberthnay stood by Florence's chair, guiding her through the intricacies of a Chinese puzzle, that I saw in his countenance something I had never seen in any other's, not even in Gilbert's;—certainly not, in Gilbert's.

I can scarcely tell you what it was, it was so spiritual, so aspiring, so pure, so real, yet so fervid. Something that made me blush for the material, earthly kind of existence that I led—I, a woman, who ought to walk in heaven's ways, leading men with me, not to stand afar off wondering at it in another's. The same look, with less of determination, more of tender humility, equally pure, but more spiritual still, was always shining out of Mary Allen's sweet hazel eyes. While I watched that light in Carlton Aberthnay's face, my cousin Hal had evidently seen the same in Mary's, for I saw him sitting by her, with more of interest and refinement in his appearance than had ever been won from him by the brightest "belle of the ball."

"I can never do it," at last sighed Florence, looking pitifully up to Mr. Aberthnay.

"Really? why, Miss Georgie did it at once. She can explain it better than I;" and he turned to me, much to Florence's disgust; she, however, maintained a show of interest while I coldly and rapidly explained.

To get her away from me, Mrs. Graham called her to the piano, but Mr. Aberthnay did not follow; he sat with me by the low French window, looking out on the river.

He talked well, better than usual, for Florence had rested his intellect, and it was ready for a fresh start.

His manner had always suited me as a relief from the cold, unenthusiastic, undemonstrative ways of the North; and, now that I was becoming hardened from the joyous-hearted, impulsive girl, to the stately, sarcastic woman, it did me good to mark the flow of his impetuous nature. It amused me, leaning back in my chair, refusing to lose myself in poetry or romance, to hear him, excited to the utmost, paint for me his dreams of the future. His especial ambition was military renown; the pomp of battle was to him earth's grandest romance. "I shall wait," he would often tell me, "until some oppressed nation, with whose principles I can fully sympathize, rises against the oppressor, and join them, as Lafayette did the Colonists, as—"

"Byron the Greeks," I once interrupted him. "No, no. Earth has many ways to fame, and honor should be every man's aim ; but war is butchery, slaughter, adorn it as you will."

But I never moved him; and was nearer being converted myself, for, after all, what man or woman is great and good enough to be deaf to the fife and drum, or blind when "Horses prance and lances gleam"? I found refuge in the magnetism of his cheerful nature from my own thoughts. So I bore, listening to him, without a word of complaint, the dull, hard pain that was gnawing all the sweetness and blessedness out of my life. I meant to be true and just to Carlton Aberthnay, that he might never suffer, if indeed men ever do suffer, as I was suffering then. I knew that his ever courteous manner had a shade of reverence in it for me that it had for no other; mine to him was ever frank and cordial. Beyond that I meant that neither should go. I was tired of love, tired of hearing of it, tired of reading of it, tired of living for it, and I meant there should be none of it between Carlton Aberthnay and me.

Indeed Florence was determined on the same point, and so contrived it that Carlton would have been more or less than man, could he have had a whole heart to offer any other than herself.

My cousin Hal, who, weak as he was, was beyond his excellent mother's control, had "paired off" with Mary since the first evening of their meeting. Kate and Gilbert were almost equally exclusive, or I fancied so; Emma, Uncle Tom, Aunt Graham, Mr. Aberthnay, and myself were left to be as entertaining to each other as possible under the circumstances. Gilbert Stuart came and went very much as of old, and among so many *affaires du cœur*, my little trouble passed unnoticed. How weak I must seem when I confess that my heart still ached for Gilbert. If by so doing I could have preserved his present esteem, and the hope that even yet was not dead, I would have considered it happiness to follow him around the world as the meekest of servants, living years on a smile, braving death for a loving look. Only that I knew he would despise me for it, how I would have knelt and begged for his love!

But well for me the delicate face, Kate's idealized face, was always before me, standing, like the Angel with the drawn sword, between me and paradise. And Kate herself—! Sometimes I almost pitied her in her faint prettiness, as my uncle's rich-set mirrors flashed back my royally-cut features and my deep autumnal coloring. I asked Kate nothing. I asked myself nothing. I never analyzed my feelings, only, when severed from the being in which my own had been so long absorbed, and the responsibility of my own life and happiness came back to me, only then I longed to throw myself into his arms, hide my head on his heart, and pray him to take me back to the love which I still believed had been, still was mine.

Was that my greatest folly?

Well, at least I kept it to myself. I went through the almost daily agony of meeting and parting, with a self-possession that astonishes me now, and must have completely blinded him.

During the earlier summer months Gilbert had often been my escort, on Sundays, to church at the convent where Mary Allen was then at school. Her vacation had commenced during the week, but on the first Sunday after the strange conversation with Gilbert, I proposed going to church there, as usual for afternoon service.

"Who are for the convent?" I asked, with less indifference to the answer than became a polite and impartial hostess. "Now, don't all speak at once!"

"I am at your service as usual," answered Mr. Stuart, looking steadily at me.

"As I did not want to speak all at once," Mr.

Aberthnay said, before I had replied to Gilbert, "I have lost the opportunity of putting myself in the way of getting an inside view of that mysterious building. Do pity me, kind Miss Vane."

"I do," I said; "but there is no reason why you should not go to-day, the larger the party the better."

"I am restored to happiness," Mr. Aberthnay said, smilingly, and began an argument with Kate on religious life, which was conducted with great spirit on both sides, for Carl's religion was a quiet part of him, and Kate was the most rigid of Presbyterians.

"Stop arguing," I had to say, at last, "and let us decide how we shall go."

"Miss Mary is going with me in my buggy," Hal answered, promptly; "I will show her a horse as is a horse."

"You will very likely see too much of that horse, Mary," I said. "If you have any regard for your friends, go with me in sober style."

"Mr. Graham says *Lady Louise* is as gentle as a lamb under his guidance," Mary answered. "I am not afraid, and I like to drive fast."

"Very good beginning for a novice," I thought, but decided not to interfere. When this important matter was settled, it was proposed that the two gentlemen and I should walk, and then began some little ceremonious politeness between Messrs. Aberthnay and Stuart, which showed each wished the other a thousand miles away.

Finally, Mr. Aberthenay came privately to me and gave me to understand that some other day we could go, but that as I had generally gone with Mr. Stuart, and so on. He should not enjoy a pleasure at the risk of interfering with Mr. Stuart's rights.

"Rights!" I echoed; "this is the first I have heard of Mr. Stuart's rights!"

"How shall I express my meaning, then?"

"I do not know your meaning, nor care. I have known Mr. Stuart ever since I can remember, but if I had known him a thousand years I should not consider he had any *right* to my society."

"On that account, no."

"Not on any account. He visits here as uncle Tom's friend, and, some people think, it is just possible my cousin—"

I felt ashamed of having said so much. Mr. Aberthnay saw that I did, and very quietly said:

"I had no idea of annoying you; I beg you will forgive me."

"There is nothing to forgive. Come, now, it is time for us to make ourselves ready for church. After vespers very likely they will show you around that mysterious building."

Our arrangements ended without including Mr. Stuart, who chose to find excuse for withdrawing for reasons of his own, perhaps because Kate, who could not be persuaded to put her foot inside a convent, came down, looking quite as pretty as usual, just as we were talking.

I have always thought if I should wake up after days of sleep or unconsciousness on a Sunday, that I should know the day by the very freshness and stillness of the air. A sweeter Sunday there could not be than that one on which Mr. Aberthnay and I took our first walk together; and took that walk over the very ground where Gilbert Stuart and I had wandered a hundred times, in the easy joyousness of the bright years of my life. Nothing, not even that revelation of his, had seemed to show so clearly our broken trust, as that I walked there with another man at my side.

How different it was! Yet my present companion was one any woman could be proud to be with, and against whose cheerful society and gentle deference few hearts could find it in them to rebel. No more reference was made to Mr. Stuart; and Mr. Aberthnay had never been more interesting.

"This is really a charming town," he said to me in the interval of graver conversation. "I keep liking it more the more I see of it. I remember your speaking of it to me the summer I met you at West Point, and my thinking to myself that I had seen all New England when I saw M—— and G——, for it is the usual remark that every New England village is a fac-simile of every other. I did not think then that my fate would ever station me so near to it, any more than I imagined that I should ever have courage to speak a dozen consecutive sentences to the 'Miss Vane,' who was so fair and stately, that we cadets trembled at our own audacity in asking her to dance."

"And Miss Vane, I assure you, looked upon each particular cadet as a mountain of wisdom, wit, and majesty. So our illusions leave us at every step."

"Some we say good-bye to with all our hearts," he answered; "some we would rather die than lose. I have lost one to-day; I trust it will not come back."

"Oh?" I said, but I did not ask him what it was.

"Yes; but it is terribly selfish in me to be glad."

It struck me just then that he meant something in regard to Mr. Stuart and me. We had been quite often spoken of as engaged, and, no doubt, Mr. Aberthnay had had information to that effect. I thought I had undeceived him, however, for the future.

"Do you really mean that sweet little girl serious-ly intends becoming a nun?" Mr. Aberthnay asked me, when, a few minutes later, Hal and Mary dashed by us at a rate not at all in vogue among New Eng-landers on Sunday, and no more in accordance with my own views of proper respect to the day. Mary, I knew, would never venture to express any objection to Hal, up to whom she looked with great respect and perfect ignorance of any fault possible in him. Her little mind had never been exercised in separating the true from the false, the real from the seeming; certain things were articles of faith with her; certain other things she regarded and shunned with holy horror, just as she had been taught.

"Yes," I said, "she does intend to become a nun."

"Miss Mary seems just made for a nun," Mr. Aberthnay remarked. "She is just our ideal nun; tender and sweet, simple and meek; she might have sat for Tennyson's St. Agnes."

"Surely if there is any truth in a vocation, Mary has it," I said; "she knows of no world outside the convent, and I do not think she will outgrow her present ignorance; it is to be hoped for her own peace of mind that she will not. But herewe are at the convent."

We found Mary kissing nuns and girls indiscriminately. I myself could not deny that there was a certain pleasant charm around the pale-faced sisterhood who had dragged me through the "elements" of English, French, German, Italian, music, and drawing, not to mention embroidery. The parlors were crowded with girls and their visitors, my heart ached for the poor lonely ones who had none, and leaving the parlor I found my way to the long class-room, and for the sake of old times tried to endure the confusion that was the natural consequence of a hundred and fifty girls all talking at once. "I did not go crazy *then*," I thought, remembering my school days. "Nothing will drive me crazy now."

A few words here and there, a glance at my old desk, and a glance through the window by which I had lived so many feverish lives, and my mission there was ended. Just as I left, the bell rang for afternoon service, and the tumult was in a measure hushed; white veils fluttered from all parts of the room, while I hastened to join my cousin and Mr. Aberthnay in the parlor. Mary was taking her old place among the girls.

The beautiful chapel was still as death as we entered, nor did the long procession of white-veiled girls much disturb its silence.. Here every thing was saintly, calm, and sweet. My lost girlhood, my proud, ambitious girlhood, with its wild aspirations, its grand imaginings, its royal hopes, rose up before me, until I cowered before the memory. And while the nuns' sweet voices blended with those of the girls, had all the world been there I could not have repressed the tears that seemed wrung out of my very heart. I had been wishing for them ever since *that* night. I felt better when they came.

"Only a few weeks more," Mary whispered, as she bade the nuns farewell. "Only a few weeks more and I shall be always with you; but it is a long time to wait."

"Patience, my child," one answered. " Our Lord will repay you tenfold for waiting. It is better you should see the world, and know it, so that if you should be ever tempted to wish for its vanities, you may remember what they are worth. Go, dear; God in heaven bless you, and his holy Mother protect you from all the snares of the wicked."

I fancied, as the nun said this, that she had had at least a glimpse of Hal's well-trimmed whiskers.

"I suppose they are sincere," Mr. Aberthnay said, as we left the convent. "They live on another plane .than ours, speaking after the manner of the 'spiritualists.' I believe they mean all they say."

"Indeed they do," I exclaimed. "No one could live so except sustained by the faith that God wills it. Who can tell—do they become mere machines, mere creatures of habit, after a time, or is their self abnegation a perpetually offered sacrifice? As we have seen them, how near to heaven they seem! And oh! who would not throw down life's burdens to possess the repose we saw there?"

"Not I, for one!" cried Mr. Aberthnay; "I thank God that life *has* burdens. Repose is not for me; no, nor for you either, Miss Vane. I thank heaven for the energy and the activity that scorns rest."

" You are wrong there, the greater the activity the sweeter the repose. Who sleeps best, the hard-worked laborer, or the listless, languid 'child of fashion'? If any graybeards were here they would laugh at us for thinking, at our age, of rest, either to scorn or to woo it. Yet what right have they? *The heart knoweth its own bitterness.*"

"I want a regular pow-wow with you to night," said Hal to me on the way to tea.

"What is a pow-wow," I said to Hal.

"A pow-wow," he answered, "is a thundering big talk. A consultation like."

"Oh!" I said, and promised. As soon as I had opportunity I led the way to my own special sanctum, in which foot of man had never entered.

"Well, Hal," I said, as he sat down.

"But, Georgie, *do* go somewhere else; I want to smoke. I never can get it out if I don't smoke."

I looked at my snowy curtains, my spotless carpet, my neat books, my delicate flowers, my pictures, and my hundred little "femininities," and wondered how it would seem.

"Harry," I said, "you may smoke."

"Georgie, you're bully," Hal said, looking for a match, "a regular P. B.;" and having lighted his cigar, he put his boots a little above his head, breaking only a vase and an ornamental tea cup in the operation. I have noticed that when men open their mouths to smoke, their feet, as a seemingly natural consequence, seem to go up to the highest resting-place at hand. I have never been able to explain the phe-

nomenon. "I tell you why," Harry went on, "there
isn't any humbug about you. I tell you there ain't
any thing like a woman with a heart, who's got enough
natural fire not to be put out by a little smoke. You
know very well if you weren't my cousin—I would,
I'll be dashed if I wouldn't. Nice little girl this Mary
Allen—eh ? "

"Very."

"Dashed pretty eyes—have you noticed?"

"Yes—rather."

"Georgie"—this very solemnly—"I always was a
good-hearted fellow—wasn't I, Georgie ? "

"Yes, Hal; I'll answer to that."

"That's you! Coz you're a team. You always
know what to say to a fellow, and get him off when
he's stumped. That's the sort of woman for me. Now,
just as sure as my name's Hal Graham, I will do it;
I will, I tell you; and when Hal Graham says he will,
he will. I will do it. I'll do it if it kills me. If the
landlady kicks up a muss, or the governor refuses to
come down like a P. B., I'll do it in spite of them !
I'll sell my gun, I'll give up Lady Louise, I'll give up
the club, I'll stop smoking—I mean I won't smoke so
much—and I'll do it, wouldn't you ? "

"Decidedly ! "

"She's just perfect, just as pious as any angel; will
get me to heaven, sure. I'll do it—but how ? There's
the rub."

"Oh, that's easy.

"The dickens it is! Did you ever try it?"

"No, Hal, I confess I never did."

"That's the plague of it; *how* to do it? I have asked her out to drive to-morrow, and I'll ask her then. What shall I say?"

"Let that depend upon the way things come around. Just as if an old flirt like you would have any trouble!"

"But this is different. I positively believe I'm regularly in this time. I should feel confoundedly bad if she shouldn't see it as I do."

"Perhaps you had better give her more time."

"Nary. I must know at once. Bless my soul I should be dead in love with her in a week. You wouldn't have me in love with a girl until I was sure she liked me, would you?"

"How can she help liking you, Hal?"

Hal stroked his whiskers. "I'll tell you to-morrow," he said. "I know you want to get rid of me, so good night—but I vow I'll do it. I'll sacrifice myself. I say, won't she look first-rate when she is Mrs. G——, with a nice morning costume on, and a white table cloth between us? A fellow could afford to reform for such a pair of eyes, I tell you. Good night. I don't—suppose—she will stick to the convent idea, will she?"

"Not if you can contrive to get her in love with matrimony."

2

"Somehow it does not come natural to talk that sort of thing to her. But to-morrow must decide. Adieu. I'll do it, you may swear to that. Bon soir."

Hal was as good as his word, and plumply proposed to her at the end of their drive, and was, of course, decidedly refused. But Mary was a perfect novice in the affairs of the heart; and when Hal told her that he had an income large enough for two to live on, with a little economy and some help from the Governor, and that rather than see her immured in a convent he would sacrifice himself on the altar of matrimony, Mary thought pretty much as her hopeful lover did himself, that he was the most generous of men, and assured him, without the least embarrassment or flutter, that she never meant to marry, that she was going to be a nun, that her "vocation" was decidedly to a religious life, in which she would always pray for him for being so good as to be willing to sell his house and stop smoking for her, when she had never done any thing for him; and then she talked so beautifully about the sanctity of single-blessedness and convent shades, and dwelt so tenderly on the sinless life of prayer and meditation before her, that Hal was, at the end, almost ready to emulate the knight of old, who built a hermit's cell under the windows of the convent in which his lady love had, in a moment of despair, vowed to live her earthly life.

"It doesn't seem to me to-day," Hal confidentially

informed me, "it doesn't seem to me to-day near so much like a sacrifice as it did yesterday. I believe now I could stand seeing her face at the other end of the table, day after day, year in and year out, and I'd almost like, 'pon honor I would, to see her fooling with a big-headed baby in long dresses. Hang it! I am not the first man that's said I'd never marry, and then went and did it, am I Georgie? And I've held out longer than a great many others. I couldn't tell you half of the right down pretty girls that I have disappointed. I wish you'd tell Mary about that smashing French widow; you saw all that yourself at the Springs, and you know I never encouraged her at all. Then there was Lottie Jane, with a big fortune in her own right, and expectations ditto, I might have had either of them as easy as winking; supposing you tell Mary so. I don't think she appreciates what she's throwing away."

"Leave it to me to teach her; don't say any thing yourself about other ladies to her. I'll do what I can for you, Hal; but, after all, how can I be sure that you will be in the same mind a year from now? I should not be overmuch pleased after winning her for you, to find you were running off on some other track."

"I vow, cousin, I'm in earnest this time, and I'll stick to what I say, if I die for it. Oh, dear!"

"Will you help me, Hal? will you work with all your might and main for her?"

"You may bet your money on that."

"Then Hal begin; when Mary comes down stairs she must find you in a state of melancholy, from which you must make spasmodic efforts to arouse yourself; you must be rather distant to her—"

"And flirt with Emma Lewis?"

"No—no—that would never do; Mary's kind heart would suffer nothing if she saw you seemingly contented with anybody else."

"How *can* I ever do the melancholy?"

"You *do* feel badly, don't you, Hal? You do think it a thousand pities that a pretty girl, with the sweetest eyes in the world, should go and bury herself in a convent just when a handsome fellow like my cousin Hal is all ready to throw himself at her feet?"

"Yes, of course I do, and I told her so; or something like it."

"Didn't she melt at that?"

"Oh, no, not in the least; she threw the Bible at my head; that is, she quoted Mary and Martha; that dished me at once. She said marriage was good for some—"

"Oh, she did? Very condescending on her part I must confess."

"I don't think you'll be a nun—eh Coz?"

"I don't think I shall."

"I wish you'd coax Mary to think like you. Now, you know, I don't claim to be a saint myself, and I must say it don't seem just the thing. I a'nt sentimental, but 'pon my honor I do think a nice little wife is about as good a passport to paradise as a man can have. Jack and I used to say that, if it wasn't for the expense, matrimony was the best school of reform; and sometimes, when we've been to see some of the fellows that have gone into that blessed state, I'll be hanged if we haven't felt like dashing the expense. I can't talk much, but you know what I mean, and that's more than I can say for most women. If I'd had a sister like you, I believe I'd been something, I do positively. Now, if I could talk like you, cousin Georgie, I know I could bring Mary to my way of thinking; but I can't, and there it is."

"'Faint heart never won fair lady,' Hal. I'd rather Mary would marry the greatest goose in the world than go into a convent, so you may be sure I will help you."

CHAPTER III.

"What a bore this world is," half yawned, half growled Hal, as the end of the week satisfied him that his 'sacrifice' was not to be accepted. "What a bore this world is, especially the part they call the country."

"Which seems to be the unanimous opinion of the company," Kate said, after a pause which brought no contradiction to Hal's assertion. "What is the matter with everybody? Mr. Stuart, you look as blue as a church mouse, what ails you?"

"Nothing, I assure you; I was never in better spirits in my life."

"And Georgie never in worse; what dose it all mean? Is it because Mr. Aberthnay is going away to-morrow?"

I don't know which said "no," with the least truth, Gilbert or I.

"'A penny for your thoughts,' Mr. Aberthnay," Kate continued; "speak your mind and receive your reward," and she displayed a shining "one cent" piece.

"My thoughts, Miss Kate? Not worth a penny, far less your kind interest."

"Oh, then I am sure you were thinking of something you would not like me to know; you Southerners do not rate your thoughts so cheaply."

"Poor. as my thoughts are, Miss Kate, I'll take your penny; never yet did a Northerner fail to get the best of a bargain with one of us, rate we ourselves ever so highly. I was thinking, then, that to-morrow I must up and away—to see you all again, who can say when? I was wondering, too, where all this pleasant company would be this time twelve months! There was more sadness in the wonder than you think, Miss Kate. Have I earned my penny?"

"Twice over," she answered readily. "Well, I for one expect to be immured in solemn Salem-walls, unless Uncle Tom sends for me, in which happy event I shall probably be here—giving away pennies to make moody young gentlemen agreeable; who knows?"

"And I, ditto, or something not much better," said Hal, "unless I emigrate to China, Australia, Jersey, or the Fejee Islands, as I am sorely tempted sometimes. This is such a dull world. Say, Carl, can't you get up a nigger row down South to give us some excitement?"

"Keep your energies, Friend Hal, for something more than a 'nigger row.' Hermetically sealed they won't spoil, and, perhaps, will pay for the keeping," Mr. Aberthnay replied.

Kate made a comical face. "I question that," she said. "What can he ever do with them, unless in domestic spars; and Hal is always going to be an old bachelor, ain't you Hal?"

Hal looked dolefully at Mary, but answered not.

"Even so," said Mr. Aberthnay. "Ours is a glorious Union. You at the North are the hard-fisted, strong-minded, close-handed husband; we of the South, the impulsive warm-hearted wife;—here's chance for domestic spars, even for old bachelors like Hal."

"We have heard of these things before," remarked a visitor, "and have learned to appreciate them."

"You do *not* appreciate them," Mr. Aberthnay answered hotly, "or you would know better than to sneer at them. Some day you will appreciate them."

"Pray keep your politics for your after dinner cigars," I said, rising. "Let us have a walk in the garden."

Mr. Aberthnay was the first to accept the invitation, and we together led the way. Finding even the porch cooler than I expected, I returned alone for a shawl. I found quite a group around Kate.

"Hang these officers," one said with more emphasis than politeness, "they give themselves so many airs."

"I hate Southerners," said Kate, to humor the spirit of the company; "they are too conceited for any thing."

I lingered to hear Gilbert answer: "You should except Mr. Aberthnay, he is perfectly unassuming and unselfish; how could he have said less?"

Years after Gilbert Stuart owed his life to those simple words. I only thought, hearing them, that he did not care enough to be even jealous, for there was no superhuman virtue shielding a rival in that calm voice, I thought.

"Mr. Aberthnay must feel almost a stranger among us," I said, as I returned with my shawl, "and since he has been ordered to our part of the country has done all in his power to please us all. We ought not to visit the sins of his country upon one who has so few of his own."

I did not look at Gilbert, but passed on to the porch where Mr. Aberthnay awaited me. I had spoken incautiously loud, and I saw at once that he had heard me. He drew my hand over his arm.

"It is such words as those, it is such women as you, that piece the broken links," he said, rapidly; "that bind us firmer together than all the parchment scrolls on earth! Something more than political cords, something more than even social bands must be broken first, our very heart strings must be torn apart, before it can be done!"

2*

I looked at him in surprise.

"You do not believe it," he continued, "no one does. You laugh at me for an enthusiast, a dreamer, a mad prophet. There's a cloud above us, a cloud no larger than your hand; it will cover the sweet blue sky above us, and flood this fair land with blood as with rain; I tell you it will!"

"How dare you," I cried, turning to him; "how dare you, Carlton Aberthnay, in the face of this glorious night, through whose gleaming you can see the proud strength of Bunker Hill and Fanueil Hall, tell me they will ever be less yours than mine? In the face of these brave forests, no stronger, no firmer than the hearts that guard them; in the face of these fields of plenty tilled by the brawny arms that will never shame their toil, how dare you tell me they will ever be needed for less peaceful labor? You stand in the very home of Freedom, and talk of danger to its loved and cherished land!"

"Yes, I talk of danger to that very land, for fair as it seems it is black with crime. Think of it, Miss Vane, I do not say as I see it, a soulless despotism, but as you see it every day—a land of extravagance, of social luxury, of utter political rottenness and corruption, and tell me what but a miracle can save its pillars from crumbling to dust, and its proud temple from falling to the earth a mass of blackened ruins."

"Then the miracle will come, for God holds us in

His hand, preparing us for humanity's greatest mission. It is ours; it has been decreed ours from all eternity; it is ours, we claim it, we will have it, and fulfil it. God never built us up so nobly, to cut us down so soon."

"Not as we are now. From our ruins shall arise the nation of which all mankind have dreamt. The veritable land of promise."

"Not from our country's ruins; but from the ashes of the brand of evil in our midst. Burn out that vile outrage on humanity, and we are purified. Now we are not worthy to think of our mission."

"You are an abolitionist, I see."

"I am a human being, and must needs share the degradation of my kind. Their tears cry to heaven for vengeance, and justice demands tears for tears, blood for blood."

There was a long silence.

"Always met with that," he said, at last. "Because that is beyond our power to change. Is it always to be so? Is life always to be a helpless struggle? Are we always to be seeking a glorious haven, and forever dash our heads against the rocks?"

"God knows," I answered, thinking just then of my own life, of the years passed in security floating with the current, and now, the sudden breakers.

"Always met with that," he went on. "Oh, why

was that curse ever fastened upon our land, our bright, glorious Southern land; our land of plenty, of romance, art, and loveliness! There is no other land that can compare with it. God speed the day when it shall take its rightful place among the nations of the earth. It will come, but its way will be strewn with broken hearts instead of roses. You will think of that some-times, will you not, Georgie, while I think of your kind words in there? You will, will you not?"

"I do not more than half know what you are talking about," I said. "I know it sounds somewhat harsh, after all that you have been saying so poetically, to confess my ignorance, but tell me what it all means."

"It means nothing or it means every thing," he answered, excitedly; "and it means besides, that—"

It is useless to repeat the rest. To save him, per-haps myself, I turned away as if in anger.

They had nearly all returned to the parlor; as I passed by the open windows I saw Kate and Mr. Stuart standing by themselves away from the others; she arranging some flowers in her hair, and he bend-ing down to assist her. I looked back, I could just see the dark outline of a figure leaning against the fountain in the garden. I went back, and gave him my forgiveness—nothing more; had I looked twice at the tableau in the parlor it might have been more, but I did not look.

Mr. Aberthnay sprang from his place, and pressed my hands to his lips. "I thank you a thousand times even for this," he said, with his Southern impetuosity. "I shall never forget it."

I did not see him after that.

I was glad to reach my room after the tedious remainder of the evening was over. I had to be alone by myself, or, at least, away from Mr. Stuart and Kate, to fortify myself, to assure myself that I had done right.

How he loved me! Of course I had known it all this time. I had felt it every day; revelled in it as a slight revenge for Gilbert's wound; had sought it, when Gilbert's coldness had been more than I could bear; and now I had thrown it away. Was it right? Was it right? How he loved me! How his face had grown radiant in my presence! I had seen it day after day, and contrasted it with Gilbert's cold, calm demeanor. How eagerly he had sprung to meet me! I had listened for his quick step, day after day, and each time thought of Gilbert's slow, steady walk. How he loved me! I might kneel in vain to Gilbert. One word would bring *him* to me, to be forever mine.

I tried to write that word, but proud, vain girl though I was, I was still woman enough to try in vain.

"I will go and talk to some of the girls to put this thing out of my head," I said to myself, and turned toward Kate's room; but how could I hope to conquer myself with her against me? I was not good enough to hear Mary's eager hopes, so I went to Emma's room. It was very seldom I ever did so, for until lately—perhaps the change was my fault—Emma had always come to me.

"It is I, Emma," I said, not waiting for my knock to be answered. "May I come in?"

There was no reply, the room was quite dark; for a moment I was almost frightened, the next I thought that the silly girl was probably in some cozy corner dreaming of her lover over the seas, as we always called him.

I lighted the gas with careless freedom, and, as I anticipated, quickly discovered Emma sitting by the window with her head on her arms.

"Dreaming, awake or asleep," I asked, raising her head.

A tearful face tried to hide itself from me.

"Tears!" I exclaimed, preparing myself for the story of some lover's quarrel. How small, how childish seemed all other griefs compared to mine! "What has gone wrong now? What right has anybody in this house to cry away from me. What is it?"

"I cannot tell you, I can never tell any one. Please put out the light; I don't want it."

I put it out, and drew Emma nearer to me, and, by and by, she told me her "little tale."

"I have been deceiving you all the time," she said. "I have let you believe all about that man you thought I cared for, but it was not true; I do not care for him."

"But you care for somebody; everybody cares for somebody?"

"Everybody? Then you do; tell me is it—"

"After you, my love."

"It is so silly; so like every thing else; just like a hundred stories; how I went around and saw so many people, and fancied one here, and one there; and said things that I did not mean, and had them misunderstood; and said things in fun, and had them taken in earnest; until one day, oh! such a lovely, beautiful day, when my mind was all full of other things, I was taken into a room full of company, and as many as a dozen gentlemen were all introduced to me at once, and I just bowed to them all, and was tired and wished them all gone, when one said something that made me look up to his face, and—now I know you are going to laugh—but it is true, just as we read in books, and never believe, I felt some one say, that is, as plainly as if some one whispered it to me, 'It is all over now—you must love him always.' But I can't put it into words. I did not think much about it then; I accepted the conviction. He seemed to understand it; so did everybody else, and no one interfered with us. Oh! how I should love to tell you all about those blessed days, I remember every hour of them.   But it would tire you."

I protested against this, but she was firm.   "I did not want to tell anybody while every thing went on well, but it seems to me that I should believe it all if I talked too much about it.   I never coquetted with him; perhaps it would be better now if I had.   I was too truthful, too trustful; men never love you half so well as when you are indifferent to them."

I almost thought so too.

"I was too happy, too secure; I did not suppose any thing could happen, but something did.   He would not listen to me, or when he did, in so cold and incredulous a way that I could not justify myself, and, after all, I had done nothing wrong."

"How long ago was this?"

"Oh, long ago—about two years."

"Well, and then?"

"I ought to marry somebody else, oughtn't I, Georgie?   You know whom I mean.   Of course *he* does not love me now."

"Of course not.   Do you suppose if a man loved you he could leave you two months, not to say two years, in doubt?"

"I don't suppose he could.   But I know if I should ever meet him again, it would all be as it was.   I keep turning this over and over in my mind until I am half wild.   I have argued it from every point of view, and what to do I cannot say."

"You have no right to marry any man feeling so," I answered decidedly. It is so easy to decide for another.

"But I might love him afterwards?"

"It is too great a risk."

"But I am afraid that, in my foolish despair, I have made it too late."

"You are not married; it is never too late until then."

"And then, Georgie, what do you suppose women do?"

"Die; or pray to," I answered, in my old way.

"It is not too late yet?"

"No; but you have no time for hesitation."

It is so easy to be strong for others.

She relit the gas, and wrote a short note, which she handed me to read. It was a decided refusal.

"After all, I feel relieved," she said, sealing it slowly, "and shall be more so when it is out of my power to recall this answer. But it is hard; *am* I right to stand by that which may be only a delusion, and sacrifice half my life for it? Who knows?"

After a silence she said:

"I never doubted your fate, Georgie, until that night you told me you thought Mr. Stuart was engaged to Kate. Now, I do not know what to think, only that it does not seem so to me. I know Mr. Stuart is not quite so fascinating, and rich, and polished as a certain somebody not a thousand miles away, but I never imagined wealth, station, or mere accomplishments, would weigh a feather in the balance with you!"

"Of themselves, never," I replied. "I do not care one iota for wealth or station, but I *do* care for the mind that commands position. I do care for the spirit and the enterprise that walks boldly up and claims its own from the world. I do not believe these things are mere accidents, or the reward of impudence. Fate and Fortune are not so blind as they are represented. Now, I do not think any combination of circumstances could make a great man of Gilbert Stuart; it is not in him to be more than he is: calm, generous, and reliable, always trusted, always respected; never a leader."

. "Who would be a leader if such qualities did not make him such? Who would be a crazy enthusiast, mad on one idea, whirled along to-day in a triumphal car by an excited populace, and thrown in the street to-morrow to make way for some equally mad successor? Not I, indeed. No, give me the man of even mind, of practical thought, quiet, calm, reliable; for, after all, he is the real leader. What a man to trust to, to live for, to die for! Why, Georgie, if such a one loved me, I should worship the very earth that held him, and you do not?"

"I do!" almost burst from my lips, but I answered indifferently. "I am not given the choice. Well for me that I am not, perhaps, for all women are fools, when it comes to that. I should be false to all that is strongest and best in myself if I did not seize, at all hazards, the place where my work would be the hardest and greatest—"

"You talk all sides, Georgie," interrupted Emma. "You would have me sacrifice life for love, and throw love to the winds yourself. How often have you said 'the marriage rite is woman's best right?'"

"For other people."

"For you, and me, and everybody. There isn't any one to hear us; I will even put out the light if you wish, so that we may not see each the other's foolish face as we confess that the world, with all its pomp and show, its wild and thrilling romance, its power and luxury, its grandeur and beauty, has no life to rival the life of a loved and loving wife; say it, Georgie."

"The power and the luxury, the grandeur and beauty, the romance, the pomp and show, we all of us know more or less about—have all seen something which was real and tangible in them; but who ever saw a loved and loving wife?"

"Don't be ridiculous, Georgie."

"Grant that such a thing can be, is it not, after all, a refinement of selfishness, the life she leads? Is it any merit if she secures her husband's comfort and happiness at every cost, since securing his is securing

her own ? She makes no sacrifices, she has no sorrows;
what seem such are merely small prices that she pays
for immense joys. But for her who denies self, who
throws every gratification beneath her feet, how infinitely holier the destiny !"

"Then you justify Mary ?"

"No, it must be done for some work," I answered,
confusedly; for, truth to tell, I was arguing down
myself, not Emma, and was venturing on unknown
ground, "some work that puts her talent out to interest."

"And all this to prove that you are right in sacri-
ficing one of the best and most generous of men to
your ambition ! It just amounts to that."

"If by *one of the best and most generous of men*
you mean Mr. Gilbert Stuart, permit me to inform
you that it is not, and never has been in my power to
have the slightest influence on his destiny, one way
or the other."

"I never thought you so unreasonable," Emma
said. "You know the man loves you; everybody
knows that. Only yesterday your jewel of a housekeeper, Mrs. Glynn, gave me a glowing account of the
way in which she and your uncle would marry you
off, and could not tell me enough of the charming generosity with which you recognized true worth—that
is, Gilbert Stuart—and was undazzled by outside glit-
ter—that is, Carlton Aberthnay."

"Mrs. Glynn was very impertinent," I replied, quickly, "and I would thank you, Emma, not to discuss my affairs with my uncle's housekeeper."

"Now, wherein have I offended your ladyship?" Emma cried, quite undaunted by my remark, the hardest that had ever passed my lips. "It can't be Carlton—"

"Why not?" I asked, haughtily, and asked without knowing why. "Why not Mr. Aberthnay?"

"There! Now, I see it all! Oh, Georgie, I thought you the truest, bravest, and sincerest woman in the world! So fall our idols at every step! You a flirt, a coquette, like all the rest! just as ready to throw aside a brave, true heart, for a heavier purse, as any of the rest! Where is your cousin Florence? I will make her my next idol; she fights under no false colors, at least. Just like all the rest, Georgie; so strong and brave for me, so weak and ambitious for yourself!"

So she drew away from me, and judged me with her half knowledge.

Who drew away from him, who blamed him when he wrung my heart with his deception? Who blamed him when he came in his manly strength and vigor to poison my fresh, young life? Who blamed him when he sought, in deliberate cruelty, the wild, devoted love for which he could not return even the semblance? Who blamed him when I writhed in my anguish in the solitude of the night, while he played with the roses in my garden?

Who blamed him? Who dared? Close in my heart I held his secret; those who would not let the winds of heaven blow too roughly against my cheek loaded him with honor. So it should be. Till I died no one should know of his wrong to me, say what they would of me.

"Come," I said, "come and see if Mary is better contented than the rest of us."

We entered her room softly. She was sleeping sweetly; the rosary she held in her hand under her head had gently indented her rosy cheek, fair and soft as that of an infant's.

"She must be dreaming of angels," Emma whispered.

"While we have spent our thoughts on *men*," I added, ashamed of myself. "Who knows, Emma—it seems almost wicked to question it—who knows but, after all, Mary has chosen the better part?"

"Who knows?" Emma echoed; and her eyes, as they turned from Mary to me, had a look in them that haunts me still.

CHAPTER IV.

"Why did you ever let that handsome young soldier off without warning me?" my aunt Graham said to me the next morning, when it became fairly understood that half of the officers, among them Mr. Aberthnay, who had enlivened our little town for the past two years, had been ordered away. "Why did you not let me know?"

"I was not aware such an item would esspecially interest you," I answered.

"Really? You are very short-sighted, I must say. But I won't scold you; I have had enough of that with Florence."

"What has Florence been doing?" asked my uncle. "Not flirting with our 'handsome young soldier,' I hope, because I shall, then, have to scold too."

"My daughter never flirts," Mrs. Graham answered. "In truth, I almost wish she would, occasionally. She is too indifferent to please my fancy. I was just saying to her that she has treated Mr. Aberthnay very unkindly."

I felt my eyes were dangerous, and looked out of the window. What strange fate was it that made me always Mr. Aberthnay's champion? Was it merely contempt for Florence and pride in myself that made me angry that her name should be mentioned in connection with one who was so much my friend?

"Very unkindly," Mrs. Graham rattled on. "Although Florence is the gentlest creature, and the most artless in the world. At least, I think so; for Mr. Aberthnay seems to me a very superior young gentleman, and it has pained me very much that Florence—"

"That Florence, what?" I asked, turning suddenly, as she made a pause—a pause which said more than words.

My aunt played with the tassel of her morning dress and smiled.

"You are in a very bad humor this morning, Cousin Georgie."

"What were you going to say about Florence and Mr. Aberthnay?" I asked, not noticing her opinion of my humor.

"About Florence and Mr. Aberthnay?" she repeated. "What have I to say about them? I have always made it a point never to influence my children in any way, not even by a look; and whatever I might have wished, I give it up cheerfully, believing it to be all for the best."

Of course I did not believe one word of her insinuations; but Florence was one of my aversions, and every thing her mother said angered me.

"So, Florence would not see Mr. Aberthnay with your eyes," I said, at last. "A thousand pities! Supposing Mr. Aberthnay should shoot himself, or do some horrible thing, how dreadful it would be!"

"Are you two women going to fight?" Uncle Tom said, looking from one to the other with comical bewilderment. "Because, 'pon honor, I can't allow it."

"Georgie is only a little out of humor this morning," my aunt answered. "She cannot help her nature, you know. I do not know but I rather like her little tempers; they are amusing. Florence, you know, never changes: she is always the same sweet-tempered child. I often wish she was not so much so. But I'll leave you, Georgie, to find your smiles again. Bye-bye."

As she went out she dropped a letter from her lap on the floor, but passed on without noticing it. Uncle Tom picked it up and threw it carelessly into my work-basket. I would no more have touched it than if it had been burning coal, but I could not help seeing that it was addressed to Florence, and was in Mr. Aberthnay's writing.

. "What! another!" I thought; and remembering her last words, her comparison between Florence and me, I knew she was not satisfied yet, would not be satisfied until she had taken my all.

"What did she mean, Georgie?" Uncle Tom asked, after nearly fifteen minutes' silence, and throwing down his paper with a tired gesture.

"She wants to take every thing from me; she wants to turn everybody against me. Against me, because I am fatherless, motherless, and—"

My uncle was not given to sentiment. He laid his hand on my mouth to stop me, then took me tenderly in his arms.

"Your father neglected your mother," he said; "left her, night after night, and day after day, without a friend or a comforter; and when I interpreted her silence as pride, and begged her to accept my sympathy as that of a brother, he piled insult on insult upon her glorious young head, until she fled from him in terror, and the morning found her dead. Your father has never asked for you from that day to this. To whom do you belong most, eh? Whom would your mother trust you with if not with me? And do you think you can ever get away from me? Try it! that is all."

CHAPTER V.

SLOWLY the long summer came to an end. Our
boats rocked idly on the river, which the falling leaves
were already choking; our horses neighed unheeded
in the stables, our voices echoed dully in the parlors,
for our guests had departed; not all the splendor of a
New England autumn could enliven our lonely house,
and I knew not how to face the sadness of the cold
but gorgeous sunsets, so mournful even when our
souls are at rest.

"Uncle," I said, "let us follow the birds."

"Aha!" he exclaimed, "set my Georgie's thoughts
in *that* quarter? Verily, a few days more in this
deserted house and I shall learn all her secrets."

"Let us have no secrets, uncle, no thoughts, no
cares, no feelings; let us leave them as the birds have
left their nests, once loved now forgotten. Let us
lead a gay, *sans souci* life, until the sentimental summer
brings us new thoughts and feelings."

"New cares and new secrets too, eh? Why, child,
I thought no life was gay to you, except that of your
books, your music, and your rides."

"When I was a child you know, uncle. I want to be a *young lady* for the little time that is left me before I settle down to spinsterhood. I want you to buy me a new Saratoga trunk and fill it with handsome things, and—"

"For a season."

"Let us be merry before we go."

"Want to empty this, do you?" holding before my eyes his well-filled pocket-book. "Want to empty this, do you, you young *extravaganza?* That's the way with you women!"

"That is our mission, Uncle Tom. If I have hitherto neglected fulfilling it I hereby promise amendment, certain that you need never complain of me in the future."

"Beauty unadorned—" began my uncle.

"Belongs to a past era," I interrupted. "Am I good looking, uncle?"

"'Pon honor, really, you embarrass me. Well—now—'pon honor, can't say I was ever in such a fix before. All women are handsome."

"But in different degrees; what is mine?"

"Well, really you are hard upon me, not but what I've done such a thing as tell a lady she was pretty. In my younger days I might have staved off your question with a compliment, now I leave it to younger heads; what do the young men tell you?"

"No man living ever dared speak to me of my looks!"

"No one ever told you you were handsome?"

"Of course not."

"Then you may be certain that you are."

"I don't want that kind of certainty, I want your candid, unbiassed opinion; I suppose you are a judge?"

"Thank you, dear, I believe I am; Jack used to say I could tell a pretty girl as far off as I could see a church spire."

"I am not *pretty*, I know that."

"And as for the other—let me see," and he put on the eye-glasses he never wore before any one except me, whose discretion he knew. "'Pon honor, Cousin Georgie, I never knew before what a dashed fine looking woman you are! But how is this—the last time I looked at you you were a red-cheeked, round-faced lassie; where have the roses gone?"

"The summer has passed," I said, so mournfully that my own voice startled me. "So your judgment may be considered favorable?"

"In the highest degree."

"May I ask you one question more? What is the first duty of a handsome woman?"

"Ahem! Upon my honor, I am again embarrassed. The first duty of a handsome woman is—to make the most of her beauty."

"By—?"

"By dressing, dancing, flirting, and making fools of her natural enemy, mankind."

"Put that down in your note book. You say I am a handsome woman whose duty is to flirt, dress, dance, and fool mankind; it is your duty, as you stood sponsor for me, to see that I perform my duty."

"Bless me! What a logical mind it has!"

"Now, once more, uncle, do you know how old I am?"

"'Pon honor, no! Never knew a lady's age in all my life; never knew she had one."

"In society of course not, but just privately, between ourselves, I have an age; do you know it?"

"Impossible!"

"Guess."

"More impossible."

"Calculate."

"Most impossible."

"Think."

"I can't!"

"Then I must tell you,—I am twenty-one."

"Bless me! How shocking! Have you no respect for my nerves? Twenty-eight—"

"Twenty-*one*."

"Which means five years more."

"Not in my case."

"Well, as you say; never contradict a lady. Is it a fair question to ask how long you have been twenty-one?"

"Long enough to learn I can be twenty-one only a

month or two more; long enough to know I ought to
be fulfilling my mission."

"Oh, indisputably."

"Then when do we begin ?"

"Does that apply to me, or to my pocket-book ? "

"To both."

"Then, at once, what can the former do ? "

"Escort me after the birds, as I said."

"The birds are sorely scattered, and the Eagle

> ' Clasps the crag with hookéd hands,
> Close to the sun in *southern* lands.'

In a Louisiana fort, I believe."

I did not especially fancy this, my uncle's distant
allusion to Mr. Aberthnay, who was my uncle's
favorite of all young gentlemen who visited us; so I
answered quickly:

"Who cares for eagles, uncle, save the respectable
bird that upholds our national honor ? "

"Well, then, whither shall we wing our flight ? "

" Wherever the harvest of heartlessness is the
plentiest."

"I don't like this," he said, changing his tone; " we
have carried the jest far enough. I believe there is
something wrong under it."

I left my seat, and going to him, said: " Look at
me, Uncle Vane, is there a line in my face, a shade,
even, that speaks of folly, wrong, or deceit beneath ? "

"Bless you, child, no! no! Don't I know it? Can I not read it as plainly as if in a book? Earnest, truthful, high-toned, and conscientious. Do not ask me, did I not know your mother?"

"Then for her sake trust me. Take me with you to some of our large cities, anywhere where the world is in motion. Let me make the most of my few gifts, and gladden your old heart by my success."

"My 'old heart!' faith, Miss Vane, you are peculiar in your choice of adjectives. The heart may be older in the breast of a girl young as you, than in that of a man of twice my years."

"And it is, uncle," I murmured; and then distinctly, "I judged by the good it has done, not the years it has lived."

"There! there! Very well put! very well put! But what was that you said first?"

"One word, Uncle Tom; no answer, no comment: mine is like Niobe, turned to stone."

"By overmuch weeping? I admire your good sense, Georgie, in keeping your tears there; they would have ruined your eyes."

"Thank you. Where are we to spend the winter?"

"Where ever you will. Washington is dull, always dull to me, but I think you would like it. I wish we had an intriguing, diplomatic, courtly capital; there would be your element. Let us try a little of New York first."

"So be it, and I will commence my shopping at once. Give me lots of money, uncle, it may be my last effort; let me go gorgeously through it."

"Insatiable girl! You will ruin some poor fellow yet, by your extravagance."

"Woman's mission," I answered, as he gave me a roll of bills. "I should not wonder if I had found the real solution of that grand problem *Woman's Rights.* Thank you, Uncle Tom."

"Will it soften—" he began.

"Hush!" I said, and left him.

3*

CHAPTER VI.

WHO glories not in the activity of real city life!
The never-resting crowd, pushing, jostling, pressing,
hurrying each for his own particular goal; what life
can be called life beside it? How the sluggish blood
starts up and tingles through our veins! How the
languid nerves spring into action, as we mingle with
our kind, straining like them, for power, wealth,
fame, and happiness, each man for his own idol! I
love the sweet, green fields, the far, blue sky, the
dark, forest crowned hills, the murmuring brooks, the
gushing rivers; but I revel in the noisy, rattling,
stirring town, where God's last, best works are living
out their lives together.

I felt my life renewed, even as the pent-up city
denizen renews his in the summer vacation. I
returned home, from those few days' shopping, stronger, braver than I had been for months before; I
could even think of meeting Florence, and my old
enemy, my aunt Graham, with equanimity. A trial
which I was, however, spared, for they had flown off
to the South for the winter and spring.

I remember very well the night previous to our departure. I came down to our cozy little sitting-room, which was the favorite of all our lower rooms, in my travelling dress, alone, and with that peculiar feeling one has after locking drawers and packing trunks. My uncle Tom was in his library, deep in his papers, and giving directions to everybody for the care of the house in his absence; a thorough old maid in this was my dear uncle Tom. A long dreary November storm had desolated the streets of our never very lively little village, and fearing no intrusion I wandered around the room in a listless way, a little softened by the loneliness of the once gay household.

Old memories came creeping to me, as I sat down, at last, in the firelight; little speeches, isolated sentences, pleasant meetings, tearful partings, quiet evenings, and dashing parties; little things, but full of meaning to me. Round school-girl faces, even now, some of them elongated to suit the dignity of married life; some dead, all scattered! What hopeful projects we had planned, what blushing tales confessed, sitting around that now lonely fireplace! They softened me, hardened as I had made myself since then, and finally, yielding to their influence, I knelt down in the red light, sighing my requiem over my lost girlhood.

A step at the door startled me. I arose quickly, and advanced to meet my visitor. It was Gilbert, just out of the rain and dark; I could not help a little start of surprise.

"I felt as if I should do something desperate if I stayed at home another day," he said, half answering that start. "These rains are stupid. I find I cannot see Mr. Vane quite yet?"

"No," I said, "he has laid us under orders not to venture near him for two hours to come."

He took the chair I offered him, and leaned cheerfully toward the fire. He had made us but few calls since the summer and Kate had left us, but it had made no difference in his manner, which was still that of an old friend and favored guest, only that now he seemed to avoid the large chair always placed near my little work table, which had formerly been his usual seat.

He would not let me light the gas, preferring the softened light from the hall, he said, and said with the same apparent confidence in my consent with which he would have made the request a year before. I would have resisted, but he turned his eyes undauntedly toward me, with manlike consciousness of power, scattering my frail defences like chaff before the wind, and I yielded with what grace I could, and essaying a half indifferent, careless glance, I took my usual seat by the table; but under his fearless eyes, though I brought all my strength to aid me in the contest, mine wavered and fell.

I could not help it, I struggled hard, but his eyes could have led me through fire and death, with but half the mingled emotions that were in them then. What if the past six months could be blotted out, and the old times back again! Could I be deceived; in spite of all did he not love me, had he not always loved me? What right then had any other to come between us?

I heard his voice, some every-day words, but it was a reason to meet his eyes again, and for the burning blush and quick-dropping eyes to own him conqueror. He knew enough not to proclaim his victory too soon, not until he had played the vanquished. I could not help it. What, if years or oceans had separated us, could I refuse, meeting, to those dear eyes? By and by he came to his old place, and soon my work basket came under contribution, for his amusement, as of old; it did my heart good, though I made a great show of opposition, to see him clipping my thread, entangling my silks, twisting my ribbons, and notching my spools, as he had done so often in the olden time. I lost not a word he said, not a sound of his voice; there was no power within me to remember that miniature, which he, too, seemed to have forgotten.

It seems to me I never sang as I did that night, with that one listener, who never praised, but only dreamily heard.

"Your next audience will be a fashionable New York crowd, I suppose," he said, as I turned around on the piano stool. "How can you care for any thing better than this?" glancing around the cozy room.

"Because I want life, action, work. I should petrify here."

"Do you call dancing, shopping, and having a 'gay winter,' work?"

"There is more than dancing, shopping, and having a gay time in the city," I answered. "There is downright work for every man, woman, and child there."

"What an amount of energy you have! I could never dream of going after work, it would be bad enough to have work come to me."

"Are you not ashamed? You are only half a man while you talk so."

"It's true, Georgie, I *am* only half a man, and my laziness is the key to my whole life. I can't get out of old ways, I can't break through old customs. I am not half what I ought to be. I feel all the time that if I would make one great effort, one firm wrench, and stand to it, I could do an immense deal; but the least show of resistance proves too much for me, and I give up rather than fight the battle."

"Perhaps it would not be so if you had any thing worth fighting for," I suggested.

"I *have* something worth fighting for," he replied,

less lightly than before, "which would make me indeed a true and happy soldier to win. I see others pressing in, I do not wait to be jostled aside, I move away, and watch others win the prize that shōuld be mine."

"You're a good for nothing, lazy fellow," I cried, "and you will have to suffer for being so, depend upon it. And with so much power as you really have if you only knew, and would use it!"

"Have I power?" he asked with a meaning there was no mistaking.

"Are you not ashamed to ask that question, Gilbert Stuart? Are you indeed devoid of manliness?" I exclaimed indignantly.

"I think I am, Georgie, but I am going to get righted one of these days. Will you not sing for me again?"

"No," I answered coldly, and left my seat.

"Then I shall have to sing for you," he said, gaily.

"You are very kind," I returned with increased coldness, and leaned back in my chair. I had never heard him sing, and did not suppose he could.

"I am afraid I cannot manage an accompaniment," he said, after striking several chords. "Will you not help me?"

"I beg that you will excuse me," was all the answer I felt it in my power to give, for I was deeply hurt.

"Then I must help myself. Please listen to the words. It took me a week, nearly, to get them to jingle."

I did not hear any more for some time, and was half lost in reverie when a rich, deep voice, broke in, or rather mingled with it, singing:

"Your brow is set with woman's pride,
　　Your eyes refuse a melting smile,
　But oh! how check the heart's strong tide,
　　That rushes wildly all the while?
　How cold are all the words I win!
　　And colder still the tones I loved,
　How calmly pale that once bright cheek
　　Whose color each new feeling moved!

"I may not even speak of days
　　O'er which I brood with strange delight,
　Nor may I ask the simplest grace,
　　That then seemed mine by true love's right.
　But vain is all the world would say,
　　To rouse perchance my jealous fears,
　I bowed not to that gentle heart,
　　Till I had known its truth for years.

"Ah! do not think I could believe
　　My darling's heart less true than then!
　Ah! do not think that I could fear,
　　Her eyes can droop for other men!
　Though never in this world again,
　　One of the dear old looks I win;
　The fault be mine, but to distrust
　　That constant heart, were gravest sin.

'I know I've wronged that faithful heart,
　　Half failed its tender worth to prize,
And I to whom they trusted all
　　Have dimmed with tears those peerless eyes.
Too many are the ways that lead
　　Our rougher manhood's steps aside,
'Tis thine, sweet eyes, 'tis thine, dear hands,
　　To virtues paths our steps to guide.

" I cannot speak of all I've seen,
　　Nor how each gloomy road I've past,
But made thee seem the brighter still,
　　And led me to thy feet at last.
I cannot speak of all I've erred,
　　Nor yet of all I fain would be,
But if I gain a place above
　　I gain it love, dear love, through thee."

"And now," rising, and coming behind me, "having completed the measure of my enormities, I suppose I must go ?"

"Yes, go," I said rising in my turn; "I thought that measure was completed long ago, but your invention is wonderful, and I know not how many new insults you may have in store for me."

"Are you serious, Georgie ? Make me so, then; make me forget that we are not boy and girl together still, and you will be fully avenged."

"I have forgotten that we were ever boy and girl together. For the future, at least, I am not to be other than *Miss Vane* to you."

I was getting him in earnest, I could see.

"It is useless for me to beg pardon in detail," he said. "If I ever become wholly a man I will entreat it all at once."

"With the full expectation of being forgiven!"

"I expect nothing; I hope but little; I deserve your taunt, nevertheless."

He turned slowly from me, irresolute, it seemed to me.

I was angry enough for any thing then, and I called him back.

"You have more to say, say it."

"I *have* more to say, but I cannot. Some time, perhaps, I shall be serious, earnest, and what I ought to be, now it makes no difference. I do not suppose you will believe me if I say I would not have offended you for the world."

I hesitated a moment.

"You remember what you told me one night, last summer. Did I understand you rightly?"

He bowed.

"It is the same now?"

He bowed again.

"And yet you would have me believe you have a grain of truth in you!"

That was enough; if he had forgotten it for that hour, it was only to make him remember it ever afterwards.

The bright light in the hall shone full on a face that was pale and full of sadness, as he lingeringly prepared to leave.

"Good night, Miss Vane," he said looking into the room, but not at me.

"Good night, Mr. Stuart."

I could not realize even when the door closed behind him that he would not come back, and explain all this mystery, and win the forgiveness that was only for a moment out of his reach. It was harder still to think, after so many years of trust and faith, trust and faith that had not died in all the past months, that faith and trust had been met, not only with indifference but with insults. Even yet, such is woman's folly, with all my pride I could find excuse even for that, could believe he meant more than he could say.

The next day I was to leave; I had seen the last of him, and hope was over.

And then—Kate!

Did I, therefore, tear him out of my heart? Did I blush that I had ever yielded him a moment's thought? Did I place hatred and contempt in the place where he once had reigned?

I was no strong-minded heroine. I was a strong woman, perhaps, but strong only for others; the merest schoolgirl, crying over her first love, could shame me, weeping, *de profundis*, over mine. I was no strong-minded heroine: I opened the great door softly, and listened for the echo of his footsteps splashing down the wet pavement; I found myself gradually leaning farther out, until the rain fell around me, and on me, listening still—holding my breath to hear that step once more. I went in, when I could no longer catch even its faint, far away sound, I went in to the now dull room, lately so brilliant with his presence. I stood by the chair in which he had sat, by the piano at which he had sung, with such earnestness and pathos, those strange words; longing to caress each object which had been blessed by his touch. I took my basket, just as he had left it, with its notched spools and twisted ribbons, and locked it in the little black cabinet where I kept my letters and journal. I sank down on the floor, with my head in his chair, and there shrined my life's young dream in my heart, as a blessed memory, a glimpse of heaven before the celestial gates closed upon me; I buried him deep down in my heart, never to see him, with lovelit eyes, until the appointed day of Love's resurrection.

I might well go to my room that night as from a great and solemn funeral.

CHAPTER VII.

Society opened its arms to us, affectionately to my uncle, cordially to both. Affectionately to my uncle, for there was not a silver hair among his curly locks, not a glimmer of frost in his abundant whiskers, to whisper of the coming winter of his life; for the which be praised my uncle's own immaculate hair-dye. And, too, my uncle was trim and lithely made, preserving the happy medium between superabundant flesh and gout on one side, and leanness and dyspepsia on the other; for the which be praised my uncle's energy, and his great, warm heart.

Joined to these rare advantages of figure and whiskers, my uncle had a still handsome pair of clear, dark, youthful eyes; a massive nose, of the New England type, which just intimated there was a rough road somewhere that my easy uncle Tom might have trod; a good voice, excellent taste, and his own teeth; so that it was not wonderful that in long parlors, and in crowded halls, Mr. Vane's person, or Mr. Vane's income—which, by the way, was in an equally flourish-

ing condition—was the object of admiring eyes innu-
merable.

As for me, though I had none of these latter claims
upon society, there was still a prospect of something
from my uncle, the good world thought. There was,
too, a lingering remembrance of a brilliant heiress
who had flitted across the sky of society, meteor-like,
about whom there had been a story, deepened into
mystery as years glided onward and saw no more of
her, until a daughter came to revive her image, and,
thanks to a wealthy uncle, to raise it above the slan-
derous tongue of envious society. A little mystery is
piquante sometimes.

I am not writing my uncle's biography, or I should
dwell, half with amusement, half in disgust, on the
many incipient courtships of my tender-hearted uncle,
during that gay winter. Incipient courtships, for it
was not in the power of my generous uncle to confine
himself for more than a few evenings to any one pretty face; it never had been, hence his bachelorship.

"I own it," he would say; "what then? Must a
man make himself a boor for the sake of consistency,
when his fickleness makes him only the more interesting to others, and agreeable to himself?"

Just here, in speaking of my uncle, I am reminded—I can hardly say why—of a dear and honored
friend, who once said to me, speaking of a mutual acquaintance, "Do you know the secret of G.'s worldly

prosperity? I will tell you: When he was about starting on his worldly career he came to me for advice. 'My dear young friend,' I said to him, 'life and your profession are not all made of roses, as you will too soon find. When adversity presses hard upon you; when every thing is dark as midnight, without a glimmer of hope or comfort; when your friends look coldly upon you, and every thing, in fine, seems driving you to despair; go then, expend, if need be, your last dollar, and buy a new pair of light-colored kid gloves, and put them on.'" Therein is a world of meaning associated always in my mind, spite of the New England nose, with my uncle Tom.

And we two lived in the same house, eat at the same table, walked arm-in-arm, sat side by side, read the same books, and lived our separate lives! So goesthe world!

I cannot understand those who say that sorrow or disappointment, such as mine, embitters the mind, and sours it to the world. The power I had for loving, sent back upon my heart, ran no longer in its deep but narrow channel; it diffused itself over my whole nature, becoming weaker, perhaps, by the diffusion, mingling, as it did, with my lighter, less noble, every-day character; but it made it kinder, more charitable, more generous to all I met. I did not hope that those loving tides could ever be gathered together and secured in their old sweet, unseen bounds. So I lived for society as best I could.

Feel kindly, friendly to humanity, and humanity rewards you by its efforts to appreciate and become worthy of your regard.   It is only the selfish, the useless, or the wicked that declaim against the injustice of mankind.   Just it seldom is, for humanity is human; but it does its best, and the true man tries in other ways than angry remonstrance to make that best better.

So I gathered to myself many a heart-offering from those who surrounded me, and strove here and there to say a word or two that might fall in the right place. I, a woman, honor women.   I know they are vain, frivolous, extravagant, and capricious, with a thousand faults beside; but I honor them still.   I say nothing of the false state of society, the folly and blindness of parents, the flattery of friends, that make them what they are.   Would you have me dash my head against a wall ?   From now until the day of judgment, I verily believe young girls, fresh and sweet, and pure and lovely, with the dew of heaven on their lips, and the music of angels in their voices; with holy inspirations, saintly virtues, heavenly dreams, and martyr endurance sleeping in their breasts, waiting the time for woman's work to need them, will be led like lambs to the slaughter, after systemized boarding-schools and contentious homes have labored day and night, by open blows and concealed undermining, by every power known to man or woman, by appeals to every woman-fault and woman-enemy, to deaden and destroy that heaven-born nature before its first sweet slumbers are broken. We may write books, we may preach sermons, we may deliver lectures, we may call conventions and establish associations, we may found nunneries, and our reward will be only ridicule, and fruitless labor, for the world will go on just as before, and woman will dance, and sing, and make merry, for a brief season, before she resigns her throne for the nursery; because, maimed and crippled, spiritually and physically, she has not found that both can be held at once. From the patient endurance, the tenderness, the unselfishness, and the strength for which women fight, and which they so rarely lose, through all the power and skill of the world, what may we not hope?

I honor them still, these very girls—light, vain, and capricious—who rattle nonsense till your head aches, and imagine they are clever; these very girls who would measure Tennyson by the cut of his coat, and Browning by the style of his whiskers, who count men and women by their dollars, rather than by their virtues, these very girls, aimless, missionless as they seem, are panting every one of them, like tired children, for the lost path. One of these, delicate, pampered, idle, luxurious as they are, will stand by your bedside day after day, night after night, and dream not that she is doing any thing. Your stout, hearty brother will do as much, perhaps, and you can never be enough grateful to him; a few sweet words, a loving smile, a caress more ^ tender than usual, is *her* utmost reward. One of these,· weak, silly, thoughtless as they are, will find you a way through the labyrinth of cares and fears, in which your last friend has left you, hopelessly ensnared. One of these—what use is there to talk—neglected, misled, misunderstood—there is something pure and good, and strong in the worst of them all. I honor them still, I long to take them in my arms and say: " Oh, you frail little creatures, wandering, like lost children, on false paths, what mighty ways you might tread! How beautiful, how great, how lovable you might be, if you would strive not alone for the path of beauty, but of strength and goodness; if you would only follow the divine light not yet, never extinguished in your souls, and make it a halo for home and for the world, a fireside glow, and a beacon light !"

False, but so unconsciously false to themselves. I love and honor my sex; and when I see one bright, and sweet, and good, with a warm heart, and cordial hand, cherished at home, honored abroad, bringing sweet homeways into society, and grateful social charms into the home circle, then indeed have my eyes beheld a lovely sight.

And in this spirit I took my place among them, and together we danced through one gay winter in New York, while my uncle grew younger and gayer every day, and was, perhaps, less glad than I when fashion decreed that we should leave the dusty city for summer's sweetest home.

Yet I did not like the prospect of another summer in L——. I scarcely knew why, and my uncle reading my half-formed thought proposed a tour through the East, finishing, as in duty bound, at Saratoga, where every thing was as it always is; crowded hotels, brimming over with flirts and fortune hunters, and for the rest neither interesting nor picturesque in any degree.

CHAPTER VIII.

THERE comes a time in nearly every woman's life, I believe, when she is like one waiting. She is not married, perhaps she does not care to be; she has no especial work, perhaps she does not desire to have; she has no particular ambition or object in life, perhaps does not know where to seek one. It is a trying time; society is all in all to her no longer. She is too unsettled to study, not knowing the need, and any straw in the balance may turn her fate. Great misfortune, some unexpected change, may rouse her and decide her for immense good, or monotony may conquer, and she turns to a listless routine, from which the chances are few that she will ever move.

Such a time had come to me, and I faced it, for I knew its meaning. Now, or never, a work, a mission, a destiny, or a placid existence made up of books, music, dancing, and embroidery. I tried many things. I tried to write, I failed totally; I hardly know why, I had education enough, and my imagination had entertained me many an hour. I tried charity, but I merely made myself notorious, and was terribly imposed upon. I tried a " Young Ladies' Mutual Improvement Society," but the third meeting ended in exchange of embroidery patterns and fashion plates, and as I would not lose my esteem for the minds of my friends, I withdrew, and the whole thing fell to the ground. I tried teaching, and adored it, but I had never known confinement and my health gave way—I was not sorry. What right had I, with a happy home, to take the place of those who count it a blessing from heaven to find a place, however irksome, in which they could toil and earn their daily bread?

"I wish we had an intriguing court," my uncle said, "and troublesome times. You would be in your element then."

We were walking down Pennsylvania Avenue as he spoke, and I smiled for answer, for feet on desks, pocketed hands, and tobacco-stained mouths had not much increased my admiration of the rulers of this glorious Republic.

I was walking in my Yankee trust and simplicity, in an honest road; how strange it seems to me now that the very men I voted past redemption dull, were plotting and planning over their wine, with a skill and a daring for which history furnishes me no simile!

We turned, my uncle and I, into a public hall to see an exhibition. The rooms were almost empty, but a small group of gentlemen were gathered in one, around whom the few passing visiters lingered, apparently listening. Uncle Tom was in some manner drawn aside, and as I stood waiting for his return, some words of seemingly eager discussion caught my ear. Presently one voice, deep and impassioned, fixed my attention.

"A little more of this indecision," were the first words I heard, "and the work is lost! A little more ease, a little more pleasure, and every thing will be gone! Is there no strength, no energy left us? Is it a few words here, a vote or two there, that is to work out our salvation? Is it now and then a man, earnest and willing to labor, that is to do the work?"

There was a mingling of voices, and I heard no more; but something in the voice I had heard haunted me. I really hungered for it as I wandered around the building. I have heard stray notes of music, passing tones that have lingered with me in the same way, but this was intensified, and so real that I gladly saw my uncle depart, leaving me, with many remonstrances, behind. I cared not for the words, I would not even look at the speaker, but I would go back and hear its music again. I was standing near a large window, the crowd was whirling by beneath, rattling, thundering by, but it did not prevent my hearing and distinguishing the voice that had beguiled my fancy from all the rest. They were passing me on their way out of the house; I turned slightly toward them, the speaker was leaving them. I turned back to the window just as you do when a sweet song is ended. Some one stood beside me. I turned, and a pair of eyes, so blue, so bright, so glad, so tender, looked into mine, that I received their gaze as if all were a dream. So blue, so bright, so glad, so tender, that I can never forget that moment's meeting.

"Am I forgotten? Am I to be introduced, and begin all over again?" It was the voice I had heard, and though the tone was apparently light, there was a deeper earnestness in it than when speaking before. The same voice, and the speaker was Carlton Aberthnay.

"Forgotten?" I repeated dreamily. "No, I have a vague, indefinite idea of having met you somewhere before—in some other world, perhaps. It seems a lifetime since, but it will serve for an introduction."

"Take my arm," he answered, or rather asked, "and let us bring up the books for that lifetime; for a new lifetime begins now!" This last half spoken, half murmured, wholly exultant.

So arm in arm we paced up and down the long rooms, and in his rich voice, his radiant beauty, in his joyous words I found such pleasure as I had not known for many a day.

"Ah, I have been roving around everywhere," he said, answering my inquiries. "It seems rather absurd to talk of a soldier's life in such times as these, when our eagle looks so dovelike, but mine has been almost a live existence these two years past. It is quite promising, I assure you! But do tell me by what strange chance Mr. Vane was ever induced to put his foot into this city of abominations; has he gone into politics?"

I laughed for answer.

"O, he scorns them," he said, interpreting my laugh. "Don't let him grumble, then, if things don't go to suit him. It's a burning shame, the indifference with which Northern men let the 'vulgar crowd' settle all affairs of state. Why, after a little it will be highly disreputable for a respectable man to hold a government office, which will be bad for us."

"Government rolls along comfortably enough," I answered. "I can't blame men like uncle Tom for being unwilling to worry about its incomings and outgoings so long as it comes and goes as prosaically as at present. But don't let us waste our precious time upon subjects so unworthy. I am more than disgusted with Washington already."

"And how is every body in L——?" and so on, gossip, small talk about works, paintings, music, men, and women, now and then something a little graver; so our talk ran, until my uncle Tom returned for me, and as Mr. Aberthnay was of old an exceeding great favorite with my uncle, he lacked not the most cordial invitations to become almost domesticated with us, invitations which were most quickly accepted.

As I thought now, sometimes, of the days when I had looked upon Mr. Aberthnay as a lover, it seemed as if they were days in a dream. No word, no look that could bring back that time ever fell from him to startle me; and enlivened by his ever-animated spirits, interested in his plans, as no one who heard him talk could help being, I soon found myself yielding to the magnetism of his cheerful influence, and counted every party dull of which he did not make a part. No woman will believe me if I say I saw with pleasure that he had overcome his boyish fancy for me; no one will believe me if I say I saw, with unmixed satisfaction, that however much we were together the old feeling gave no sign of reviving. We tell these men to forget as a matter of duty, but we are not expected to see, without a little surprise or mortified vanity, how readily they obey us.

He was called my lover everywhere: there are few greater annoyances than this of having one's name always coupled with that of one who is more than friend, and less than lover; to whom the world will positively engage you, or absolutely demand that you shall count him not even an acquaintance.

He was not my lover, yet I knew he had a reverence for me that I had never seen him yield to any other. I knew he recognized me at my best, with a tender, protecting, manly forgiveness for all my weaknesses. I knew if he *did* love me, he would love

4*

me as I had fancied I loved Gilbert—as far as a man conscious of his manhood can so love—as if mine not his were the greater soul; an unhappy love for both man and woman, for it is her sweet right to lose herbeing in his.

One day, it was the last before I was to leave for our summer home, there had been a meeting of influential men, apparently for social enjoyment, but really for graver purposes. My uncle and Mr. Aberthnay had gone, and I was alone nearly all day. It was a restless day, warm before one is ready for warmth, a day with summer's languor without summer's beauty, a day in which one's life hardly seems worth fighting for. That day, at twilight, after the meeting, Carlton Aberthnay, with a rush of words which I could not stay, told me that he still loved me—not timidly, almost hopelessly, as of old, but powerfully, determinedly, with a love that would never cease. Gently he told me, but terribly.

I could but beg him to hush, to spare me.

"Spare you, Georgie? Is it so dreadful to love and to know it? One word—"

"No, no, I cannot say it." I moaned, thinking of his pain, and the wrong I had done him in letting this thing go on.

He saw, at last, my heart was not for him; and when he saw there was pain beyond any maiden coyness, he stayed his words of entreaty, asking me only to tell him why it pained me so.

"Because," I answered, "because I should have known this; I should have been strong enough to deprive myself, for your sake, of the society that has been so pleasant to me."

"Do you imagine you could have done any thing to change me? You could, indeed, have taken away the joy of being with you, but you could have taken away none of the love wherewith I have loved you from the first, and will love you as long as I live in this world, and, if God so permits, in the next."

"I must not listen to you," I said. "I am incapable of loving any one, and it is not right that I should hear such noble words. I have done you wicked, bitter wrong; you should do nothing but hate me."

"I can do nothing but love you, Georgie," he said, "but love you and reverence you all the days of my life. Not incapable of loving! do not say that, but not loving because there is no one worthy of your great heart. I, least of all; I have never for one moment dreamed myself worthy, but I did dare to think my love for you might make me less unworthy. I have tried to think if I knew one better than I who loved you, could I stand by and let him take what I dared not hope to win, and I knew I could not do it; I must seek you, you only. But do not look so frightened. I love you, I seek you, I wait for you, but I shall not persecute you, in word or thought; do not think of me as of one sorrowing, but as one glad to have loved you, even though loving in vain. This is all. I would not pain you for the world."

Had he said more I could have resisted better; but my own reproaches, his resolutely-suppressed words, his gentle forbearance to probe my wound, were almost more than I could bear.

Soon I spoke more plainly, telling him, not that I had loved any other, for I had persuaded myself that I had not ; but that deepest, firmest friendship, was all I could ever give him, or indeed any one. Then he plead for that in exchange for the love he offered me, and I strove with him for himself against himself, implored him not to let me weakly consent to do him this terrible wrong. But my words no longer availed; and so, at last, wearied with the day's languor, and listening to the voice that pleaded so sweetly, believing I could make him a true and trusty, if not a fond and loving wife, I choked down the expostulations of my conscience, and the forebodings of my heart, and became Carlton Aberthnay's promised wife."

"Not promised," he said; " nothing more shall you promise me than that I may love you, may be near you, may live in the light of your presence. I will not do you the wrong to take a promise so urgently entreated, so almost forced from you. But I will love you, I will follow you, I will live for you until such day as your heart turns against me; and then, dearest Georgie, do not hesitate to send me away."

"I shall never send you away," I answered; "so long as you are satisfied with that which I told you is yours, has long been yours, so long shall I, too, be yours."

The duty was less wearisome than I had feared; I ground down my conscience, and at last it ceased to reproach me; I began to forget that I did not love Carl, and to live willingly, eagerly even, in his love, his ardent, unselfish love.

Time went by lightly enough, when, sitting under our brave Massachusetts' elms, I poured out all my thoughts to him as I had never done to any other. Often and often had I longed for this; a manly mind in communion with my own, not for love, but cultivation. His letters were treasures of literary taste, and full of thoughtful interest, apart even from the unvarying devotion which was the undercurrent of every thought and expression. I lived in the varied scenes through which he passed; I felt that I knew those whom he met and cared for, and scarcely considered if the myriad fancies which clustered around our correspondence were mine or were his. But here it ended; mine was only an intellectual pleasure in writing; he, poor fellow! opened his heart and showered its wealth of love on me, and received never a word of love in return, for I was scrupulously exact in all I gave, or seemed to give. With his native delicacy he made no complaint, although it must have pained him deeply. Once he wrote. me, however: " Your letters are beautiful ; were they not even from you, I think I could never tire of reading them. They are really works of art, but works no more for me than they might be for any other."

And again : " Among all these fresh, fragrant flowers of your fancy, what unutterable joy if there should be found one little heart blossom that had bloomed for me only; one leaf or bud from your great wealth of such to be worn ever in his heart whose life is in yours."

Still I did not realize the yearning which thus murmured to me. I lived in a cold, selfish mood, rather proud of the fervid, romantic way in which he loved me, never thinking love could be forced, however gently; never questioning to which my heart were best given, never straining to the higher soul, the knightly soul that loved me, " not Lancelot nor another." I was startled into momentary warmth only when I was obliged to feel that no man's love can be long preserved without some slight hope of return; clinging to Carlton as my all in the world, this thought always frightened me. But I kept even that passing glow out of my letters. I meant to be just to him, and never to deceive him, never to feign what I did not feel. It did not occur to me to feel what I would not feign.

CHAPTER IX.

THERE were gay times when "Miss Georgie's" engagement came to the knowledge of the household. Kate in a silk so stiff that her every motion made my headache, came down especially to congratulate me. Of course, she had known all about it all along; she always knew I liked him; she had said to Mrs. Glynn, "Just you take my word for it, Mr. Aberthnay's the man;" *some* people had thought that I was going to have Gilbert Stuart, but she had known better, she had: I was never going to be a farmer's humdrum wife, with two new dresses a season, and one silk for Sundays, not I—I was no such fool as that—I had played my cards well, Kate thought, had got a real nice husband, and now she had only to hope my wedding dress would be a beauty. And then to think how many would be jealous, and what Mrs. Graham would say who had tried so hard to get Mr. Aberthnay for Florence, and what Mr. Stuart would say who had tried so hard to get me. The hypocrite! If she but knew how well I understood and scorned her for her duplicity!

Mr. Aberthnay had resigned his position upon my uncle's demurring about my marrying an officer; officers, you know, take excellently well with the ladies, but when I was young, guardians, uncles, and papas had a holy horror of the army; but Mr. Aberthnay's resignation removed my uncle's only shadow of objection, and as I could raise none, our marriage cards were ordered.

I went down to L—— for a few days before the time, while Kate, who was to be my first bridesmaid, kept house for my uncle in New York. Kate might well congratulate me on my marriage, for she was to take my place, a snug one enough, in my uncle's homestead, as she had already taken my place elsewhere. No, not that; she could never fill my place in either capacity. It rained nearly all the time I was there, dull, dreary November storms; I was glad enough to leave the old house that would never see Georgie Vane again. Mrs. Glynn, the housekeeper, would not let a thing be taken from my room; it must always look just so, she said, to welcome me when I came home for my visits. We went all over the house together, I giving her some little memento for each of the servants, until we came, at last, bonneted and cloaked to the hall, when she said: "Please, Miss Georgie, you've been so good, you've remembered all—even poor Christy—there's one who you might remember."

"Whom?"

"Mr. Stuart, Miss Georgie."

Turning toward her angrily, I answered: "I have nothing for him."

"Oh! any thing, Miss Georgie, that I could give him some time; I needn't say you told me, Miss."

My eyes fell wistfully on the little black cabinet, I even put the key in to open it, but I remembered. "No, Mrs. Glynn," I said, rising and speaking resolutely, "I am going to marry Mr. Aberthnay, I must not think of any one else. But here," I added, taking off a ring that Mr. Stuart had won at a Fair, years and years before, and given to me, "give this to Miss Kate on her wedding-day. Tell her Mr. Stuart gave it to me." She took it wonderingly.

"But Mr. Stuart—" she urged.

"*I hate him!*" I answered, stung by her perseverance. "I hate the very sound of his name!" She sprang toward me, holding her hand before my mouth, a freedom which startled me more than words or shrieks could have done. I saw that she turned her eyes toward the parlor door. I had not time to ask her what it meant, before a pale face passed between me and the light.

"I did not intend to hear—" he began, then paused. "You are quite right, Miss Vane; I did not know you were going so soon. I hoped to have made you a call earlier, but was detained. Shall I see you to your carriage?"

He did ; for I had no power to move or speak.   He pushed in my dress gently, closed the carriage door, raised his hat, and the carriage moved on.

I looked at Mrs. Glynn.

" Please don't be angry with me," she said half crying, " I always fancied you had a liking for each other, and I thought may be at the last minute it would come round ; so when he came past the house this morning I made bold to speak to him, and to tell him you was going away ; he said perhaps he would find time to see you, only perhaps, he said, you'd be too busy ; but I said no, and told him to come ; but I didn't mean no harm, only—"

" Life isn't a novel, Mrs. Glynn, and I hope you are convinced now that Mr. Stuart and I do not care for each other ? "

" Yes, Miss, now I know, but I didn't used to think it would come out so."

" You see he does not care for me," was all I could say.

" Yes, Miss, I seen it now ; but I hadn't then."

" What did he come up to the house for, then, if he didn't care for me," I exclaimed.

She looked at me amazed.   " I think it was my fault, Miss Georgie," she answered ; but I had regained my self-control, and said no more, hating myself, hating her, hating him, hating all the world.

But it was different when Uncle Tom and Mr.

Aberthnay met me at the depot, as glad to see me, both, as if I had been gone a year. My trousseau was almost finished; Mrs. Giddings had sent for more lace for my dress, and Mrs. Varney said my wreath would be superb—this was Kate's greeting, of course.

I had a grand wedding; my uncle looked upon it as the climax of his life, he wouldn't have had any thing wanting that money or labor could get, for the world. He and Kate seemed to feel very much more excited about it than we who were the most concerned; indeed, Kate seemed ever on the point of thanking me for my kindness in getting married, as if I had done it all on purpose for the gratification she found in fixing and fussing for it.

I do not know of what other people think when they are about being married, I know I thought more connectedly of the fitting of my dress, the trailing of the skirts, the falling of my veil, than any thing else; and I am sure if Mr. Aberthnay had told me the truth about his, it would have been of the ugliness of a modern man's "wedding garments."

At last I was dressed, and left alone, haunted by an undefined dread, nervous and restless.

But when I heard Mr. Aberthnay's eager step on the stairs, knowing that he had come for me, my heart almost failed me. He came in, every feature radiant with happiness.

I went forward to meet him, holding out my ungloved hands for the bouquet he had brought me, while he gazed upon me with pride and delight. Somehow his trust and happiness shot like arrows to my heart.

"Oh, Carl," I said, with more warmth than I had ever shown him before, "forgive me for this wrong to you."

"Wrong! oh, Georgie! Can you call that wrong which makes my whole life a song of thanksgiving for my unutterable happiness? I am not worthy that you should permit me even to love you—you, my peerless Georgie,—how infinitely less worthy that you should give yourself to me, to be mine, all mine, darling Georgie, forever and forever mine!"

"Hush, Carl! Only too soon you will find that I am only common earth, common clay; and you will blush for shame to remember that you ever thought me otherwise. Only too soon, Carl, you will become tired of me, reproach me for my coldness,—become negligent, indifferent, and then, Carl, what is to become of me?" For, with it all, I was fearfully jealous of his love; knowing my small claim, I was ever in terror of losing that which was all the love the world had for me.

"Reproach *you*, my pride, my joy, my love! How cruelly you judge me! Say, Georgie, do you think that man lives who could woo you from your happy home, where every love and care were lavished on you, even to look upon you with less than unutterable gratitude and adoration? Trust me, Georgie, my love is warm and great enough to shelter you forever. Every day it must increase, for every day, already, I love you more than before. Come to me, then, fearlessly, Georgie, as to one who only prays to spend his life in loving you."

"You will tire of that, Carl; and how, then, can I keep you—I, who am so cold, so undemonstrative? Oh, no, Carl, it must not be. I cannot return you any thing worthy of your great, boundless love."

"It wishes no return, dearest Georgie, save your own free return. Is it not of itself happiness beyond words to be with you always, and to love you always?"

"Always!" I repeated, clinging to him, whose caresses, in a few hours I could no longer refuse.

"Fear not," he said, fondly; "when the blessed words are spoken, God will turn your heart to me, and we shall be forever happy."

My conscience was not satisfied, my fears were not calmed; the more he told me of his love the more I longed for it, trembled to lose it, and yet felt my own unworthiness. I felt old in the ways of the heart, feeling like one who takes from a child his fresh, trusting innocence.

Looking down on me, he seemed startled.

"Georgie," he said, "tell me, are you forcing yourself to this? It is not too late. Georgie, fear not to answer. Would I not die here at your feet, and count it bliss so to die, rather than cause you one instant's pain? Would I accept any happiness at the cost of a pang to you? And perhaps it is better; who can tell into what sorrow and pain I am leading you? who can tell what shadows, dark and heavy, may gather around the home to which I take you? Oh, Georgie, I have not dared think before that even blood and death may fall to my lot, for you to share with me. Now that I feel how dear you are, I tremble before the thought. How I have wronged you!"

This was enough; I shrink from danger or grief! I fear to breast life's angriest wave by my husband's side! If there were storms ahead, then well for him to have the one he loved by him. "Danger or sorrow will but bind us the closer," I said, and hid my face against his heart, pressed his hand firmly in mine, and when I looked at him again every shadow had passed away, his eyes were misty with unshed tears of joy, and his lips trembled with gratitude.

And so we went down through the long line of bridesmaids and attendant grooms; went on until we stood before the high altar in the crowded cathedral, —in the crowded cathedral, fragrant with the choicest flowers, brilliant·with myriad lights, melodious with the richest music.

The last echo died away, every breath was hushed

as the words were spoken. His deep " I will " rolled on my ears terrible as some loud, prolonged thunder-peal. My own, spoken low and firm, they told me afterwards, sounded to me as if echoed by a thousand mocking voices. But the words were spoken, there was no recall, and we went down the long aisle *man and wife.*

CHAPTER X.

It was hard to see my poor Uncle Tom breaking down at the last, and pushing me into the carriage with something between a blessing and a jest; harder still to hear Kate's violent professions of sorrow and affection; but I forbore resistance, letting her have it her own way, wondering if she fancied I could be so easily deceived. All the partings came to an end, at last, and Carl and I departed.

We went down to the plantation, and lived happily as might be. More loving and more tender bridegroom could not be. Every luxury that the most boundless devotion could devise was lavished upon me by him, who, though my husband, was still my lover.

There were all the novelties of Southern institutions to interest me,—the freedom of Southern life to employ my energy, curiosity, and love of scenery; while each particular negro seemed a "character" to my unaccustomed eyes.

Nothing at first struck me more forcibly than the

wonderful capacity of the negroes for enjoyment. Notwithstanding their hard-working, aimless lives, so burdensome as to seem calculated to deaden every spark of spirit within them, they entered with the zest of children let loose from school into all the festivities designed to celebrate their master's marriage. Never shall I forget my first sensations as their dark faces suddenly appeared before me, intent, no doubt, on no thought but a fair look at the new " missus," but seeming to me ominous of shadows and clouds in my new home.

I could not enjoy their hilarity; it was to my views so forced, so soulless, and unnatural. All shams were and are alike to me; no clown ever aroused my laughter,—no circus antics ever gave me any feeling but of pain for the performers; and so now I breathed freer when there came an end to the "festivities," that is, the well-arranged farce, in which the expert manager exhibits his sable troupe for the especial edification of benighted Northerners visiting the sunny South, who seeing, return and write ponderous volumes about the gay and affectionate negro, as seen in the charming light of the patriarchal system. We know better.

They are a sensitive race, these poor black slaves, quick to see through your actions and your motives, through your mask to your heart; and although I treated them with uniform consideration, never over-working them, never letting them suffer for any care in health or sickness, never speaking harshly to them, never even raising my voice in sternness to them, I found they loved me not half as well as they would others, whom I myself have heard talking to them with a vehemence which would shame our sharpest tongued northern virago; and not only *talking*, but I have seen fair and gentle women, soft-eyed, sweet-hued, angelic-seeming women, like the blue-eyed heroines of men's novels, redden their lily hands by repeated applications to dark, offending faces, in spite of which the affectionate victims are ever ready to sacrifice their lives, their all on earth, to them, to these same relentless persecutors.

My husband only smiled at the horror these "fair ladies'" conduct excited in me. My husband, who would have forgiven me any crime upon earth sooner than an unfeminity; who would have avoided as he would a scorpion, the daring woman who stepped enough from' her sphere to be observed, to be criticized, to be lauded even; with his delicate, sensitive, refined, fastidious nature, smiled at the things which would have turned away the roughest northern farmer! It was the inevitable consequence of the "institution," he said; "the women were as kind-hearted gentle creatures as need be; the thing was necessary; a negro takes to whipping, he don't know how to get along without it."

That might be; but no lash fell on woman's shoulders, no hard words, no harsh voice on any ear, while I was their mistress. My conduct was actuated by the pride and self-respect which scorned to insult those who were beneath insult and beyond the power of resentment, and in due time they came, meekly as lambs, under my government, fearing my quiet voice as much as they feared the cellar or the lash. My heart never warmed to them. I knew it was our own sin which had brought them there, our own sin which we must expiate in tears of blood; but I could not forgive them that, innocently, they had caused the sin. They felt this, they knew my heart was sealed to them, poor creatures, watching my every movement with a painful desire to anticipate my every wish. One who had governed them in the same way from kindness instead of pride, would have been almost as a goddess to them, led as they are blindly by their hearts, out of which the warmth never dies.

But beyond all horrors, and, Yankee-bred, I found plenty, was that inspired by my first sight of the field-hands as they came slowly in,—men and women together, staggering from heat and exhaustion, the latter scorning to moan, though visibly almost sinking to the ground; a stern, *morne* set of women, looking as if they had become too hard even to curse their fate. I felt something like sympathy for them, standing upright, upheld by innate strength, statue-like, awaiting each her turn to have her work weighed and her day's toil ended, to be free to throw themselves, like logs, upon the floor, muttering now and then a bitter oath or two before they turned sullenly to the wall. I went down to them and spoke to them as one woman to another. I could do it easily to them, easier than to many a fair white lady in her beauty and wealth.

"Carl," I said, one night, "you must not have women work on the plantation. It is cruel."

"They only work when we are pressed, and are worth as much as the men."

"It is not a question of their worth, but of your humanity."

"Nonsense, Georgie; you must get these Yankee ideas out of your head, or they will make you trouble. Nobody on my plantation has much to complain of. Grimes says the rascals are as fat and lazy as the day is long. I am not a hard master. Will not every slave I have tell you there is no easier master than theirs for miles and miles around?"

"But it is not other men's actions that you should take as a standard, but your own sense of right. It is an outrage upon Christianity, upon human nature itself, to allow a woman to work at such labor, under the burning sun, and your barbarian overseer."

"Forever down upon poor Grimes! Why, Georgie, you ought to have unqualified admiration for him; he is a countryman of yours, that is, a New Englander. He gets more work out of those lazy fellows than any other overseer in the county, beats us Southerners all hollow."

"I do not doubt it. A Northern man, bred to Northern morality, never sinks to such dirty work until he has thrown away all ideas of civilization and decency."

"You are hard; but, come, have one of Jack's cobblers, and let the niggers go; too hot a subject for such a confounded hot day."

"But I cannot let it go, Carl; I cannot sleep while those hard faces are.in my mind; they perfectly haunt me. I supposed it was only the Legrés who had such assistants."

"You are too kind-hearted Georgie."

"I am not kind-hearted. I come to you in the extremity of dread; I cannot dare to think of peace here or hereafter, while such things go on. Do, Carl, for my sake, if not for a better motive, send away Mr. Grimes; let the women leave out-of-door work to the men, and—"

"You and I take to farming,—eh, wifey mine?"

"You shan't laugh at me, Carl."

"And you *shan't*," mimicking my broad Yankee *a*, and laughing up to my eyes. "And you shan't worry me about these things. There isn't such a long life before me, that I can afford to lose one sweet minute in any thing but happiness with my queen of wives. Hush! not a word. I am too good-natured and lazy;

the first I know, you, with your terrific Yankee energy and *vim*, will prove a perfect despot over me."

"You shall not turn me away," I answered; "I am not going to be put off with pretty speeches; I am in earnest, speaking from my heart."

"Well, Georgie, I do not doubt that many things strike you, a stranger to our ways, as rather hard, more especially as just now we are in such a state that we have to work things harder than ever before; but when you know us better, you will see that we do our best considering the circumstances. Fancy now that I should do as you ask me, and you know, Queen Georgie, there is nothing that you could ask that it is not happiness for me to do, if it is only in my power; fancy now that I should in this, our busiest season, send away Mr. Grimes and release those few women, what would be the consequence? In place of the women for whom there is no other possible work, I should have to get some more men, which is a thing out of the question,—I cannot afford it. Next I should have to find a successor to Grimes, no easy matter, and all the time spent in searching so much time lost; the best I could get would, I am certain, be so much inferior to him, that half a dozen extra hands would not more than make up the difference. When times come better and things get easier, you will not have to ask this twice; but now it will not do. Grimes is a good fellow; he knows I would discharge him in an

hour if he was cruel to the hands; he is a thorough
and a superb manager; he takes a world of care off my
shoulders; so let us leave him to get things through in
his own way; and now, Georgie—

> ——'Since in wailing
> There's naught availing,
> But death unfailing
>   Must strike the blow;
> Then for this reason,
> And for a season,
>   Let us be merry before we go!'"

"But, Carl," I urged, "what do we want of so
much money? Do you suppose I want useless fine
things obtained by money coined out of the tears of
my own sex."

"If there's one thing that I hate more than another," interrupted my husband, "it is to hear you
call those black beings of *your* sex. Let me implore
you to spare me that pain. You, the very perfection
of beauty, grace, and intellect! God's fairest, proud-
est, noblest handiwork, and those——. There's your
Northern cant—'Am I not a man and a brother?'—
good enough for your Garrisons and your Phillipses,
but thorough cant—what man or woman of those
abolitionists ever meant a word of this? I hate cant;
but I answer your question, 'What do we want of so
much money?' Georgie, we have a use for all our
money, which it would make your blood cold to hear.

'Coined out of tears,' you say,—it will be coined out of better life-blood than that of black slaves one of these days. But not yet, perhaps never; do not think of it. Forgive me, darling Georgie, if I seem unkind to you,—you, who are dearer than life itself; but, trust me, I am not hard-hearted, and what I can do for my slaves I am glad to do; but to make any change, however slight, in their condition, might endanger more than my property."

"How so, Carl."

"A certain set of men in the South, Georgie, in order to prevent the people from being disgusted with slavery, and to keep the South united in one interest, in order to further their own ends, social and political, have taken advantage of the Northern detestation of slavery, and the imprudent expressions of a certain set of fanatics at the North, to make our people jealously, morbidly sensitive on the subject which is our perpetual bone of contention. Lately it has become imperative on us to be as one man,—this, our common interest, is the tie that binds us in spite of all opposing thoughts and feelings; we have been worked up on the subject more assiduously than ever, and now it is not safe for one to do a humane or Christian act toward his slaves, especially if he is known, like me, to have a Northern education and a brave Northern wife; my smallest act would be magnified into an enormous abolition tendency, the crime of crimes down here."

"I never dreamed of this, Carl. I thought we lived in a free country."

"Not yet; but we shall make it so; the hour is almost at hand."

"Carl, I do not wish to penetrate your secrets, but let me entreat you to beware lest your enthusiasm and love for your own section, may be used to make you a tool in the hands of ambitious and designing men."

"A tool! Do I look like it? No, Georgie, wherever your husband goes he goes as a leader, be sure of that. I do not go into any thing blindly; this is no new thing, we have been brought up to it, to work for 'Southern rights.' You are amazed; you remember our conversation at your uncle's? I did not know then how much of reality there was in what I said. You laughed at me for a dreamer then—so would all your Northern friends; they have been too busy making money up North, to think what we were doing here; too much elated with their annual fleecing of the Southerners to see that we were not the easy fools we seemed."

"Carl, you terrify me."

"It is that which terrifies me. Oh! Georgie, if any thing should happen and you an exile from your early home, turned against this, and hating me, hating the fate which brought us together, perhaps! Oh, Georgie, how easily, how cheerfully, how proudly I could brave the world and death itself if you but felt

5*

with me, but sent me forth with your smiles and your blessings."

"Whatever you do, Carl, so it be nothing unworthy yourself, I, if you care for my poor prayers, shall never cease to give them."

"Bless you for that! But how can I ever hope to convince you of the justice of our cause while your Northen education and your Northern prejudices force you to see only that which is misled or mistaken in our lives? How can I show you the South as I see her, to-day writhing under the heel of the North, to-morrow baptized, it may be, in blood and tears, rising resplendent to her proper throne, radiant and pure, mistress of herself, queen of the far West?"

"Never, Carl. I see no picture of the kind. I see only that you, my husband, are following a will-o'-the-wisp to worse than death. Of what can you complain? The North for all its superior strength and talent, for all its greater power and position, is ever ready to kneel in the dust for you. Our Government has long been in your hands; we helped you elect the present President on purpose that no Northern influence should be used against you; he is bound by his office to administer his government fairly and impartially, knowing no North, no South. Has he done so? Who has a right to complain—you or the North? You give us our Presidents, we say humble thanks; you dictate our policy, we kiss your hands; you fill our places in the Cabinet, in the Army, at West Point, we are duly grateful, and now we are in the dust crying to you—'what more can we do?' You yourselves laugh at us for our servility, and dictate to us with all the arrogance of contempt. What more would you have?"

"That may be as you say, Georgie, but it does not suit us. The North outnumbers us, any day that it chooses to unite against us we are lost. But let us once become free of her, free to stretch *our* empire, and then!"

"And then?"

"Why, then, we shall become a great Southern Republic, and Madame North will have to be on her good behavior."

"Like the prodigal you want your share of the substance, and freedom to go off on your own hook awhile? Don't try it, Carl, or you may search in vain even for the husks of the corn which the swine did eat. Reflect, it is not one man who goes, nor ten, nor a thousand, it is the Union that is a Union no longer; and the sin, a terrible one, will be on your own heads."

"I deny any wrong about it. If South Carolina, or any other State which of her own choice went into the Union of her own accord goes out of it, my duty to her requires that I go with her."

"Is not Calhoun dead yet, or is it that the 'evil men do lives after them?' It *may* do for some to deny that our Union is a nation, but it scarcely does for you, Carl, a commissioned officer of the United States, educated by her to whom you have sworn allegiance, to plead any States Rights' sophistry.

"I have resigned my position in the United States Army; when I again take up the sword it will be as the—" he paused.

"As the enemy of the Government to whom you are indebted for that sword!" I added.

He did not seem pleased. I did not imagine my words were so little wide of the truth.

"Let us be happy while we can, Georgie," he said. "Leave arguing to your cousin Kate, and tune your voice to the music of which I can never tire," and he sent me to the piano.

CHAPTER XI.

Days came and went; dull days; little to do, little to see, little to read. I tried to interest myself in the new scenes around me, but, the summer gone, my heart pined for the white fields of snow the ice-hung trees, and the clear, cold starlight of dear New England—ever dear, but never so dear as when, sitting in my own new home, my hands clasped so as to conceal the wedding-ring, memory brought back the rosy skaters, the merry sleigh-bells, and the shouts of the boys dashing down the hills on their swift sleds, which had so often aroused my mirth. at home; *at home,*—would any place ever seem like home to me again! Thinking of the old days when a bright, somewhat hoydenish girl, I tramped through the snow to school, made snow men, or glided through labyrinthian snow-caves with a bright, red-cheeked boy, my constant companion, torment, and champion,—thinking of this, how tame and aimless seemed my present life!

"Your heart is not with us," my husband would say, if a shadow rested on my face; "patience, Georgie dearest, let the fierce March winds go by, and my prisoned bird shall breathe her native air again."

And for that I seemed to live. I counted the days until the spring should be at hand, and I could be once more in the arms of the old house.

No change had come over my husband's tenderness, but I was far from being his sole engrossing thought. Deeper things than I was permitted to know were being woven in my very house, which I, hands tied, could make no effort to sunder. .

A day or two before we were to leave, it was not long after the Charleston Convention, my husband brought some of its members home to dinner.

"Do not invite any one," he said to me; "let it be really *en famille*, and do try to keep that Grimes away. He has lately adopted a fashion of intruding his vulgar face whenever I have gentlemen here; I don't like it; and, Georgie"—this very wistfully—"Georgie, darling, it kills me to keep these things from you; I cannot deceive you, and we so much need your help, your quick observations, your tact, your ready woman's instinct; I want your brave heart and your noble soul to uphold and steady mine. But I have to shut up every thing in myself, away from you,—should it be so?"

"You can trust me, at least. It may be that I cannot agree with you, that I shall even be forced to condemn your work; but I can respect *your* motives.

I do not flatter myself I could aid your cause if I would ; but I can guard your honor."

"Then I need not fear to speak before you ?"

"Carl !"

"I mean that I did not know but you would consider your duty to your country would require you to betray your husband."

"I have been too often tried, as you know, and been proved too weak for any such Spartan virtues for you to fear me now."

"It is a great relief to me," he answered; "I am always afraid of your heroic, Puritanic New Englanders. I do not care how hardly you blame us to our faces, so you keep our secret. You will have to meet all sorts of men, Georgie darling, men that I hate to have to breathe the same air with you, men that I shrink from meeting myself; but I know you will understand that it is necessity."

"I never mind that sort of thing, Carl; if men are vile and base, I feel it if they are ever so smooth and polished; but most men have something endurable in them, so do not worry for me. Are you to have a set of *diplomats* to dinner to-day ?"

"They will be somewhat in that line, I must confess; insignificant, common-place men they may seem to you, and they probably are not broad-minded, but each has his allotted work, and through that may one day be famous. I shall tell you no more of them or our plans, but let them develop themselves; only this, whatever is said, answer as you choose; I will not have my wife restricted at my own dinner-table. There are things that will seem strange, perhaps repulsive to you, but I trust to the largeness of your intellect to know such things must be, and to make allowances for all; and, remember, we see our own side of the shield as clearly as you yours."

"You do not seem to have succeeded over well in your conventions," I said, at dinner, to relieve an embarrassed silence, or a more embarrassing attempt at small talk among the gentlemen. "Are good men and true men so scarce that you could not find a worthy candidate among them?"

"It was a sad affair," said one, without lifting his eyes.

"Mrs. Aberthnay," said my husband, significantly, "although of Northern birth, is very free from Northern prejudices; and though she will not let me, quite yet, call her an earnest friend to our cause, she is, at least, a noble and trusty foe."

Every one looked relieved, and a gentleman next me offered me his hand; "such a foe speedily becomes a friend," he said, "we welcome you."

"I shall not allow myself to be called your opponent," I said, "until I see something I must oppose."

"We shall not break our hearts over the fate of the Charleston Convention," one said, who seemed to be their leader, and whose name was Layton, I think. "We are going to be good, and let the North elect her own president for this term."

"Provided he is of our choosing," said a Lieut. Gwynn, one of my husband's classmates at West Point.

"I don't think we need trouble ourselves," answered Mr. Layton; "Abraham will be an excellent patriarch for us as for the North. He was especially made for this emergency, if I know the man; we'll let the North have him to its heart's content."

"But he is the Republican choice," I said.

"Most fortunately, we think, some of us—most fortunately, Mrs. Aberthnay, for us, they have chosen the very man who will help us best," answered Mr. Layton again. "We think him, some of us, an obstinate, self-willed, ignorant third-rate attorney. You mustn't mind our saying it, you know, because he may turn out a second Washington, whom, by the way, I never considered any very great shakes of a man. Yes, he is the Republican choice, and if we can only get him elected we are all right."

"But even granting the man to be a fool," I said, "how can you be willing to have a Republican President?"

"Because, my dear lady, we want only one more wrong to perfect our plans. To speak plainly to our *trusty foe*, every thing is ready for the explosion; we only want the match to start it."

"And the insult of a Northern President—" began Lieut. Gwynn.

"Stimulated, encouraged, and completed by yourselves," I added, "is to furnish that match? It strikes me, gentlemen, that a work commenced with so much —duplicity" I intended saying, but seeing my husband's anxious face, I changed the word to "address," "cannot but succeed. But do you think Mr. Lincoln will be elected?"

"Beyond a doubt," answered a small-featured fiery seeming little man on my right, who had not before spoken. "They will elect Abraham Lincoln; they will dare force on us a Black Republican President; a rail-splitter, a low-bred, vulgar backwoodsman, for our ruler!"

"Good!" cried Lieut. Gwynn, "work that up into an editorial to-morrow; it will tell; it is very suggestive, that is; one could make a lot out of that."

"Not so fast," interposed Mr. Layton, "who knows but the Yankees will take you at your word, and be afraid to put up a vulgarian, like Abe."

"There is no danger; Abraham is the New England Coriolanus; they like the idea, it is a new one, and they will stick to it. Besides, too, many of my beloved brethren of the press know what they are about."

"That's your department, friend Risley," Lieut. Gwynn said; "you wield the pen and I the sword."

"It will not come to that," remarked Mr. Layton.

"It may," replied my husband. "At all events we must expect it. We may never need to strike a blow; but we must be prepared to strike many, and perhaps to lose our heads for it."

"Very improbable," returned Mr. Layton, who was evidently a man of peace. "I doubt if it will be more than the settling of a few law questions, and the display of a few tricks by that excellent attorney, Abraham Lincoln. What think you, Mrs. Aberthnay? Will the North let us go in peace, do you think?"

"How do you mean ' go ?'" I asked.

"Orderly, quietly, and according to law, if they will let us; with flourish of trumpets and roll of drums, if they will not."

"This is something so unexpected and unsuspected at the North," I said, "that in the first surprise she might forbear immediate violence; but the peaceable separation of one State from the Union can never be."

"It is rather late in the day to talk of the chances," said my husband. "For my part, I want no peaceable separation. I am for war—war to the knife."

"And I!" cried the Lieutenant.

"Easy, easy, gentlemen," Mr. Layton said; "better any thing than war until our new Confederacy is well bound together. What we want is to establish the precedent, make the Union acknowledge the right of a State to secede, and we have the Southern and

Border States sure; by and by we will take in the Middle States, and sweep downward to the Gulf. Then we may fight any nation on earth, not now."

"So you don't mean to take in New England?" I asked.

"Not if we know ourselves. New England has been the skeleton in our closet long enough; if we take her in ever, it will be by conquest," said Mr. Layton.

"Then you bid her an eternal farewell!" I exclaimed.

"New England, indeed!" broke out Lieut. Gwynn. "Better than sweeping down to the Gulf, as Mr. Layton says, would it be to see South Carolina and Massachusetts arrayed for a fair field and fight against each other. I'd bet my all on the issue."

"The Massachusetts men will make the best fighters in the North," my husband remarked.

"I should judge the Western men would do better," I said; "they are so rugged."

"For some reasons you are very right, Mrs. Aberthnay," said Mr. Layton, who, courteously, made me all the explanations. "An army must fight for a principle, and the better the principle is understood the more it will affect the fighters. Besides, the *morale* is half its power, and a New England man, whose will is stronger than any other emotion belonging to him, must fight well if he fights at all. The Westerners are more hardy, it is true. If I were to lead an army

I would rather have moral courage and physical cowardice than the reverse, to command. How is it, Captain, am I right?" he added, to a gentleman who had
spoken but little, and that altogether to my husband.

"Right, sir!" was the laconic reply from the Captain.

"I count very little on help from the North," my
husband said, after some minutes of silence.

"And I every thing!" cried Mr. Risley; "we have
many zealous friends at the North, initiated and otherwise; but for them our glorious undertaking could
never come to its culmination."

"How is that?" I asked.

"Northern merchants supply us with arms and
ammunition—"

"Has it come to that?" I exclaimed.

"Come to that? Why, my dear lady, it has been
at that this many a day. As I was observing, or about
to observe, the Northern press, partly with knowledge
and partly in ignorance, form public opinion, and
there is often a big swing around our way; Northern
merchants, who would sooner lose all the flags in
Christendom than the patronage of one Southern firm,
are on their knees begging to serve us. We have not
been these twenty years building a grand conservative
party there for nothing. We have made it, formed it,
moulded it, and fashioned it round about, and now
hold it in our hands. You will find in a few months a

host of Northern writers, speakers, and demagogues generally, fighting lustily for us."

"This thing has gone far," I said.

"Almost to the end," one answered.

"And, gentlemen, just among ourselves, what do you expect the world to say of you?"

"As it does of all schemes: if successful, just; if unsuccessful, infamous.

"And your consciences?"

"Applaud us!" answered my husband, enthusiastically.

The Captain here showed some interest in the conversation.

"And history?" I continued.

"Will judge us as the world judges," replied Mr. Layton, "according to our success."

"Successful or failing," I asked, "will it forgive you for the infinite misery your movement may cause? Will it forgive you for the blood of the bravest and the tears of the purest? Will it forgive you for the loss of the noblest country whose story has even blessed its pages? Will it forgive you for rights invaded, for principles disregarded, for honor desecrated, for broken hearts, for lost lives, and vanished souls? If you have wrongs, remember no state or society ever had less; remember, to right them would infinitely multiply others; if you are ambitious, remember ambition may soar to heaven or lower to hell, choose yours. Let the good of humanity decide you, let the tears of countless widows move you, let the sorrow of unborn generations plead with you, for, successful or failing, truth and justice will pronounce you rebels and traitors."

My husband looked at me aghast; the Captain was silently balancing a spoon; the others looked not over-pleased, and in this manner we left the table.

"I have given my homily, and eased my conscience," I added; "Mr. Aberthnay will give you cigars, and by and by I will give you coffee and music, which I hope you will like as well as either."

The Captain went to the door with me, and even followed me out into the gallery. Here he paused and handed me a letter. "I have not quite known whether or not to send it," he said; "you have decided me not, and you deserve to know your victory. After reading, please destroy it."

I understood the letter moderately well: it was the resignation of his commission. I remember the name very well, *James Belton*, written in large round letters, perfectly characteristic of the Captain, as one knew at a glance.

"For God's sake, Georgie," whispered my husband, preceding the others into the parlor, "atone for that cruel speech."

I saw already its uselessness; I understood that I was endangering, for no purpose, my own and my husband's security. Poor fellow! had I not already wronged him enough? So I did my best to make up for that which I had said. I promised the Editor letters from the North; I played chess with Lieut. Gwynn, let him beat, and complimented him on his skill. "It may make you a General one of these days," I said. I sang Mr. Layton's favorite songs, and when they were all in better humor with me, I went into a heavy political argument with them, and allowed myself to be almost vanquished, which is as much as one can expect of a New England woman.

"We shall have you an enthusiastic Southerner soon," said Mr. Layton.

I shook my head.

"I am sure of it," he added; "I never ask more than to find my opponent open to conviction. You would be a good friend now, only I perceive Mr. Aberthnay has not set the arguments before you."

"Ah, you must not convince me," I said.

"We will let you off after that, Mrs. Aberthnay," the Lieutenant said; "that one sentence half promises surrender. The North itself will finish the work."

So, on the whole, they went away pleased, as men always are when they have demonstrated their superior minds.

I watched my husband long after the others had gone, as he lay back in his arm-chair lost in thought. He seemed to have grown years older in the few months lately passed. How he must have suffered, been suffering, while I, his wife, his only friend, kept her heart closed to him.

I went around to where he sat, softly, and laid my hand on his forehead; it was burning. Smiling up to me with that love which never failed, he laid his head over my heart. "Let me take a little of its care," I said; "I who give it so much."

"No, no, Georgie; it was of your care I was thinking; if we could only bear every thing together. Religious differences between my wife and myself was the only thing I used to fear; who would have thought so small a matter as politics, a subject which we once, do you remember, pet Georgie, thought unworthy of a few moments' careless thought, should now divide us!"

"I did not mean to speak so strongly," I said; "the words surprised me as much as they did you."

"I was not thinking of that; you could not help speaking as you did: they honored you,—Southern men always honor frankness; they respected the feeling which dictated your words. All of them, except perhaps Captain Belton."

"Did he not like it?"

"He was the only one who spoke of it. He said it was very doubtful if our fears had foundation; but that if they had, and this came to any thing, it was to be hoped Mrs. Aberthnay would be spared any contest

6

between her feelings and her actions; or some rounded, set speech of that import."

"Yet he spoke to me, and gave me a letter to destroy."

"He will have time to change his mind around again," my husband answered, after reading the letter. "I am glad he has left us; we want none with us who are not heart and soul in our cause. I am glad he has found courage to leave us."

"Oh! Carl, if you—"

"It is not possible, Georgie; my fate is firmly fixed. Do not worry me with pleadings. I have decided. Before we return from the North, it will be pretty clear what is to be done. If there is danger of trouble, I want you to remain with your uncle; to arrange every thing pleasantly for you will be one of my greatest comforts, one which you must not deny me."

"I must. Either with you here, or with you there. I shall not leave you under any circumstances."

"Georgie, do you remember once, in Washington, when we were dining at Mrs. Gaynor's, some one made the remark, that until a woman would lose her soul for one she loved, she did not love? Do you remember how shocked you were, and how much more shocked when I said you were just that manner of woman?"

"As I had a right to be. You know me better

now than to think me any such mad, passionate woman."

"Still, Georgie, can nothing make you love
me?"

"Can nothing less than such wicked folly content
you?"

"I do not want you to make sacrifices, more than
I can help, for me."

"If you loved me, Carl, you would know there are
no sacrifices in love."

"Then you will not leave me to battle this out by
myself?"

"Am I not your wife?"

"Always that! I hate your heroism! I do, indeed. I wish you were a great big baby of a woman,
who would fret at me, and cry, and scold, and go
into hysterics; any thing but this passive endurance
of every thing; this complete submission to my will
and my wishes! Isn't there any rebellion in you,
Georgie?"

"Not a particle."

"Then I'm to have your bodily presence, without
your sympathy? Well, I ought to be grateful!"

"You're a barbarian!"

"There, that's something like! If I were to fret
very much, perhaps in time you would call me a *brute*,
and then my happiness would be complete! What
are the chances, Georgie, pet?"

"That it will be well deserved, whether said or not."

"Better and better; have I driven you off? Well, to-morrow for the North. I have work enough to do there."

CHAPTER XII.

WE were not destined to get away without one more meeting with political men; for all day, nearly, my husband had visitors, and three joined us at our early dinner.

They had already discovered my existence, as I learned by the indiscreet loudness of a coarse voice, that, on the way to dinner, pronounced my name and and spoke of my natural qualifications as sufficient to do something which, I surmised, their arguments had failed to do. I did not hear my husband's answer, but I was convinced it was only a reply in words, and not at all prepossessed in favor of my guests by this little interchange of thought, I received my husband and them.

All three were strangers to me; an open-faced, soldierly man, Major Montreuil, sat on my right; a rather shabby but aristocratic-featured man, introduced as Mr. Beames, supported me on the other side; while a Mr. Miles, to whom the rough voice belonged, completed the number. I saw my husband was tired and worried, and I felt, myself, impatient to have the coming hour go by.

I was cross, which always, among those I dislike, makes me suspicious; and it was not long before I discovered that somebody was wanted to be added to their friends, who had, so far, resisted all allurements; and it was thought, as this somebody was socially inclined, a few womanly persuasions, properly disguised, might attain the desired result, and it would be, I fancied, a result of great importance to my husband's side. My well-known Northern birth and generally supposed Northern prejudices, and perhaps some natural tact, made me, I suppose, chosen to apply these " womanly persuasions."

Having quite satisfied myself of their desire, I amused myself watching their plans of attack. The Major, who was clearly an ambitious, dashing man, recognized something of similar qualities in me, and only doubted "if I had the grit to do this thing." I think Mr. Beames was a man of a higher order of mind, and must have known that I could not work except in conformity with my own convictions. Mr. Miles had implied his motive-key in his half-heard speech to my husband; for, after all, people judge us very much after the fashion of their own order.

"Well," said the Major, "things look much as if there was a prospect of a lively time before a year has passed. The days are approaching; they have already commenced, I may say, that make history, Mrs. Aberthnay. We are coming to the days that will make heroes of our countrymen, and days that raise up Rienzis,"—a half glance at my Roman-like husband—"and Ninas beyond the skill of any Bulwer to paint. What Scott, what Shakespeare, will ever exhaust the theme ?"

"If not Scott or Shakespeare," I said, "a Sylvanus and a Southworth. If you do no more, Major Montreuil, you will give the foundation for a new American literature. What is the old line: '*Blanche, Sweetheart, little dogs, and all,*' will have their bark at you, or the other side. There was a woman whom nobody knew, in New York, who saw fit to marry her father's coachman, who, likely enough, had as fair a start in life as many a worthy friend of the lady's father. One could not undertake to tell the books that were written on the subject; the veritable history of half a thousand, more or less, heroines, black-eyed and blue, tall and short, learned and simple, who devotedly loved and frantically married into the interesting social class designated as *grooms.* Think what a relief to our authors to have a GRAND SOUTHERN REBELLION to chronicle, instead of the now well-worn theme of domestic revolution."

"There is a world of meaning under Mrs. Aberthnay's jest," said my husband. "Our movement, be its end what it may, will give us a national literature.

We have very few late American books,—living, breathing American works; no hash of English and French romance, or ridiculous imitations of European society, but outright American books, with just such tastes, thoughts, and doings as we see surrounding us. I believe half of the success of Mrs. Stowe's *Uncle Tom's Cabin* lay in the fact that it was a genuine American book, which, even though it was hard upon *us*, we read because it belonged to us. We shall have a history, a national history, not a humdrum, worn-out story of Pilgrims and Plymouth Rocks. We shall have heroes now that will not only suffer and be patient, but toil and be strong. Altogether, I think we shall put some new elements into the minds of men living now, and leave something more than a name for ages yet to be."

"Who knows," said Mr. Beames, "the legends yet to cluster around our names,—the names of us who sit here, under Mrs. Aberthnay's eyes, that are half ridiculing and half inspiring our enthusiasm? If I can do no more, I will, at least, write a song, some of these days, for the populace to sing; for there's more power in the jingle of some popular rhymes than in half a hundred speeches. Witness the revolutionary 'Yankee Doodle!'"

"We are laying a glorious foundation," the Major now told us, having been too long kept from the charge by our skirmishing, "as Mrs. Aberthnay, under all her fine sarcasm does not fail to admit. I would like to get through all our coming battles with my life and my eyes, for the comfort of one day reading the attempts to do justice to the history that, as I said before, we are making. But who can ever do justice to the boldness, skill, and courage of our men,—to the wit, the beauty, and the heroism of our women?"

"You let in the woman element?" I asked.

"I should give up our cause as hopeless," he answered, "were there not in every rank and degree brave and beautiful women, with the address and the courage to aid us. Never was there a wider sphere for womanly work; and I know our Southern women will be behind none, Spartans though they may be, in showing this to be so. What a scope for their tact and their talent, their courage and their tenderness, while the weak are to be nerved, the vacillating to be steadied, and the opposed to be converted!"

The Major had opened his battery, but paused for ammunition, and in the pause Mr. Beames commenced his attack.

"Not common pride and ambition merely," he said, "should nerve and lead us in these days, but the thought that, through all ages, our names will be watered with the loving tears of a grateful people: the thought that our hands are sowing the seed that will ripen into eternal fruit."

"I fear, a poisonous fruit," I answered; "what bet-
6*

ter can spring from such seditious seed ?" Mr. Beames
had shot wide of the mark, and I saw my reply had
staggered the Major. Mr. Miles dashed into the conversation perfectly unconcerned by any thing I could
say.

"It ain't every one as can understand them high-
flown sentiments," he informed us. "Some do, perhaps, but we all has our motives. Some goes in, like
the Major, for the ' grit of the thing,' and for promotion,
like enough. Some goes in, like Mr. Beames, because
they hate the North, and do kind of believe the old
Union ain't exactly the thing."

"You make shrewd guesses," said my husband.
"How about the rest of us ?"

"I should say you, Mr. Aberthnay, take to the
thing because it's grand and romantic, and sounds like
Bruce and William Tell. I hope you'll get the glory,
sir. Some goes in, like Mrs. Aberthnay—"

"But I don't ' go in,' " I interrupted.

"But you will," he answered. "You've got the
nerve, and when your husband gets in a tight place
you ain't the woman to leave him there. You ain't a
going to crowd down all your fine ideas of things, and
leave Mr. Aberthnay down here among a parcel of
traitors, as you called us the other day."

"So you heard of that ?"

"Yes'm; and we knows very well it's what we'll
be called for a while yet. So you'll go in, Mrs. Ab-

erthnay, and you'll be worth a dozen men; and when you see what you can do you'll stay in."

"What takes you in, may I ask, Mr. Miles?"

"I go in, ma'am, for a beef contract the Major has promised me. That is in my own line, ma'am. We all has our motives."

"You are an observer of things, I see, Mr. Miles."

"Yes, ma'am; it ain't my way to go through the world with my eyes shut. I looks around and I sees heaps of things that maybe other people don't think big enough to count: I counts them." ·

"As you have seen so much of the world," said the Major, "suppose you tell us how we can take Fort Blank, in case we need it?"

"A dashing assault by a smart woman, and nothing else," he answered, clapping his hand upon the table. "The Captain is as afraid as death of women."

There was an awkward silence.

"I suppose you have travelled a great deal, Mr. Miles," I said, to break it.

"Never outside of Virginny until now, ma'am. Virginny's a likely old State."

"There will be lively times there one of these days, if we ever come to blows," my husband remarked; "Virginia and Kentucky will be our battle-grounds."

"I hope not," Mr. Beames remarked. " Virginia's more than a likely State, as our excellent friend observes; it is a noble old State, which even the Yankees admire. I cannot imagine such a thing as soldier-tents in view of those grand old mansions, unless placed there for a holiday parade. I never could see why any fault was found with Thackeray's '*Virginians*.' I think he gave the spirit of the State truthfully, and in a way to do her sons honor."

"I wonder if Kentucky will come over?" the Major asked.

"Has not our excellent going-to-be President an interest in Kentucky?" Mr. Beames interrogated.

"If so," my husband answered to both questions, "the worst will be that it will be neutral, which will do very well as a means of communication with the North, should harsh measures be used."

"You talk," I said, "as if your Mr. Lincoln were already elected, and had declared war against you."

"Elected he is pretty sure to be," responded the Major, "only you must not allow your Northern friends to crow over you in advance; declare war he never will, I am afraid."

"Afraid? You officers are so bloodthirsty!" I commented.

"It will be almighty tough work to carry Virginny," said Mr. Miles; "she's too near Ohio to have much pluck."

"Ohio is near enough to keep her straight, that's true," said the Major; "but we can count on one of her sons," smiling upon Mr. Miles.

"If Virginny goes, I goes," answered that gentleman; "I goes with my State."

"May every State that hesitates pay dearly for her cowardice!" the Major observed with emphasis. "Let them choose at once, and be open about it."

"No doubt we shall all pay dearly for our course," returned Mr. Beames. "No one ever attempted a reform of the most moderate dimensions without paying for it; but we have the glorious consolation of knowing that we buy our liberty cheap at any price, and we must be prepared for whatever may come."

"We shrink from nothing," my husband said, with a fire that made me proud of him; "we are prepared to sacrifice every thing except the principles which are dearer to us than life, even than those we hold dearest. I bid you farewell now, my friends, in doubt and indecision in regard to the future; but about one thing there can be no hesitation among patriots— *we will be free!*"

So we said good-bye, checked our trunks, and started for Boston.

At this point I am requested by an interested and evidently appreciative listener, to state what dress I wore upon this occasion. I am very sorry to disappoint any who have counted upon a blaze of diamonds,

but truth compels me to state that my dress was a
gray travelling-dress, very slightly trimmed with blue,
and that I had my hair plain, ready for my bonnet,
which had not then, you remember given place to
the present jaunty style of head-dress.

CHAPTER XIII

I WENT home to the North, but home to the North did not bring me childhood and its buoyancy, and I was still a weary woman, fighting something I called fate, but which others, if they knew, would call my perverse will.

I had a trial I had not anticipated; the world, my world, saw proper to go into raptures over my husband, so good, so brave, so accomplished! One would have supposed they wondered how he ever chose me. Then I was told, at every step, of his ·indulgence, his generosity, and his kindness to me; no one seemed to recognize that I was his equal as well as his wife, and that I took liberty and care as my due. Are our men savages that one should comment with surprise and admiration upon their every approach to civilization?

Oh! what aggravating people there are in this world! People with their little minds and their restless tongues, who make more misery than wars and famines and pestilences; people whom you cannot challenge to fair fight, nor satisfy with less then half your happiness, nor dose, nor doctor, nor diet! These were the people that widened the little brook between Carl and me, until it became, I feared, an impassable river. I feared, for, strange to say, I had not yet learned to hate my husband; I was not even careless of his love; whether it was my pride or my vanity, or some unknown emotion, I clung to his love; I was more tenacious of it, more fearful of losing it, than I could have been had I loved him. To have Carl's heart shut to me as mine was to him, was the one most agonizing thought of my married existence; and these people, with their homilies and their exclamations, their raillery at Carl's devotion, and their congratulations to both of us, bade fair to realize that burning fear of mine. I knew that the time must come,—all the world knows it finds a foothold often even where love has been, and never fails to reign in the unprotected places where Love has never set up defences,—the time when I should weary of Carl, should hate him really, long to have him out of my sight, and pray, if I dared, for the day to come that would remove every vestige of his influence, every sign of remembrance out of my life. I used to think, as by some strange fascination, of that day, and to picture myself bound to this man whom I no longer simply endured, but actively detested. You may think it drove me to an attempt at loving him, who was in every way so worthy of love, but I had long before resolved I could not love him; I had married him with his eyes and mine wide open to the fact; of course I could not change.

Few people will fail to start when I call that summer of 1860 a weary summer, for it was generally a gay season; more people went travelling than usual, and as they were warm but healthy months, the change of air and change of scene benefited all who had them, and looks and spirits prospered accordingly. Wide-Awake processions made the nights brilliant outside, and theatres and parties kept brilliancy within. People were lively, confident, and seemed to hold money lightly in their hands. How many, it hurts my heart to think how many, took their leave of joy, and ease, and sunshine that summer, to them so beautiful, and forbearing to prophecy aught that could dim its brightness. I toiled through it as best I might; I listened to the hollow talk of those around me, and I fancied I felt what prophets feel, when they stand within the gates of a city unconscious that destruction and wrath is coming speedily.

Carl and I were growing more and more distant to each other; the constant presence of visitors at my uncle's house kept us apart during a greater portion of the day, and when we found ourselves, without our will, in each other's presence, it was only to realize how far we were from that happy trust which the

world imputed to us; and we sat constrained and often
long silent, trying to think of things to say, which, if
thought and said, sounded so forced and hollow, that
we, as by a mutual agreement, came at last to give up
the attempt at conversation. I think Carl had greatly
counted on my visit North to bring us closer together,
by throwing me more upon his care; but it had had
the opposite effect, and we were both wearied nigh
unto death. And now Carl no longer sought my
love; more and more I saw he no longer let his eyes
rest on me with wistful tenderness, and that more and
more he grew abstracted and self-absorbed. It was
easy to see how it would end,—indifference on his
part, hatred on mine. I was not yet twenty-five years
old, and the prospect was not a pleasant one. My
husband,—through all he would be my husband still,—
might replace me with enthusiasm for his country, but
I had nothing to put where his love had been; and
while every hour that love was slipping like sand
through my fingers, the world cried out, " Oh, incom-
parable pair! Oh, noble husband and devoted wife!"

Just about so much does this world know!

Of my old friends nearly all were as I left them.
Kate was not married, and was travelling somewhere
•among the mountains; Mr. Stuart was in business in
New York; Mary Allen and Emma Lewis were both
in convents; Emma, among the Sisters of Charity. I
went to see her; I love these dear, Martha-like sisters.

There is magic in the very tones of their voice, magnetism in the touch of their hands,—those patient, never idle hands; and comfort comes with every step of those willing feet vowed to walk in ways of sin and sorrow and pain, untouched, unhurt, as the children in the fiery furnace.

"How did it come into your mind?" I asked Emma.

"I thought of it first," she answered, "that night at your uncle's, when we went in to see Mary Allen, do you remember? and for a while I thought of it as a pleasant dream, until it grew a longing, then a hope. I am a woman too much after the manner of Martha, and it was natural I should choose to join the Sisters of Charity, who have the love and the faith of Mary and the activity and solicitude of Martha. There is nothing,—I mean when I was in the world,—nothing touched me more than the simple unaffectedness of these dear Sisters; there is no bitterness, no contempt real or assumed, of the world they have left; it was a good world, they say, and they liked it, but they liked this life better; they are still a part of the world, still toiling in it, still breathing its air, though purified by prayer and good works. Another thing which is characteristic of our Sisters, they never affect to have been any thing while in that world; there are no half-dropped sentences, no conscious glances, no affected interest or indifference which intimates,—*I once was a lady with all these things that delight you, and more than these at my command.* Our Sisters have forgotten they ever lived a life of gaiety and of fashion; simply and quietly they have put on the dress of the Sisterhood, and if worn with old-time elegance, or with unaccustomed awkwardness, it is the same."

"You are right, Emma; I have seen these things, too. God bless dear Mother Seton, who brought these dear black caps to show us what women may be! These little things are mighty indexes, and they are so winning that one thinks no more than the lady herself of her position passed, but sees in her only a ministering angel, sweeter and lovelier in her charity than all the gold and gems of earth could make her without. If any thing should ever happen to Carl, I shall come here for rest, *rest*, the blessed, blessed word!"

"And you will not come in vain, Georgie; a nun's life would kill you I am sure, but our sisterhood will use all your talents and fulfil all your ambitions; there is no stagnation here. I am teaching now; by and by, after I have taken the black veil, I may be sent to some hospital. I long for that; my work is too easy here; this sentiment, however, lays me open to self-commendation; the first lesson we learn here is submission. And now, Georgie, of yourself; do you like the South ? What a question to ask, as if you would not like a desert *now*."

"Not in the least should I like a desert, married

or unmarried. I like the South as well as I expected; my life is very quiet and monotonous; nothing ever happens; my husband is never sick, and I am always well, so we are spared even the small excitement of an occasional visit from the country doctor."

"Is there not more than usual excitement about the elections? I hear the school girls talking about them occasionally."

"Yes, there is a great deal; the South threatens to secede if an abolition President is elected. Do not imagine, Emma, if you were fifty times a nun, that you have no duty left to your race and your country; the smallest duty you have is that of interest; you are to teach not merely a b ab, and 2 and 2 are 4, but to teach that fidelity to God absolutely requires loyalty to our country, a loyalty that binds women as well as men, Sisters of Charity as well as members of the Cabinet, girls at school and men in business, all ages and classes. A Catholic priest has no more right to give absolution for disloyalty unrepentant, than for robbery or perjury. You do not forget these things?"

"I may be a Sister of Charity," Emma said, "but I have not lost my country or my sex. More than ever am I taught to do my duty scrupulously, and next to my God is my duty to my country."

"You are a true, good woman, Emma, and I see that you will be elevated, not repressed, by this change in your life. I am going to say good-bye to you now, God only knows when I shall see you again, for no one knows what may happen within a year, nor where I may be, nor what wounded men, Northern or Southern, you may be nursing. Pray for me, Emma; I have some trials, I am hard and sadly in need of softening grace."

So I left Emma, one out of my old circle of friends, joyous and contented. Mary Allen I did not see; she belonged to a community of nuns who lived entirely within their convent walls, and lacked the genial light-heartedness of the Sisters, and I had no desire to see Mary growing "old and formal, fitted to her petty part."

My Cousin Florence, to my Aunt Graham's unbounded satisfaction, was married to a wealthy New York merchant. Hal was pursuing some other idol with the same ardor with which he had at one time followed Mary Allen. I saw Hal; he was fast approaching that period in the life of a gay young bachelor when the portion of parties that comes before supper, proves very tedious, when sweet eyes and graceful forms no more delight, when the last novel becomes stupid, the new singer a flat, and things altogether a bore, or as Mantalini elegantly observes, a *dem'd horrid grind.*

Uncle Tom, dear Uncle Tom, how much he loved me! was the same hospitable old bachelor as before, but he complained bitterly that Kate never gave him a decent cup of tea. He joined my husband in his solicitations to me to remain at the North during the winter; not that he believed there would be any trouble—for he pooh! poohed! the idea—but to ease Carl's mind, he said.

I was not so fierce against staying as I had been, for Carl was now so distantly, politely kind to me, that I sometimes half fancied he wished me out of his way, for his sake as well as for my own. Sometimes I thought if he were separated from me the old love, the old yearning, would spring up in the absence, and make him again my lover; but there was a possibility that he might like his freedom better and better, and that the separation begun in affection might end in life-long estrangement. You know I had not yet reached the point in our lives when I was to hate Carl, and so this possibility frightened me,—I could be frightened,—and made me shrink from the dreadful picture of myself, a mark for every one's wonder and astonishment: a woman neither maid, wife, nor widow. Considerable of the old spirit had died out; I could think in quite a listless way of Carl's going alone into danger and death, and of myself resting in peace and security; for after all, I was not sure I could make the danger and death less real and sorrowful by my presence.

You must not think Carl was unkind to me, for he was only too kind; every arrangement was made with special reference to my will and pleasure. He himself was always at my disposal to go or come as I chose, and he intended to prove himself kinder still, by never asking me of my heart any more than he would had I been another man's wife, a deference that was gall and wormwood to me. How could I break it? I certainly could not say, "Carl, make love to me." I could but wait, patiently as long as I could, then in anger and indignation.

Partly because I thought it might move him, and partly because I cared, or thought I cared very little what became of me, I yielded, coldly enough, to their wishes, and said, that as my duty was to obey my husband, I would of course remain at the North if he wished it.

"I do wish it," he said.

"I submit, of course," I answered, and turned back to my book.

"I do not wish to offend you," my husband said, when we were alone, "but I must insist upon your remaining here; I am confident there will be war between the two sections, and the safer place will be the North, and the happiest place, certainly, for you whose sympathies are with the North."

"I thought we had settled the question before we left Charleston. I was not aware, nor did I in the least suspect the trip North which was to give me so much pleasure, was intended merely as a trap to lure me here and leave me."

"It was not intended to leave you; but since I have been here I have learned the insecurity of a home at the South, and it has made me most anxious to have you left here."

"You are very solicitous about my happiness."

"I wish to do for you the little that I can. I know I once thought it in my power to minister more fully to it, but I know now that I must be grateful if I can secure you against bodily discomforts."

"Then you do not love me any more," I forced myself to say.

"What is my love to you? A constant annoyance, a source of vexation to us both. Perhaps when we see each other again we may understand each other better; I shall pray God that it may be so, as I never prayed for any thing before."

"I have tried to do my duty to you, Carl."

"Only too well; but it is no pleasure to me,—rather a pain,—to be the cause of so much constraint to you. I must go back early to-morrow; you know, of course, that if at any hour your present home wearies you I will come for you, be it through what it may."

"You are an excellent husband, Mr. Aberthnay; a lady told me the other day that for dressing in style, and attending to my wishes, you were unrivalled. I shall not write for you to come; you can choose your own time; this home has always been a pleasant one to me,"

"I do not doubt it. I have arranged the money affairs with your uncle."

A pang went through my heart. "It sounds as if you meant to leave me forever," I said.

"Not at all, only until such time as you say. It is not safe for you at the South."

"Then I am decidedly to remain ? "

"You are your own mistress, of course, but it is my wish that you should do so." And he took up a book. I sat some time in silence, then I went into the next room, our sitting-room, dimly lighted from the light in the room I had left.

My thoughts were intensely bitter; I could only believe he wished to get rid of me, and the two kinds of pride, the pride that would not force myself on him, and the pride that would not be flung aside like a broken plaything, chased each other through my mind, while I lay on a lounge in the darkest corner of the room, and watched my husband in the clearer light, reading just as I had left him. Very handsome, even to a degree that might be called beautiful, was my husband; fair, very fair, with eyes as blue as a summer sky,—bluer still, more like that sky in its deep starry splendor,—eyes that could glow with love, scorch with contempt, freeze with coldness, kill with indifference ; eyes that, unstirred by any thought of the morrow's parting, read quietly while I lay and inwardly writhed. Over and over again with a persistency that angered me ran through my mind those lines in the *Princess:*

> "Oh, tell her, Swallow, thou that knowest each,
> That bright and fierce and fickle is the South,
> And dark and true and tender is the North."

Bright fierce and fickle though he might be, I resolved he should not escape me; stay I might until he had gone, and then I would go too; I would track him night, noontide, and morn, in some disguise always near him, not from love, but pride, the pride that hated him who oppressed it so.

I knew an evil spirit possessed me, and I tried the charms of music to exorcise it; but it moved neither the evil spirit nor my calm husband reading in the library, for I could hear the slightest rustle of his book, although the change of my position hid from my view his Roman-like face. By and by out of my irresolute chords there was moulded an air, and out of my restless thoughts some words that sung as I sung them had both point and force, though weak enough, perhaps, as I give them now, unpolished, or in any way bettered from that rough dash:

> "Oh, your sternness becomes you well, mon bràve,
> And goes to my poor heart,
> And cuts with agony too deep to tell
> So well you act your part.
> I'm grieving in a sad, sad maze, mon bràve,
> I'm but a woman weak,
> One on whom it is but only right and just
> You should your vengeance wreak.

"I hold my heart 'neath aching lids, mon bràve,
    Once mine you called sweet eyes,
Now must they weep if coldly he but bids,
    To whom their duty lies.
I've prayed to God that I might die, mon bràve,
    No more to mar thy life;
I've prayed in my white shroud to lie, mon bràve,
    No more to move thy strife."

Before I had finished I heard my husband lay down his book, then he came across the room and stood by me.

"Georgie," he said, standing there, "I cannot bear it, not even for your good. Will you go back with me?"

"Yes," I answered, "I will."

CHAPTER XIV.

WE were back South just before the elections; the excitement was terrible, but I liked it better than the old calm. Men like my husband who looked deeply and were prepared for the worst, were the only calm men one met; the women were fierce for war, for war, as we read of it, is romantic enough, and in our long, luxurious peace how could we realize its horrors? My husband had had me do enough shopping, while at the North, to last us for a ten years' siege, it seemed; and now he was busy superintending every thing on the plantation himself. Courteously and tenderly he cared for me; but it was with the chivalry of an old-time knight for the lady under his protection, more than the ardent love for her whose colors he wore. He built every manner of defence around me, but never warned me, cautioned, or denied me in any thing. When he went up to Charleston in the winter he attempted no remonstrances against my accompanying him, although I was sure he knew there were dangers at every step for me there. Mostly all of those of Northern principles who could, had already left the South; in the country towns a few had been forced away; and as violent demonstrations were not modified for the sake either of rank or sex, it was wonderful that I walked as safely as I did.

A great many sad scenes passed under my eyes, in which I could not interfere. I saw one, one day as I was passing by one of the hotels, shutting my ears as best I could to the swearing crowd which had collected on its steps. A "Yankee" was being examined by the self-constituted court of inquiry, pretty certain of the sentence usually given to all "spies," or those suspected of being opposed to the South. Just as I came near the little knot of men, the victim, whom I could not see, appeared to have succeeded in imposing a kind of silence upon them, and to be addressing them in his own defence. Something in the matter or manner of his language made me pass very slowly by.

"I tell you I am not a spy," he was saying; "I have nothing to do with public affairs; I came here on my own private account; I have seen nor heard nothing that I care to remember. My ears and eyes have been only for one whom I came here to find, and whom I must find."

This was as much as they allowed him to say; but even the Northern accent would have won me, so obeying an impulse I stopped and looked at the crowd, who were laughing and swearing heartily; fortunately I recognized among them a man who had done some work for my husband.

"What is the matter, Taylor?" I asked of him.

"Only another spy; we're going to give him a little airing, ma'am."

"It's very foolish," I said. "What is one man, especially one man who does not care for either side? Yes," I continued, seeing I had attracted the attention of one or two others, "it is very foolish; such things won't frighten the Yankees; it will only make them mad for nothing. Wait until old Sumter comes down if you want to scare them. This man can't hurt us. Let him find her;" I said *her* designedly; "there's a kind of romance in every man's heart. We shall have work enough by and by; who minds one man?"

"Is he a friend of yours?" one asked.

"I have never even seen him," I answered; "but I want you to keep your fight for better use."

Two or three grumbled, one or two laughed, and they all stared; one spit out his tobacco juice and swore I was right: "The d——d Yank might go to hell and be d——d for all he cared."

I gave this one some money to drink confusion to the Yankees, and with one or two jests and threats the group separated, to straggle into the bar-room. As soon as they were gone I went back to the man, and spoke to him. "Do not trust to a second chance of this or any kind. These men will soon be back, mad with liquor; there will be no rescue then. I do not know who you are, but I will do for you what I can. Go to the next street. I will drive and meet you there; and if you take my advice, you will let me send you at once to leave the city. You have not an instant to lose; do not lose time talking thanks; for the sake of the little a Southern woman has been able to do for you, go back and speak with as little bitterness as possible of the South."

As soon as I had rapidly spoken these words, we separated to meet again as I had arranged. The carriage had been left at a store where I found it; at my hasty gesture the stranger entered it, and I—I had no choice—followed. I expected to save him, having commenced, and I knew a private carriage, especially with a lady in it, was protection.

When we were face to face, and the carriage had started, I for the first time really looked at my companion's face.

It was Gilbert.

I thought I had forgotten having first hated him; for a moment I remembered him intensely; the next I remembered all that stood between.

".You have done a strangely rash thing, oh man of exceeding great calmness!" I said.

"Yes," he replied; "but it has repaid me well,

and I owe you my life. I owe you more than my life; I owe you joy that you did this thing, and for—me."

"I did not know you, did not dream who you were until five minutes ago."

"And had you known, would you have left me to their mercy?"

I felt his dark eyes bent upon me, burning into mine, as of old; heroes have faced death with less courage than I faced him there.

"I could not do less for an old friend than for a stranger," I answered quietly; "but I should scarcely have succeeded so well had I known you. We are going now to my home; supposing you a stranger, I intended leaving you here, where there is moderate safety; but as it is, I prefer to go home, and then let Jack take care of you. You see I look upon it as a matter of course that you will leave the city at once. If there is any thing toward the accomplishment of your work here that either Mr. Aberthnay or I can do, do not hesitate to command us."

"I have found the one I sought in finding you," he returned, "and am now willing enough to go. It is true the last words I heard from you were of well deserved hatred; but feeling confident you have been too happy in your new relations to cherish any but kind and forgiving feelings toward your old acquaintances, I ventured to come to you in place of your uncle, who is rendered very infirm by his late accident,

7*

yet who, nevertheless, was resolved some appeal should be made to you, some assistance given you to leave this accursed city, for it is terrible to think of the trials of body and mind that must beset you here. You of the South are deceiving yourselves with the belief that the North will not fight. I tell you the North will fight, and fight with a force and persistency such as the world has not lately seen. You at the South are rushing headlong to your destruction; we at the North are quiet in the consciousness of power. For what has the South, with the curse of treason upon its head, to oppose to the legions of the North, strong in the knowledge of right and loyalty? There is no safety anywhere in the South for Northern men or Northern principles; even Mr. Aberthnay's influence cannot make you secure, after the storm bursts, if you remain true to your country, and it is not in your nature to be false to it. Your mind is too clear a mind to be deceived by any secession sophistry; you know very well your duty to the nation before the State; you cannot blind yourself by any States Rights' arguments,—the cursed heresy that threatens the life of our Constitution, that has been fed and fostered, cherished and petted, until it has grown strong enough to poison, adder-like, the hands that forbore to kill it in its infancy. If ever you desert your country and league with her enemies, you must do it with your eyes open to the crime. Surely you will not do it.

Too well I remember you as a brave girl praying for a martyr's trials. I have heard you too eloquently and too powerfully upholding adherence to principle through all things, to believe you will do the thing you have so often scorned, yield right to expediency."

"I do not need to be told my duty," was all the reply I could force myself to make.

"I know it, dear Miss Vane; I beg your pardon for addressing you by the old name. And knowing your duty, how can you stay here? It is madness to attempt it; folly to refuse safety. We are just learning, the best of us, what it means to *love* our country, to *love* its flag. We find it inspires a love as passionate and intense as any possible emotion; by and by you will hunger and thirst to stand under the folds of our stars and stripes, when, perhaps, it will be too late. For the sake of that old flag, for the sake of the family ties it suggests, if not the principles it represents, come back to it. I cannot tell how small you were when I first held you up to see it floating from Bunker Hill and Fanuiel Hall on national holidays; nor how many years before you could add two and two together we tried, you and I, to count how many flags we could see from steeple and spire, and how many stars each one held. Can you bear to feel you can never look upon that flag again except as an enemy and an outcast? Come back to it, Georgie, while you can; do not stand apart from it in its hour of trial.

We never had a sorrow or a wrong that it did not attempt to redress; we had never a thought but of all rightful freedom under it, and it made us prosperous, free, and happy at home, and honored abroad; shall we desert it now? Can you,—you born in the very dearest home of Liberty, in the proud mansion of our country's favorite sons,—can you, with your dauntless will and heart, fear to act according to your convictions?

"This is the terror that almost paralyzes your uncle; the terror that exists whichever way you decide. If you retain your principles, we dare not think of the consequences to you here; if you are false to them, what will be the consequences in the great hereafter? At home in the North, duty and convenience will walk hand in hand; you will hear only the brave words of loyalty,—see only the glorious deeds of rightful government. I held your uncle's hand in mine, and promised I would never return alive to him until I had seen you, and with all my power and will had begged you to leave this city of traitors. Your uncle again and again made me return to him to add some argument or entreaty to those already given me in trust for you. He told me how every spot of ground, every room in the house, bears marks of your late presence, speaks to him of you; and how can he ever bear to see them with the knowledge that you have turned traitor to all that he taught you to love and reverence?

How can he, proud as he has ever been of you, bear the sneers of envious souls, the scorn of noble minds, and his own bitter knowledge that you have deserted your country and leagued with its enemies? It will amount to that if you stay now; you know it will."

"I have listened to you without interruption," I said, "not because I have heard or expected to hear an argument or a plea my own heart has not already made, but because you shall not say I feared to listen. I will not say how I may be tried, nor if I shall pass through the trial without denying my faith; but this I I can and will say, that I shall never violate my own sense of right so far as to leave the man I took at God's altar for my husband, until he himself forces me to leave him; and he shall never force me until he has first learned to hate me. He is mine, and I am his; if he were a robber or a murderer I should not desert him, no more shall I now. My home is with him, and here I stay, making my two duties harmonize if I can, if not—"

"You cannot, and your first duty is to your country. Mr. Aberthnay himself always wished you to remain with your uncle until there was quiet again. Say only that if he wishes it you will leave, and I will take you safely to your old home; or, as that does not please you, I will carry back your promise, and gaining it leave you at once, and forever if you say so.

Say that you will, Georgie, for the sake of your friends, your name, your character, your principles, your country, your religion, and your God, for they all ask it; say you will return."

"I have given my answer," I said, as we left the carriage, and stood under the shadow of the trees in the dusk of the evening, at my own door. "My carriage is now at your service; do not think of returning for any thing to the hotel, but get out of the city to-night, if possible; you must make it possible. Tell them at home that the South is firm, and a hundred times stronger than they think,—tell them that whatever I do, they need not blush for me. I thank them all that they remember me still; I thank you, too, Mr. Stuart, for the effort you have made. Whatever happens, whatever they hear of me at home, let them not dare judge me; and you, Gilbert, you must not reproach me, even now."

He bent down under the shadows of the trees, and quietly said: "You shall not be judged nor reproached; but I had rather you had left me to the mercy of those men, than that from your own words I should learn the mission which I risked my life to fulfil should have failed."

I turned to the house, and he walked deliberately to the carriage, whose hurrying wheels sounded like the angry threatenings of fate as they rumbled along the seemingly deserted street.

I had been victor in the contest, it is true, but it was a victory dearly won. It was an hour or two before I felt myself able to meet my husband, who had come home some few minutes after I had left Gilbert.

I found him in the library, with his head resting on his folded arms, and his arms on the table. He scarcely looked at me as I entered, which was strange, for he always received me as politely, and with almost as much ceremony, as if I had been a visitor. I felt tenderer toward him for the struggles I had been through that afternoon; but I said only a few commonplace words, as I made some little changes in the arrangement of the curtains and the furniture.

"So," he said to me at last, "so you have come out as a public speaker, have you? And for the benefit of Gilbert Stuart; it is very interesting, indeed it has quite a touch of romance in it. And what, I wonder, is Mr. Gilbert Stuart doing here; he'd a great deal better be at home ploughing his old Massachusetts farm. Very likely he would like to take you home with him,—why not go?"

Poor fellow! how he must have suffered before he could insult me!

"*Why?* Because my husband is here."

"Yes, it is my fault; I who brought you to this; I who keep you here. Why did I ever enter your uncle's house and partake of his hospitality to return it in this way? A fine story that man has to carry back of my brutality, of me who keep you here! Why not go; the North is at rest, it is only we who suffer; leave us to our fate.   Go, Georgie."

"I thought we had settled that question times enough," I said.   "Are you tired of me, Carl?"

"Tired? I am tired of every thing; myself and life, and with it all I am killing you with the contest between your divided duties."

"My duties are not divided," I answered, meeting his vehemence as I would a child's, and lifting the bright rings of hair from his forehead with the same kind of tenderness; "when will you cease to fear for me?"

"Never, Georgie, while I live; I took cruel advantage of your kind heart once, though God knows I thought no wrong, and the memory of that day stands as a constant reproach to me.   Oh! could I but have seen clearer the happiest way for you! had only had strength to sacrifice myself for you!   And you, Georgie, why did you ever marry me?"

"Because you asked me," I answered; "you did not expect me to ask you, did you?"

"Don't laugh; it sounds so horrible.   In a few hours we may see things that will prevent us from ever laughing again."

"What has happened now?" I asked, seating myself by him.

"There is no doubt that ships are outside the

bar trying to reënforce Sumter; they must not enter."

"But this is an old story, Carl, it may vanish like the rest."

"God grant it may not," he answered; "would to God the first blow were struck, and we were fairly in action; this suspense is killing us and our cause. Our Governor is unsatisfactory, and we only half know who are with us."

"Is every thing ready in case of an attack?"

"Ready! we have been ready too long; we want a decisive act, something that will show the men of the South, yes, and the men of the North too, that we are in earnest; we want our men to feel they are 'in for it,' past choice, past change; this they will not feel until the Federal Government has declared war against us. God speed the day! I cannot face these dangers for you, Georgie. If I were in the North now, with my sympathies as they are, I should be wild as a caged lion."

"I am going to bear it easier than that," I said. "So long as there was chance for choice I spared neither logic nor persuasion to urge you to make it with your country; you have made it against your country; you think you have done right, I think you have done wrong; but it makes no difference in my regard for you. I cannot change my sentiments; we owe allegiance to the United States, not to North or South.

Because you are my husband I shall stay here; because the nation against which you rebel is my nation, I shall love it and honor it as I always have. I shall never by word, look, or deed, do any thing that I think will aid your cause or hurt my own. I shall aid mine when I can. I do not say I shall hurt yours, for my honor to you requires me to keep to myself what I know through you. I shall try to act according to my conscience, and yet to injure neither you nor myself. Does this satisfy you?"

"It is most generous of you; but oh! Georgie, what a man I might be if I could only feel as others do, that the eyes I loved watched me with pride and encouragement."

"Dear Carl, if a man ever sinned in the belief he was doing right you are that man; and I look to you to prove as true to the cause in which you believe as if it were my cause too. May I ask you one thing: if ever you see this thing as I do, as a treason, a crime, and a curse, will you give it up?"

"As sure as there is a sun in the heavens! To draw my sword from its sheath but once, for a cause which I no longer believed just and right, I would count murder."

"You are a true man, Carl, God bless you. If ever angels wept over invincible ignorance they are weeping now, but it is ignorance so invincible that it will save you."

CHAPTER XV.

ONLY a few hours more and war was inaugurated;
a few days further and my husband came to me in his
major's uniform, proud and exultant, though he had
come to say his last good-bye. It was our very first
separation since our marriage. I had been less than
woman had not my heart ached for him, as he stood
before me in his noble manhood, his ever bright face
radiant with enthusiasm, and every noblest emotion
of human life glowing in his eyes. I did not wish to
deceive him as I might if I showed him half my feeling; for in his eager longing how could I hope he
would analyze my emotion, and say: "This she says
from pity, this from pride, this from native tenderness." I had, at least, this honor left, that I would
not give him hope I could not realize; so I bound
down my rising pity, and admiration, and intense
terror, and quietly as might be received his last
convulsive embrace. He cried like a child then,
while I played with the bright rings of hair that
clustered lovingly around his forehead, cried and

kissed my hands, my eyes, and hair, and reaching the door turned back and strained me to his heart; then the band played, and he mounted his horse, and without another word or glance, without lifting his eyes, he took his place, and rode from my sight; a purer face, a nobler form, never went to battle yet since time began.

Do not ask me of the days that followed; there was an agony in their strained calmness that has left scars upon my soul that will last until I die. The North I heard, had flown to arms as one man, but the force sent against us was far, far too small; I shuddered when I heard the number. Seventy-five thousand citizen soldiers to stand against the long-trained men of the South, fighting, every man of them, as if the quarrel were his own, and on his own strength and skill depended its issue. I shut myself in my own house as much as I could to avoid hearing the insulting remarks of the Union's foes. My husband's letters were my only society; they were rich in interest, in thought, and incident. I could not shut out the rejoicing over the battle of Bull Run, which was a grand Southern victory, and which was as fuel and flame to the " Rebels." My husband's letters did not speak of it as enthusiastically as I expected them to: "It is, in some respects, a victory that will hurt us much," he wrote; "it is the first intimation to the North that they are not out on a holiday parade; it has too many resources, her enthusiasm is yet too un-cooled, to make this defeat an *extinguisher*, as our good friend Montreuil, who is wild with joy, and very tipsy with whiskey, calls it. Our victory has come too soon for us, we shall be more easily discouraged later, for it; their defeat has come too soon for the North; it is raw meat to a hungry bull-dog, enough to whet his appetite, not enough to satisfy his hunger."

Again there were wild rejoicings over the massacre at Ball's Bluff. "I cannot rejoice," wrote my husband; "I can glory in whipping my enemy in fair and open fight, but there is little joy in a victory thrown into your hands by the stupidity of a blundering general. The greater part of the killed at Ball's Bluff were Massachusetts young men, Harvard students, who had learn-ed their law and their loyalty in the same buildings where I spent my early college days, dreaming of some-body—you know whom! Poor fellows! One man, Dr. W——, I think you knew him, he was an old chum of mine, I saw after the battle; he was shot in the river trying to save a friend, to whom his sister was engaged, and who was so wounded as to be unable to swim. There will be wailing in old Massachusetts when she hears of these things. There were some splendid things done on our side; not alone brave deeds, but things that showed the quickness and the vigilance of our officers; they are never caught napping, which, as you may divine, is worth more than much skill and strategy."

I can hardly tell how I lived through the months that followed; after every skirmish even, I waited in trembling fear for news of my husband, in more than mortal fear, for I sometimes questioned if God should be less merciful than we, how could He who had said, "Render unto Cæsar the things that are Cæsar's," receive my poor husband if he should die in rebellion against his Government, which had given him no cause for complaint.

Until June my fears were without foundation; and then one day a letter came to me by private hand, from the son of one of my earliest Southern friends:

"It becomes my painful duty," he wrote, "to inform you, my dear madame, that Major Aberthnay was quite severely wounded in a late skirmish with the enemy, and has very much retarded his own cure by his restlessness and impatience to join his command, or, since that has become impracticable, to go home. Believing it to be entirely in accordance with your wishes, I have taken advantage of a favorable opportunity to write you, although the Major earnestly opposes any thing that can bring to you the knowledge of his very painful condition, which is much more serious than he imagines. We have been so fortunate as to have the Major at our own house, where my sisters vie with each other in their efforts to assist him. Feeling confident you would scarcely forgive me should I obey your husband's injunctions, and leave you ignorant of these facts, I have taken the liberty of stating them. My leave of absence, which has enabled me to take medical care of Major Aberthnay, is about expiring, and I shall be obliged to leave him to such care as very inexperienced nurses can render; convinced, however, that the medicine he least needs is that which a surgeon can bestow. Although within the Federal lines, Major Aberthnay is in perfect security. It will, I am sure, be the first impulse of your heart to endeavor to meet your husband; and should you be able to leave home, I am requested by my mother and sisters to assure you of a hearty welcome; there will be very little difficulty in eluding the Federal vigilance." Some directions, simple enough, were then given, and with one or two apologies for the intrusion, the letter concluded.

It would have been grief enough to know my husband were wounded: to be told of it against his wishes, to realize how great must have been the danger when an almost entire stranger thought it necessary to call me to his side, were emotions impossible to describe. As quickly after reading the letter as a dress could be changed and a carriage ready I was on my way to the depot, and fortunate enough, by one hasty spring, to find place upon the train just moving from the depot.

I wrapped myself in my travelling cloak and sank back in my seat, motionless as a statue without from the very surging of my soul within. My whole life in this world and the next seemed to hang upon the chance of arriving in time, at least to hear the words I deserved so little, "I forgive."

And if life were given to him longer still, how I would pray until I had saved him from all further dangers!

I never counted that journey by hours or by days. I know nothing how I found my way. I remember only a dark night, a lonely street, a quiet house, and myself wildly begging admittance. It was very late; a white-headed old gentleman cautiously opened the door.

"Let me in, I beseech you," I said; "I am Mrs. Aberthnay."

He opened the door wider, and I sprang into the hall; the gentleman opened the door of a room at one side of the hall, and spoke my name; a group of frightened, wondering faces, instantly gathered around me.

"I am Mrs. Aberthnay," I repeated; "is my husband here?"

"Mrs. Aberthnay, is it possible? Come in, my dear," one said, drawing me into the open room.

"You are very kind," I said; "I would like to see my husband, at once, if you please. Dr. M—— wrote me he was here."

"Let me give you a cup of tea," she said.

"Is not my husband here?" I asked.

"He was wounded, you know," she answered; "and have you come all this way alone, dear Mrs. Aberthnay? I cannot tell you half how glad I am to see you."

"I know, I am sure of it, my dear Mrs. M——; but do tell me of Major Aberthnay. Is he here?"

They looked from one to the other; and with that mistaken kindness so many people use, they said a few commonplace sentences, and tried to remove my things. At last, however, I forced the truth from them.

Some one had told of my husband's concealment at their house. He discovered his danger, and being determined to die sooner than be taken prisoner, against their prayers and tears, and all their arguments, he had insisted upon leaving them. David, his trusty servant, was with him, and he had gone no one knew where. There were only women in the house; the gentleman who had opened the door was a neighbor, who had come to them the day before from the ruins of his once splendid home, burnt by the " Yankees." There had been no one to accompany my husband, only David.

Then they told me of his wound, and of the restlessness and impatience which had put him back very much; and then that he grew sad and melancholy, and
8

made no effort to rally, seeming to take no interest in any thing except the letters from me, which had been sent him from headquarters whenever there was an opportunity, and then it was that Dr. M—— became frightened and sent for me, and I was too late.

No one tried to sleep that night; good, affectionate women, they gathered around me, and told me every incident of his stay at their house; how the doctor had brought him there first, what they had thought, how courteously he had thanked them, how gently he ever spoke to them, while they could see he was inwardly fretting; how one of the girls had been his favorite, because she was like his wife. These and a thousand trifles besides, such as love and tenderness are made of, they told me with as much minuteness as if I had been Carl's own fond and loving wife; and I heard them, and thought in my heart how they would hate me could they know the coldness, the cruelty I had shown the man they honored so much.

At the first dawn of light I started under the guidance of their one remaining servant, whose assistance they forced me to accept, to find my husband; and then it was that, for the first time since the war, as I neared the city, I saw the old flag again.

I saw it again. Not the prodigal, with the weight of his physical cares and moral guilt, leaving the husks which the swine did eat for the old home luxuries, ran faster to meet his father on the way, wept with greater joy under that father's blessing hands, than I, when, weary and almost heart-broken, a rebel and a traitor if you choose, I saw once more the flag I had deserted; saw it again, the dear familiar stripes, the bright, unfallen stars floating joyously, grandly, in the soft summer breezes,—"the loyal winds that loved it well." I did not know I had so much of impulse and fond emotion left within me, as I, who had shed not a tear during all these days of terror and suspense, who had uttered not a single groan when I learned the bitter knowledge of their uselessness, sprang forward, while tears rained from my eyes, to stand once more beneath its folds.

Another lay on the ground beside me; a soldier's flag, stained with rain and mud, and oh! its olden whiteness dark with blood; torn and tattered, thrown aside as useless, perhaps, how eagerly I pressed it to my lips, and caressed it and bathed it with my tears!

Just then the morning sun burst through the mists that had hung over us, birds sang merrily on every tree, and for a few moments I forgot I was searching for a suffering, perhaps a dying husband.

"When I write Carl," I thought, "I will tell him just how the morning looks."

Then I trembled and my strength left me. I might never write to Carl again.

He was not at his old command; I had found friends everywhere to help me on, but none to tell me of him. "He was on sick leave, and we supposed him home," was my most satisfactory answer. Then I hurried back, picturing Carl already there; actually looked for him to meet me when I reached the city; so thoughtful, so courteous had he ever been to me that I could scarcely realize myself standing in the hurrying crowd without Carl's eager face to welcome me, Carl's protecting arm to lean upon. I rushed to the house; it was dark and close; no one had entered it, but the servants coming and going, since I left. Then I sat down and cried.

"Massa berry likely stop somewhere, he be berry tired and sick," suggested one of the servants, and the thought was a good one; and acting upon it I found comfort and consolation. I arranged the rooms; I worked over Mrs. Glynn's receipt-book, preparing all manner of delicacies to tempt his taste; I sprang to the door, if ever an officer passed the window; a hundred times I cried, "This is he!" but Carl did not come. Why should he? Had I been such a wife to him that he should care to come? and if he did come, would he be satisfied with tender nursing and dainty food?

But David came, and told me his story.

"Massa berry weak, me trable and no house, no nothing; I do my best. One day massa called me and say: 'I am dying this time, David, and no mistake.' 'Ah, no, Massa Carl,' I say, 'I go foraging and you get better;' but he just shake his head, and I went on a little way to find a house or some place for Massa Carl. I find some berry nice people, and we all go after massa, but de Yanks were dere first; when dey was gone, der was no Massa Carl, only just him coat he'd bin laying on 'fore I went 'way."

Two or three days after letters reached me which gave me fuller accounts; a prisoner had seen my husband brought into the Federal camp on a stretcher; several of the officers had tried to assist him, but he was too far gone. They had all felt much interested in him from his fine appearance; but the prisoner could only say he had been kindly cared for, for in a few hours there was a surprise by the Confederates in which the informant was taken prisoner. Further information came later. He had lived only a few days, but had been cared for to the last, and was buried in a portion of the battle-ground in which Confederates and Unionist had been buried together.

Every kindness, every praise of him, every sympathy possible the officers gave me; he had been widely loved and honored for his soldierly skill and daring, and his noble and knightly character.

If one ray of light could have come in upon the darkness of my heart, it would have come in the thought that he had died for a cause he had loved and honored; but seeing with the clearer light of immortality his spirit would recognize the right, while his body rested under the folds of the true flag.

CHAPTER XVI.

With my husband's death died all that bound me
to the South. I utterly loathed the war and every
thing concerned with it. Free to feel, free to think,
at last, according to my own convictions, I made no
attempt to disguise its deformity, its wretchedness,
the wickedness of its motives, and the enormity of its
sin. I went, as I had done before, to the hospitals, for
I knew how many, like my husband, had gone into
the war as conscientiously and as heroically as your
bravest Northern general; but oh! I longed with all
my heart, it was a dream beyond any hope, to stand
among brave Union men, and toil for *them!*

I did not dare look so far as my old home; I dared
not hope ever to live under the dear flag again; but I
did dream of an escape somewhere, anywhere out of
that accursed city, every stone in the streets of which
seemed to mock at me. My friendliness was complete; many who honored my husband had shown me
many kind attentions, but I felt as if I had no
right to them. I had felt always, especially since

my visit North, as if I were wearing honors I did not deserve.

How many of the pale faces that hurried past me covered the same weariness of heart, I did not ask; but as I saw their tenderness to the soldiers, their devotion to their cause, my heart cried out more than ever to be at the North, aiding in like manner the land I loved.

"David," I asked one morning of him who was now a hero among his fellow servants, "what has become of Lizzie, I have not seen her for several days?"

"Dunno, missus."

"Yes you do, David; answer me."

"Oh, lor, missus, if yer looks in that way 'specks I'll have ter answer. 'Specks Lizzie's whar George is." George was her husband, living in another part of the city.

"And where is George?"

"Dunno, missus, 'less de Yanks got hold of him; dey's awful tiefs, dey is."

"I wonder if they would steal me," I said; but forming the thought into words became too much for me, and I could not keep back the tears. When he saw that, David cried too, but so ludicrously that I changed to laughing.

"Dar now, see dat now," he exclaimed; "missus larf just de way she larf when Massa Carl and me go courtin. Massa Carl! Massa Carl! oh! oh! Nebber

go courtin no more! Him told me dis yere'd happen.
Nebber see you no more, Massa Carl! Massa Carl
him berry badly hurt last winter, nebber tell you,
missus? Him poor foot's all frozed, and when David
take stocking off de skin all come too, but Massa
Carl he only larf. Him say: David, any thing happen
to me you go back to missus; tell her I lub her just
ebery day more; tell her forgive me that thing—she
knows. And David, him say low voice, get her up
Norf, you know how."

"You know how! Oh, David, why did you not
tell me this before?"

"I 'fraid, missus, you berry big for de war."

"Can I go, David?"

"Massa Carl tell me, I know."

"That won't do now," I said, when he had told me
his plan; "things have changed since then, and whenever I do go I shall go openly and above board,—
honorably."

"Missus know best," he said, only dimly conscious
that I was beyond him. "'Taint nuffin for nigger to
run away; 'taint for poor nigger ter have dem high
semments. If Missus goes Norf she'll take David
'long too?"

"Would you like to go, David?"

"It berry cold der, missus?"

"Not all the time."

"'Specks I'd like ter go, missus."

"Then I'll take you, David."

"Missus promise?"

"Yes, David, if you don't run away first."

"I not run away, missus, I go hon'rable."

"Oh!" I exclaimed.

"It berry cold up Norf, but a man own he self dere. How much I worth, missus?"

"How do you mean?"

"How much I bring if I sold."

"I don't know."

"Tink I'se worth good deal; two tousand dollars, may be."

"Perhaps so."

"Two tousand dollars great deal money for Norf. I go Norf, I own myself, I be worth two tousand dollars; I be berry rich man. Bimeby I make more money and buy old Chloe, den I own two niggers. Bimeby—" but David's mathematical calculations had reached their climax.

The next day I left my husband's property in the hands of his old lawyer to take care of for me, and I started for Richmond, which seemed a little nearer home.

8*

CHAPTER XVII.

Iᴛ was intensely hot in Richmond and in its neigh-
borhood, but the heat was the least of our trouble;
the "Yankees" were at our very gates, and the city
seemed moulding itself into one vast hospital on
account of the wounded soldiers daily arriving, and
the constant departure of all well persons, soldiers, and
civilians, who could get away. As for those who
remained,—it may have been the reflection of my own
loneliness,—they seemed borne down by anxiety and
care; there were some who loudly spurned all fear of
a nearer approach of the Federal army to Richmond;
there were others who trembled lest at any moment
the dreaded Yankees might burst in upon us. Confusion dwelt everywhere; our army, broken and exhausted, could offer but a feeble resistance, and what
was there to prevent the Union army from dashing
into our very midst?

Many urged me to join them in leaving the city,
but I only shook my head. "What use?" I said, "as
well now as later; it makes no difference." "Her

husband's death has broken her completely," they said.

I went from place to place in a fever of restlessness. Whenever I was in the city I visited the hospitals, and gave largely of help and money, so that my loyalty was held as a model to others. But I could not rest anywhere, nor stay in any one place. Once I walked up and down a depot; some one had said a train of wounded soldiers was to pass there, and I tried to solace my feverishness by planning some assistance for them.

A young girl who seemed to be even more impatient than myself, finally addressed me: "Do you know any thing about the train? Will it come, do you think?"

"I know nothing for certain," I answered, "but it seems to be expected by very many; we can only wait."

"*Only wait!* I am tired to death of waiting; I have been here ages."

"You are expecting some one?"

"Partly. Papa has been wounded, and I go to every depot and every train to meet him. My poor papa! I *wish* they'd come! Probably, after all, papa won't be there; I have been disappointed so many times! Are you expecting any body?"

"No," I said, "I have not even the comfort of dread or fear."

"Oh! how hard!" she exclaimed:

> "'Not to dread because all is taken,
>   Is the loneliest depth of human pain.'

But it is a proud thing to have lost any one in this war."

I did not answer.

"I shall do something desperate if this thing goes on much longer," she said.

"Dear child," I could but say, "rather thank God that he has left you even suspense."

She turned perfectly pale. "If God took papa," she said, "I would—"

She could not finish the sentence. I wondered, if I had loved Carl, would I have felt the revenge and fury her broken sentence showed?

"I wonder how you all bear it so calmly," she began again: "you must be very patient."

"We never know," I answered, "until we are tried, how much we can bear. Your father for whom you are waiting, has he been long in the army?" I added, to change the subject.

"Oh, from the first; I was in New York, and papa ordered me to stay there, but I ordered myself to come here. Well that I did, or there would be no one to take care of papa."

"I have lived a great deal in New York," I said; "that ought to make us friends almost."

"I *did* love New York, but now I hate it. I would joy to hear it burnt to the ground."

She had a fair complexion, soft brown hair and emotionless blue eyes; but she spoke with a fierce vindictiveness.

"Were you ever there much?" I asked.

"Oh, yes! I was educated there. I wish we could take New York."

"If we keep half of what we have we shall do well."

"Oh, you don't know! Papa writes me all about the war and the North. He says the Northern Generals don't fight like ours, and their army cannot stand privations as ours does. They are not heart and soul in the war like we are. Papa sends me New York papers; they never agree; they are all grumbling and growling, some wanting one thing, some another; some want the army to do this, and others want it to do something else; and Abe Lincoln tries to suit them all, and so cuts up the army, and fights a little to suit the war people, and then compromises and don't fight, to suit the peace people. Papa says they will have another revolution up there."

"I very seldom see a Northern paper," I said; "what do they find to quarrel about?"

"I don't understand exactly; but papa says the Yankee rage for money-making gets ahead of patriot zeal for the country, and so there's a muss. They talk

a deal about our slaves, and our sleeping over volca-
noes; but papa says our slaves are not a circumstance
to their foreign citizens, who don't understand about
country and government; how can they, never having
had any of their own? and they make as much fuss
and talk as loud as if the whole North belonged to
them, and won't leave the Yankees a chance to squeeze
in a word on their own affairs.   Papa made me learn
some lines of a French poet in New Orleans once, that
he says have proved almost a prophecy. I do not
know if I can quote them:

<blockquote>
'Veillons! car parmi nous l'esprit des étrangers
  Menace le pays du plus grand des dangers,
  Ah! malheur à tous ceux qui, plein de moquerie
  Par la force ou l'astuce, attaquent la patrie:
  Malheur aux étrangers, s'ils ne cessent de l'être;
  S'ils veulent conserver l'amour d'un ancien maitre,
  S'ils n'ont pas un seul cœur avec ceux du pays,
  S'ils ne partagent pas les amours de ses fils;
  Si contre notre esprit leur fol esprit conspire;
  S'ils veulent un empire au milieu d'un empire!
  Veillons! car le grand flot de l'émigration
  Menace l'avenir de notre Nation!
  Car l'esprit étranger, cruel perturbateur,
  De la guerre intestine est le premier fauteur;
  Du desordre toujours il s'est montré l'apôtre;
  Et traître à sa patrie, il trahira la nôtre!'"
</blockquote>

ADRIEN ROUQUETTE.

"You pronounce French beautifully," I said,

making no comment on the matter of her quotation.

"I ought," she answered; "I learned it at Madame Chegary's, where I learned many other things not so commendable, such as flirting."

"I don't think the art of flirting is ever taught," I answered; "it is like Dogberry's reading and writing, that come by nature."

"I don't do much of that now," she said. "This war has made me very solemn. How did I come to make you that quotation? Not to show off my French, you must not think."

"I do not, indeed. You were speaking of the disturbances at the North, of which I have heard only a little now and then, and never before directly."

"I remember now. They do not know what country means at the North, where they are mixed up with every manner of nation. It is not like it is here; we are all for one side; there they are divided, and half of their generals, who are politicians, try to keep right with both sides, so that they can keep their places either way. It isn't like it is here. If a general here gets beaten, down he goes; only our generals never do get beaten. There, papa says, no matter how much we beat them, they cry '*Victory! Victory!*' all the same. There comes the train!"

Slowly it crept along with its burden of wounded men; my companion sprang forward as soon as it

neared us.   An officer in a colonel's uniform, assisted
by a servant and an orderly, was among the first to
alight from the cars; a distinct soldierly voice called
"Gertrude," and in an instant my companion was at
his side.

A winning girl she was, with all her freedom and
her careless dignity, and pretty, too; pretty, like some
one I had seen; indeed, from the first, I had watched
her, confident I had somewhere seen her face, or one
like it, before.

The wounded soldiers were obliged to be taken out
at this point, and the confusion became almost fright
ful, as Confederates and Federals, our own and our
prisoners, were laid upon the platform together, to
await removal as patiently as might be.   A young
man in a doctor's uniform, whom I had noticed very
busily watching "*Gertrude*," while she was with me,
secured me as his assistant, and won my admiration,
by his quickness and kindly manner to the soldiers.

The prisoners were under guard, but no one pre-
vented my passing among them, and doing for them the
little I could, as I had been doing for the others; but I
was rather shy of using a privilege which no one else
would have thought of taking, and occupied myself
with my new friend the doctor.   In passing through
the crowd a man rose staggering to his feet, but, unable to sustain himself, fell almost immediately.   I
rushed to break his fall, in which I was kindly assisted

by the surgeon. I saw the face of the man, and I made a desperate effort.

"I cannot stay longer," I said to the young surgeon, "but I can still work; if there is not found room for all your wounded, I shall be really honored if you will turn my house," giving him its number, "into a hospital. To inaugurate that event I will take this man, who seems to have appealed to me, with me, if you will help me; I have a carriage here."

"He's a prisoner," answered the doctor, pointing to his uniform.

"So he is," I said; "but having made up my mind to take him, Federal or Confederate, it is about the same; I presume they will be very glad to have one less in the prison hospital."

"I have noticed a very interesting soldier, scarcely more than a boy, one of our own; he looks delicate, too delicate for hospital fare; I would like to take advantage of your kind offer for him," answered the doctor.

"I will receive him with much pleasure," I said; "I will send back for him."

"I do not think you can take this man," he said, pointing to the prisoner.

"I shall and must," I answered, with the decision of desperation. And I did take him, thanks to the address of my friend the surgeon, and thanks to the lucky chance of having seen "*Gertrude*," to whom it was clear I was indebted for the doctor's good-will.

The prisoner, who was now almost unconscious, was lifted and carried to my carriage.

The doctor, whom this hour of mutual work had made better acquainted with me than months of society meetings, offered me his coupé, but I declined, and showed my intention of going with the soldier.

"My dear lady, that is impossible," urged the doctor.

"Quite possible," I answered.

"God bless you ladies!" exclaimed the doctor, closing the door for me.

"Don't," I said, "there was never less patriotism or charity—"

I could not finish my sentence. Not patriotism or charity, what then?

My patient was Gilbert Stuart.

Jack, the driver, had muttered very considerably as Gilbert was being helped into the carriage, which showed me the Federal uniform was quickly recognized even by that not over-intelligent African.

Well might the doctor have wondered; every motion of the carriage swayed my charge, too weak to support himself, from side to side. My anxiety to escape observation almost gave way before my vexation at my position; but I supported Gilbert as well as I could, and hurried Jack as much as he was willing to be hurried. Gilbert's uniform was well-worn, besides being thick with mud and blood; one of his shoulder-straps had been carried away, evidently by the ball that had wounded him; the other, a second lieutenant's strap, remained; as he lay apparently unconscious, I succeeded in removing it, for I intended, or thought I intended seeing no more of him after I had once placed him in such comfort as could be given him.

After awhile he spoke, and I started to find he knew me, and called me by my old name, "Georgie."

"I am here," I answered.

"Why don't we push on for Richmond! I shall see her. Why don't we push on? Take care, there, now!"

He spoke in a sleepy kind of tone, but at the last word his voice rose almost to a shout, and I knew that he was raving.

"Drive fast," I said, letting down the window.

"Yes, Missus," answered Jack, dutifully, and drove slower than before.

Gilbert continued his talk, which was made up of drilling directions, battle cries, army orders, meaningless words, confused scraps of poetry, and shouts of "Richmond to-night,"—once or twice he spoke my name,—a talk so wild and confused that I was terrified.

"Drive faster," I ordered.

"Yes, Missus, Nelly is berry lame."

"Come back, Georgie," said Gilbert. "On to Richmond. McClellan won't let us. Kearney is

going. I am going. When Marmion. On! charge!"
—his voice rising and sinking, and these the only
intelligible words. I was more than terrified, and I
must have shown it, for Jack, at my next repetition of
the order,—it was the first I had ever needed to repeat
to him,—turned upon the box, and looked down at me:

"Nelly hardly walk," he said.

"This man is suffering terribly," I said; "get on in
some way."

"Is yer 'fraid, Missus?" Jack asked, with a look
that frightened me more yet. For some reason Jack
was angry, and beyond bounds; all the lashes in the
South could not have subdued him then. I felt he
had stepped over the boundary of mistress and slave,
and for a moment I hesitated what course to pursue;
there was a time when I would have mastered a
wilder animal than he, by the very power of my look
and voice. I did not feel sure of myself and dared not
venture it:

"Yes," I answered, plaintively, "I am afraid."

"Missus would have de Yank in de carriage," he
grumbled. "Nebber no Yankee lady take care Massa
Carl." And more to the same effect.

"No," I said, restored a little to myself, "but I
know this man, and once when Master Carl was
among strangers, and they were against him, this man
took Master Carl's part."

"Missus know dat?" Jack said, and I noticed the

horses went faster, as he turned to them and then back again for my answer.

"Yes," I said, "and I cannot let him die as if he had never known Master Carl."

Jack wheeled around, and Nelly forgot her lameness. The humiliation of that conversation ought to balance many an hour of stubborn pride.

As the carriage went faster Gilbert's excitement arose. "They are coming! they are coming!" he shouted. "Who says retreat! Oh! they've hit me!"

. "Here, you good-for-nothing niggers," Jack cried, as at this moment we reached home, "what for you stan' grinning dere? Help."

Then there was a rushing to and fro; every room in the house was made ready for use, but in the airiest and prettiest Gilbert was placed.

Before I had time to think of what I had done, the doctor had made good his word, and the rooms were filled. Two ladies and a Sister of Charity came with them. One of these ladies I had long known well; the other, an elderly, quiet woman, was a stranger.

"You are to command here," I said to the doctor, who had hardly waited for that permission.

"What have you done with your *tyrant?*" he asked me, in a low voice.

I did not understand him, and said so.

"I mean the 'fierce invader.'"

"Oh," I said, " Jack has taken the *oppressor* under his protection. It is but in the usual order of things that the *oppressed* should turn the other cheek. Will you go in?"

"I will see him next."

I did not go with him; I asked the Sister of Charity to assist the doctor, which she did with that gentleness and readiness of perception that seem to be put on with the black cap.

"He is going to do very well," the doctor said, returning to me; " I hope you will be able to keep him here." We talked a while about the probabilities; he gave me directions about the others, then he grew red and said :

"I see your sister is not with you, I think you are right; it would not do at all, decidedly would not do at all for her to be here."

"My sister?" I repeated ; " I have no sister."

"The young lady whom you sent off when the train arrived, is she not your sister?"

"No, indeed; how came you to imagine so?" I did not say I knew of her scarcely more than he did himself; I needed the doctor's continued favor.

"She looked like you," he answered.

"Like me! That fragile, blue-eyed thing like me!" I did not at first see that it was a supposition made to find out something of her.

"Not in physique," he answered to my look of

surprise, "but a resemblance somewhere there certainly is; a shadowy, misty, fleeting resemblance, yet a resemblance, like a full bugle blast and its faint, far-off echo."

"It seems impossible; she is directly my opposite."

"No, only your echo," he answered, smiling. "She has a lovely face."

"God in heaven send her grace," I added.

He went to one of the rooms, dressed a wound, came back, washed his hands, and accepted my offer of a cracker and a glass of wine, which he took hastily, standing.

"Your friend is very lovely," he said, reässured perhaps by the wine; "'I do beseech you, chiefly that I may set it in my prayers, her name,' or words to that effect."

"*Gertrude!*" I answered; "there's satisfaction enough for one day."

"That implies more some other day? I appreciate the kindness, and shall live on the anticipation."

We three nurses, for now that the hardest work was over the Sisters had gone to the hospital, then applied ourselves to our separate charges. I sat some time by Gilbert, who was lying in such evident exhaustion that I feared he would never revive. While I sat I thought less of him than one would suppose; much, very much of the young doctor, and the strong impression a pretty emotionless face had made upon him; and while I thought I wondered where I had seen that face before: I knew I *had* seen it before. Suddenly it flashed upon me, and ashamed, yet yielding to the temptation, I went and looked in Gilbert's pocket for the miniature he had once shown to me. It was not there; but I knew now, I could not reason myself out of the conviction that it was not Kate's idealized face, but "*Gertrude's ;*" younger, more childish, fainter-colored, than as I had seen it that day, but her face surely.

CHAPTER XVIII.

It had become a settled fact in the household, that "Missus" was taking care of a great friend of "Massa Carl's," which vexed me greatly; it seemed hard that not even death could screen that noble name from being mixed in deceit.

I had told the truth when I said Mr. Stuart had spoken for Carl, for he had done so, slightly enough, as I recorded in the early pages of my life; but not because my love for my husband's memory endeared even an enemy of my country who had been once his friend, as the servants supposed, nor on account of the intensity of my charity and patriotism, as others thought, had I brought Gilbert there; nor yet because the old love lingered still. If Gilbert Stuart stood before me in health and freedom, and offered me his love, the love I had striven so hard to gain, the love that longing for had imbittered my life, hardened my nature, and almost broken my husband's heart, do you think I would have accepted it?

When, in the wounded prisoner, I first recognized

9

Gilbert Stuart, a thrill of joy ran through my very soul, for I saw the chance that I might pay him back a debt I owed him. I owed him two debts: one was a debt of hatred for the blight he had put upon my youth; the other was a debt of thanks that he had risked his life to bring me back to honor and safety; I leave it to you to guess which debt was the most oppressive to me.

Very ill and restless he was, and perfectly unconscious that I was any other than a stranger to him, if indeed he was not unconscious of everything around him. Handsome, in a strong intense way, he had always been; but, refined by sickness, his eyes bright with fever, and the bronze not yet worn off his cheeks, his was a royal face to gaze upon; and when those great, grand eyes that in old times had spelled me, glad to be spelled, and bound me, and commanded and moved and stirred my very soul,—eyes that had been for years and years the light of my life, when they turned upon me, the old habit came with their gaze.

Again and again I resolved to go to him no more; but every day I cared for him more anxiously, more tenderly, more vainly against my will than before.

In a room opening into the one I had given Gilbert, the Confederate soldier of whom the doctor had spoken to me during the discussion about taking Gilbert, had been placed; the quiet elderly lady who came with the wounded men took the almost exclusive charge of him, and we often had long talks together as we sat by the open doors.

"How hot it is!" she said one day; "if we only had ice for their wounds!   I am often grateful that I am caring for a stranger, just alone for the agony it would be to see one of my own loved ones burning with pain, and so little relief as we can give them. All the comforts go with the North!"

"They have their own share," I answered, "of sacrifices and privations, and we have our comforts, too; our soldiers are always with us.   I doubt not there is many a heart aching in the North that would count it beyond all comfort to sit as we do by the side of soldiers fresh from the battle-field.   If love, or if distance will not let us do for those who are dear to us, we feel as if, in doing it for some brave comrade, we were doing for them.   The Northern women have not these opportunities as we have."

"Little do they care," she returned; " cold, sensible, model women as they are!   There is too much knowledge of mathematics, of metaphysics, and of housekeeping crammed into them, to leave much room for tenderness or patriotism."

"I think," I replied, " the knowledge widens, not encumbers, the heart and mind.   I know from that little sentence that you have learned disgust for *bas bleus*, but is it quite fair to blame knowledge and education because they are badly used?   For my part I have always scorned to enter into discussions upon the capacity of women for coping with men, and all the thousand times repeated arguments and denunciations which go with the subject. Simple enough it seems to me. God has given us but one pair of hands, and given us all an equal number of hours in which to labor and to take our rest. If to one woman he has given a splendid talent that others have not, have we any right to abuse the talent because the woman who has that which we have not should fail to possess that which we have? If a woman wills her household duties shall wait upon her talent, she is to be blamed for a choice which would not be ours, not for the power of making a choice. If I were an artist or a writer, or anything more than women usually are, I should make my choice between my talent and household life. If I loved the talent best, I should never marry. If I did marry, I should use my talent only to enlarge my heart and fortify my common sense. It is true all women do not see this thing as I do, and they decide to make household duties second; then they are blamed, are pronounced cold, as if mind and heart were always at odds. I have lived a great deal among Northern women, of course, as I am from the North myself, and I cannot call them cold, or allow that their hearts are not large and loving. I wonder if they are just to us, or if they blame our impulsiveness, our undisciplined minds, as we blame them?"

"I cannot bear the thought," she said; "those cold, methodical, intolerant women; do you think they care for their soldiers; do you think they open their houses to them as we do? Oh, if I only knew! I had an only son, but—"

She paused and sighed.

"You, too," I said; "is there any one whose heart is not in mourning?"

"My son is not dead," she answered. "It were better if he were. He is a traitor!—no, not a traitor; no man is a traitor so long as he is true to his conscience. He would not listen to me; I had brought him up in steady faith, but it was of no use when he was tested. If anything happened to him, those Northern women would treat him like a beggar, I suppose?"

"Do not for a moment so wrong the North; let us be just to our enemies; if our cause is right, it is right, although the women of the North were angels or were barbarians. We gain nothing by intolerance; indeed, it is that bitterness, that unwillingness to believe in anything good from those that are opposed to us, which most injures the cause of our country, as it has long terribly hurt the cause of our religion. We claim for our schools, for our institutions, for our very merchants even, as much as if their perfection were an article of faith; we will not own that a Catholic can do wrong, or that a Protestant can do right, and we are making the same mistake in regard to the two sections. It is true we hear that prosperity and ease and luxury are with the North; but women, South or North, must have changed their nature if any luxury can steel their hearts against pain and suffering, and and oh! the pain and suffering incurred for them!"

"You are a Northern woman,—would you be just as kind if you believed in the Northern side?"

"Certainly, I should!"

"You know the North. Perhaps you think I ought not to care what becomes of my boy, now that he has deserted us; but I cannot. He is my son, you know. I thought, when pleading failed, that I might frighten him; and I said, if he put on the Yankee uniform, I never wanted to see his face again; and oh, perhaps I never shall! Do you suppose he thought I meant it?"

"Surely not," I answered, for maternal love and tenderness must have been ever imprinted unmistakably upon her sweet face. "It is from you he must have learned to follow his own convictions, at whatever cost, for you have shown him the example at a price which no *man* can ever wholly appreciate; he surely honors you for your steadfastness, though, doubtless, it seems to him blindness, and cuts him to the heart to remember; so you should honor him that he followed his convictions. You could not wish him to have yielded his principles either to your love or to your anger."

"*Principles!* Do you suppose they really think they are fighting for principles!" she exclaimed; and I was angrier then than when I tried to shut out the sounds of rejoicing over the Bull Run battle.

"Madam," I said, "it is not difficult to imagine that a nation honorable, liberal, and prosperous, should fancy itself upholding a principle when it stands in arms for its government against its rebellious subjects."

"That is their way of putting it," she returned; "I suppose you understand the North better than I."

"Oh! do not speak always as if it were the *North* we are warring against; we have made war upon the *United States*, and the United States, not North, South, East, or West, has declared war against us."

"North, South, East, or West," she replied; "I hate them for taking my boy from me. I have never heard one word from him since Bull Run. I would give my life to hear of his safety."

"May I ask his name?" I said. "I may some time chance to hear from or of him."

"My son's name?—James Belton; he was a captain in the old army when the war commenced."

After that we were a long time quiet. As I heard that name I seemed to see again the little group around the dinner-table, and my husband, flushed with enthusiasm, at its head; and again, pale and tired, as he was, when he lay back in his arm-chair

that night while I told him of Captain Belton's letter.
And once more I thought, if I had argued and reasoned
with him as I ought, he might have been, perhaps, safe
to-day, or, at least, his name might have been enrolled
among the defenders of that flag against which he had
fought, but under the starry folds of which he now
slept. I wondered, too, which had done right; the
mother who, with breaking heart, had torn herself
from her son to be true to her convictions, or the wife
who had been false to her convictions, lacking courage
to leave her husband. I walked, indeed, along a tan-
gled path, hardly knowing if it were my own will to
go forward, backward, or stand still; but somehow
hoping to see that which seemed all a tangle, all confusion, woven into a straight and meaning road.

The Confederate soldier whom Mrs. Belton had left
for a few moments, an hour after, called me to him.

"I know about her son," he said; "his name was
Belton, she said, didn't she? You are sure she said
Belton,—James Belton? But I know it was the one;
he was a colonel, and commanded a brigade. And this
is his mother taking care of me like as if she was my
own mother!"

"What do you know about her son?" I asked.

"I daren't tell you," he answered; "you will tell
her, and she will never come near me after."

"I will not tell her anything you do not wish me
to."

"I only done my duty," he told me; "when we goes to fight, fight we must, and done with it. I was in a company of sharpshooters, ma'am, and we set out to hit a man that went everywhere on a white horse like as if the devil himself couldn't touch him, We used to call him '*the one-armed devil*,' ma'am. Nobody thought I could do much; and says I to myself, 'Just you hit the one-armed devil, Billy Sayres, and you'll be a big gun ever after.' I was sure I had him, when there was a crowd consulting together; but up rides another man and dashes by, all bright with toggery; nothing less than a General that time; I fired, and down he went; and when I fired again, the white horse was out of sight. But I just marked the place; for, says I to myself, 'I'll get a heap of things from him, and he deserves to lose them for spoiling my aim.' We made such a pile there, ma'am; 'twasn't much use to try to carry him off, though he were Georgey B. himself, which he wasn't, for nobody ever knew that sharpshooter that ever had a sight of *him*. So, when night came, me and some others went around, and I found my man. Soon as ever I see him, I knew him for a General that once let my mother off down in the valley, and gave our folks a guard just as often as they asked. Mother was a regular Northerner, and this General or Colonel he knew it. I wanted some clothes bad, but I hadn't the heart to take his. I was very proud to take down a General, for he acted like a Gen-

9*

eral, and there was heaps about him in the papers afterwards, but I kind of wish'd it hadn't been him. I thought maybe mother'd like something that was his; she was so fond of him, she'd cook him pies, and loved him like as if he were a 'Rebel.' So I takes this note-book, ma'am; I haven't ever opened it, I've just held on to it all the time."

Mrs. Belton had put away his old clothes very nicely, as he now wore the hospital dress, and obeying his directions I had little difficulty in finding a package which I gave to him. It was rolled in a very dirty newspaper, which the soldier unwound, although he was too weak to easily accomplish the unrolling. As he attempted handing it me he dropped it, and the papers scattered around the floor and bed; I gathered them up hastily and replaced them. A carte de visite attracted my attention, for it laid face uppermost, and was one of a set I had had taken while at the North, the summer before the war. On the back of it was written, "*From Sr. M. L., Nov.* 1861."

It seemed natural to conclude it had been given him by some one of the Sisters at the convent where I had seen Emma Lewis, for I had left several there, and with real joy I felt I had lived in the grateful remembrance of one man; one person had not met trouble and pain through me.

"Will you take care of it, ma'am," asked the soldier, "and give it to her after I am gone? *Don't* tell her who done it."

Poor bright, little fellow, cheerful, grateful as he had been, interesting and winning us all, he lost his spirits after this; erysipelas came and could not be conquered; they took him to the Sisters' hospital, where there were more experienced nurses; Mrs. Belton still seeing him every day; but before either she or I knew he was really in danger he died. I had forgotten his name, which he had repeated in his story of Captain Belton's death, and could not recall it for a long time. I should have been glad to have seen or written to his mother, and regretted my own selfish preöccupation which had not anticipated this event. As all connected with him now comes back, I am reminded of some verses, I do not know by whom written, I have since seen, which are so suggestive of the many scenes we saw and thoughts we felt in those bitter days, that I trust no apology is needed for copying them here:

"SOMEBODY'S DARLING.

"Into a ward of the white-washed halls,
　Where the dead and dying lay,
　Wounded by bayonets, shells, and balls,
　　Somebody's darling was borne one day—
　Somebody's darling, so young and so brave,
　　Wearing yet on his pale, sweet face,
　Soon to be hid by the dust of the grave,
　　The lingering light of his boyhood's grace.

"Matted and damp are the curls of gold,
    Kissing the snow of the fair young brow ;
Pale are the lips of delicate mould—
    Somebody's darling is dying now.
Back from his beautiful, blue-veined brow,
    Brush all the wandering waves of gold ;
Cross his hands on his bosom now—
    Somebody's darling is still and cold.

"Kiss him once for somebody's sake ;
    Murmur a prayer, soft and low ;
One bright curl from its fair mates take—
    They were somebody's pride, you know.
Somebody's hand has rested there—
    Was it a mother's, soft and white ?
And have the lips of a sister fair
    Been baptized in the waves of light ?

"God knows best ! He has somebody's love ;
    Somebody's heart enshrined him there ;
Somebody wafted his name above,
    Night and morn, on the wings of prayer.
Somebody wept when he marched away,
    Looking so handsome, brave, and grand ;
Somebody's kiss on his forehead lay,
    Somebody clung to his parting hand.

"Somebody's waiting and watching for him—
    Yearning to hold him again to her heart ;
And there he lies, with his blue eyes dim,
    And the smiling, child-like lips apart.
Tenderly bury the fair young dead,
    Pausing to drop on his grave a tear ;
Carve on the wooden slab at his head,
    'Somebody's darling slumbers here.'"

CHAPTER XIX.

THERE came a day when Gilbert slept quietly, and the doctor, my young friend, said that when he awoke the fever would be gone.

He slept on until it grew so dusky that he could not recognize me. I knew very well that I ought not to let him recognize me, nor let him know that I had been near him; yet it seemed very hard—you do not need that I should tell you *how* hard; but he was not free, and every voice of duty, pride, and self-respect sternly demanded that I should do so. I hoped, as I sat in the dim light, he would wake and speak in his natural voice again. It would seem like a dream of home,—and more. But it grew along late into the night, so late I could not longer delay having lights, and he still slept; so I forced myself from the seat at his side, and for the last time put the bottles in order, lowered the curtains, stood by him a moment, and then gave him into Mrs. Belton's charge.

"I knew him once," I said to her, "and I do not care to have him know that I have seen him. Please avoid mentioning my name, or saying any thing that will arouse his suspicions. I will do as much as I can to avoid extra trouble to you; the only thing is, I do not wish to be seen by him."

Day after day I prepared every delicacy I possibly could to send him, and every day I heard that he was slowly gaining strength. What wild, foolish things I did, it would be as foolish to name here; how I sent him soups and jellies in my finest silver and china dishes, accompanied by flowers, and every fancy I could devise to please his taste or tempt his appetite. I searched my library for the books I thought he would like best, and when they were returned, I cherished them for that they had been with him; but I kept my resolution well, and did not once see him.

The young surgeon and myself were now excellent friends; he had known my husband and many of my Southern friends well, and besides being genial, lively, and warm-hearted by nature, was agreeable, accomplished, and pleasing by cultivation.

" Have you seen Mademoiselle '*Gertrude*' lately?" he asked me, one day. "Her sweet face quite haunts me, and is evidently intended to exercise an extensive influence over my destiny. How eagerly, three years ago, I would have followed it; but now I almost count it sin to think of any thing but those there," pointing to the hospital; "but—she had a lovely face!"

" And a face however lovely, I ask as a matter of

curiosity, can it inspire and sustain, for nearly six weeks, an interest in the fickle heart of man?" I asked.

"For six times six weeks," he answered, "when the face is as fair as hers!"

"How very absurd! How very small the worth of a heart given to a face; to no sweetness of disposition, to no brilliancy of thought, or depth of character, but simply to red cheeks and blue eyes! I should be humbled so to make a conquest." ·

"Then your pride has surely had many a fall. But ' *Gertrude* '—a romantic name, is it not?—but Gertrude, if I read her face rightly, would have no such nice scruples, I fancy."

"Well, fate seems to have decreed that you shall be interested in her, and will most likely bring you yet to her feet, and then we shall see."

"Then we shall see! Haven't I won grace enough from you yet to secure an introduction?"

"Ah! so I am to lay all this benevolent assistance to the account of Mademoiselle Gertrude! Permit me to moralize: Here am I, a woman not remarkably ugly, and, as women go, sensible; for six weeks I have worked with you in the best cause possible—that of suffering humanity; have obeyed your every instruction most implicitly; have made your patients take your bitter medicines, to please you; have watched your incomings and outgoings; have in all things conducted myself in the most humble and polite manner possible, humbly enough, one would think, to melt the heart of a tyrant; and when, at the end, I think I have won a little consideration, lo and behold! I am esteemed only for the fact that for fifteen minutes I once was seen talking with a 'lovely and accomplished female.' Verily, it is hard to say to which of us the fact is most humiliating!"

"You speak in jest, but your words have a world of meaning. It is one of the mysteries of life. That I honor and esteem you, that I bow down to you as to a noble and beautiful woman, and that it will be my pride all my life to feel that I have been a co-laborer with one so earnest, and yet that all this talent and virtue gains additional light from a pair of blue eyes once seen, perhaps never to be seen again, is a mystery which is so common one hardly notes it, and which cannot be explained. Is it humbling? I cannot feel it so. It is to me a proof of the wonderful power of the soul, that sees beyond our mortal vision, and recognizes—what?"

"Sure enough, *what?* Neither you nor I can tell. It may be a Joan of Arc, or a Lucrezia Borgia, though I hardly think it; it may be a St. Teresa or a Flora MacFlimsey for all either of us know."

"It rouses my curiosity, and I mean to know."

"That depends not upon yourself, but on her will and pleasure. We only know as much of each other in the closest relations of life, as others choose that we shall know."

"You frighten me! But Mademoiselle is apparently an amiable young lady, and, if you will give me an introduction, the stupid formula that bridges over the dreadful gulf that no heroism, no devotion, no goodness can pass over, I hope to know considerable of her. How very powerful it is, that little formula! I may have met you every day for twenty years, have known half the incidents of your life, yet not venture on so much as a bow in the street; while some stranger, never heard of before, is made intimate at once by half a dozen rapid words. Pray you, speak them for me."

"I do not know her myself. She chose to bridge over the gulf you find so impassable in her own way. I never saw her but that once; do not even now know more of her name or address than that her father called her '*Gertrude*.'"

"That is very bad. Is she a myth, think you, or an angel rather, assuming mortal guise, just to fill my head with dreams?"

"Nonsense!"

"No, dreams."

"If I meet her again, I will cultivate her friendship for your sake, if not for my own, for I perceive you are growing desperate."

"Not growing, but grown. Now I have exhausted

my daily allowance of folly, and bid you good day."

"That is consistent with your compliments! Good day."

A slight, light-haired man in a colonel's uniform now became known to me in my walks. Once I met him face to face, and he started and stared, and, I had the feeling, looked after me when I passed. He repeated this performance every time he met me, which was nearly every day. One morning, when I was a little later than usual, I found myself walking behind him. This time he was not alone; a slender young girl, dressed in a very pretty summer suit, and a stylish "jockey hat," had his arm. I knew her at the first turn of her head. It was "Gertrude." Without intending it, I followed them some distance, until I suddenly found we were at the depot. I turned back at once.

I was delayed a little by an old woman with a piteous story to tell.. While listening to her, "Gertrude" came toward me, alone, and visibly crying. I bowed, and took a step or two toward her. She seemed embarrassed, but advanced a little.

"Did you mind my rushing off so rudely that day?" she said, as if in order to say something. "It was not right, when you had been so kind as to tell me about the trains."

"I should have been very sorry to have had you

more polite," I answered. "I was glad to see your father came."

"Yes, poor papa!" she said, her tears bursting out afresh. "Now he is gone. He took his last walk with me this morning, just to show me how well he could bear it; but, indeed, he is not able to go yet. May I walk with you?" she added. "I do not know any one here that can understand how I feel to-day. I left mamma in hysterics. It makes me cross to have her feel so badly. When will it be over! Papa, poor papa! he went away so gloomy, although things look brighter than ever now."

"I am going up to the hospital," I answered. "I would like very much to have you go with me."

"I would love to, dearly; but perhaps papa would not like it."

"If you will trust to that instinctive knowledge which women generally have of each other, you may rely upon me to take care of you. I will not let you see any of the badly wounded men; we will pass through only one ward. I have some things to give one of the nurses."

"I will go," she answered. "I am not afraid of anything that you are not."

"Do you wish to see your mother first—will she be anxious?"

"Mamma?—she would not mind if I stayed away a month. She knows you by sight; a friend of ours spoke to us about you one day—some one who had known Major Aberthnay. I am so sorry for you ! ”

As we walked and talked, her depression wore away ; her nature was not one to retain any emotion for any length of time. I exerted myself to amuse her, trying the while to think whether I would do well to meet my friend, Dr. Carr, at the same time that a thought was darting back and forth in my mind, what effect would it have if I were to lure her to my house, and let her see Gilbert ?

At the hospital door we met the doctor, and I observed with much amusement that he retained his color and his composure under the unexpected gaze of my companion's eyes. With the same politeness as usual, with perhaps a shade more of ceremony, he accompanied us into the hospital, and, when my visit to the ward was over, offered to show us other parts of the building. Gertrude had told the simple truth, when she said she had learned the art of flirting ; her eyes did the work of a dozen ordinary pairs that day. She despised the ordinary glances of surprise, dismay, and affected interest ; she gave cool politeness to all the doctor's explanations, and attentive earnestness to my slightest remarks ; her blue eyes alternately fanned and kindled the doctor's already well-fired heart, while I watched the comedy with as much interest as one can who sees behind the acting.

I did not leave my new friend until she had expressed her pleasure at meeting me, and eagerly accepted my invitation to visit me.

One thing and another detained me that morning, and when I reached home, Mrs. Belton met me with a serious face, and said:

"The soldier in your front room that we have taken care of so much, is a Yankee; they came for him this morning, told me of it, and have taken him away."

"Where?" I asked.

"To the prison hospital, I suppose," she answered. "If I had known he was a Yankee, I could have asked him about my son. Who would ever have thought it,— so gentlemanly, so polite, so intelligent, and a Yankee?"

"And he is gone!"

"Yes, ma'am, he is gone. To think of his audacity, palming himself off for one of our men, and getting taken care of by us!"

"He had not such a thought; he was quite uncon-scious when he came here."

Gone! How my life sank down again! how wretch-ed the city seemed! how long the days, varied by no labors for him!

I had left of him only that one faded strap,—not a word, not a glance of recognition even; and now he was gone. Twice I had singularly and unexpectedly had him brought before me, but how could I ever hope for such a chance again?

I dragged myself from street to street of that pestilent city, thinking it my duty to toil there; to do there the only good my hands had ever found to do, and to expiate, by hourly self-sacrifice, the sins of my life.

CHAPTER XX.

I saw a great deal of Gertrude, and tried to lead
her to speak of her life at the North; but my efforts
were successful only in so far as they drew forth countless confessions of extravagance, flirting, and the usual
sins and pastimes of young ladyhood. I had quite
abandoned the fancy that her face was like the face in
the miniature Gilbert Stuart had shown me, and I was
already quite weary of her pretty vanities and small
ambitions; but she clung all the more to me. Her
father's letters she often read to me; they were full of
affection, but such letters as one would write to a
child, not to a girl of twenty. Her mother I had
never seen, but I judged her, from Gertrude's descrip-
tion, to be an inefficient, hysterical, uncomfortable
woman, with little brains and less intelligence. Gertie, whose other name, by the way, was the same as
my own had been— *Vane*—needed little urging to
escape as often as possible from the confusion of an
immense family under the capricious rule of Mrs. Vane,
and domesticate herself with me.

A thoroughbred coquette I knew her to be from the first; but I was surprised to find that, young as she was, she had been several times engaged, and now wore upon her forefinger a brilliant diamond, whose giver she declared to be odious to her, but whose ring she wore because it was pretty.

"Every thing he ever gave me," she said, "was on a magnificent scale. I believe I came nearer loving him than I ever did anybody."

"Who was '*he*'?"

"My first love; I never told any one about him; it is quite a romance; I have a great mind to tell you, if you promise beforehand never to tell any one, not to laugh at me, nor to blame me."

"A woman will promise any thing to have her curiosity gratified. Let us hear the story."

"I must see you comfortably at your work first, for it is a long story; but it is quite a romance, I assure you; I mean to tell it to some authoress some day; it would sound so nicely, all worked up into a novel, with the fixings and framing they put in. Now I've said so much, you will expect it to be more than it is, and perhaps, after all, you won't think it interesting."

"Certainly I shall, and you can make it as long as you please, only don't interrupt yourself with apologies, as you so often do, but tell the story straight on." For I had a way of thinking my own thoughts while

Gertie told her stories, and she never suspected that I was not an attentive listener.

"Well, you know, I went to school at Madame Chegary's, and, as I have told you, in spite of all her vigilance, remonstrances, and lectures, I did contrive to have a pretty good time, and one or two flirtations. I never did like to study, and was wild to go into society, so that one year I got papa to promise that I might leave school just as soon as I was sixteen, and papa never breaks a promise. When the day came, for I knew papa would do as he said, I packed up my book, kissed the girls all around the school, and positively refused to say any lessons. Every moment I expected papa to come for me, but half the day was spent in waiting before I heard a word, and then it was a note from mamma; she was at the St. Nicholas, —sick, of course; mamma's always sick,—where I was to join her, and wait for papa to meet us, as soon as ever he could get on. I did not like this much, I can tell you, for mamma always sticks close to her room, and to sing, or move, almost to breathe, sends her into hysterics; so, of course, I did not look forward to much pleasure.

"Every day we expected papa to come, and so I tried to be patient, and bear with the best grace I could the imprisonment in mamma's room, which was worse than any thing at Madame's; but of course I was dreadfully bored, shut up, like a nun, in the great
10

hotel, with lots of fun going on everywhere, and not
the glimmering of a chance to join in it, beyond a little flirting now and then, in the passages, when I could
escape from mamma.   You look shocked; of course I
would not do such things now, but that was ever so
many years ago, and I was very young and very wild;
and, you know, girls of sixteen very often do things
they blush to remember at twenty,—we won't say
twenty how much.

"After a day or two I went around to see the
girls; you may be sure I did not tell *them* what a
stupid time I was having.   I made a great deal of talk,
as if I had been having a royal time.   When they
coaxed and teased me to go with them to a concert
that night, I pretended to consider, and finally said,
if mamma had made no engagement for me I would.
Mamma had bought me some lovely new dresses, and
just the dearest opera-hat in the world; there's one thing
I *will* say for mamma, she has perfect taste in dress.

"When I got home mamma told me I had had a
call from some one who had not asked to see her; the
card was around the room somewhere, she said.   I
went around hunting for it, mighty curious, you may
well believe, to know who had called on me.   It was a
gentleman's name, mamma condescended to remember.
I could only imagine some of the day-scholars had put
their brothers up to it, or that possibly some of the
fellows we used to flirt with had found me out, and

had the impudence to call. This last supposition gave
me a good fright. At last I found the card. It was
a written card. I remember just how I felt when I
read the name. Heigho! I have read that name
many times since! Well, on the back of the card was
a note. I think I can remember it:

." 'My dear Miss Vane,

*' I saw your name in the list of arrivals in last
evening's paper. Is not Mr. Vane coming on soon?
I am very much disappointed not to meet you, but
will call again to-morrow. If I can be made useful,
in Mr. Vane's absence, do not hesitate to command me.
I am at the Everett House.* GILBERT STUART.'

"Isn't it a romantic name? I thought so then
and I think so now. I did not know the man from
Adam. There was a horrible old fogy whom I used
to know in Virginia, by the name of *Stuart*, but he
couldn't have written such a note to save his life. It
was such a round, full hand, yet so graceful and
formed,—I will show you some time,—that I knew the
man who wrote it must be nice; and I was mighty
sorry I was not his Miss Vane, for, of course, you
know, the note had been taken to the wrong room. I
knew the little note all by heart before I could make
up my mind to send it to the right Miss Vane, for you
can imagine, in a life such as mine had been, the least
little excitement was very welcome. At last, how-

ever, I got my courage up, and sent the waiter with
the little card to the other Miss Vane, while I sat
wishing. I don't suppose women, like you, ever do
such foolish things; but silly girls, such as I expect
always to be, do give way to such wishes sometimes.
I sat wishing my time had come for gentlemen to send
me dear little notes, and put themselves at my service,
when back came the waiter. There wasn't any other
Miss Vane, nor hadn't been any other Miss Vane, at
the hotel. I took back the card, and had a great mind
to let him call and see me before finding out his mistake; but I knew it would not do, so I wrote him a
line, just as nicely as I could write, and told him the
mistake he had made; before I had time to seal it the
girls came, and I went to the concert.

"Now if I hadn't been hurried off without sealing
that letter what a difference there would have been in
the lives of, at least, two persons; for Lottie Ellis,
who sat next me at the concert,—for which concert, be
it known, we neither of us cared a rush,—Lottie Ellis
somehow got out of me about the card, and as she is
always ready for mischief, she said, 'Oh, I wouldn't do
such a silly thing as to send it back. He may be some
one who has been in love with you this ever so long,
who has taken this way for meeting you, and it is flying
right in the face of destiny to do such a ridiculous
thing; wait and see what comes of it. I would act the
real Miss Vane, if it so be that it is not you he means.'

"'How can I? he will know the difference the minute he sees me,' I said, 'and that will be to-morrow.'

"'Oh, you goose!' said she, 'what need to let him see you? There are fifty places where you can be when he calls; it isn't to be expected that you can stay in all day to wait for him, and afterwards you can write a lovely little note of regret. You know you write the sweetest notes.'

"'Oh! I would not dare,' I said, 'he would know it was not her writing.'

"'Ten chances to one he has never seen her writing,' Lottie urged, 'and besides, ladies all write alike; you can write as if in a great hurry, and if it is very unlike her hand, and he knows it, he will lay it to that. But I believe you are *the* Miss Vane; he is some one who is in love with you, I know. I'll tell you; don't send the letter yet, and we can go to the parlor to-morrow and see him,—I can, not you, for the waiter would be sure to say *there is Miss Vane*,—and I will report what he looks like. You can give the waiter orders to say you are not at home.'

"I consented to that, of course, for there was nothing in doing that much, and the next day Lottie came bright and early, as glad of the fun, almost, as if she were the principal in it.

"With the most exemplary patience she sat in the first parlor and waited; with far less patience I sat up stairs and waited. At last Lottie rushed up stairs almost out of breath, and, as by good luck, mamma was all day too sick to rise, we had a grand talk. Lottie was perfectly enchanted; she said he was handsome as a prince, tall and *splendid*, a school-girl's beau ideal, tall and splendid and dark. No schoolgirl's hero ever had any but dark eyes and black hair, nor did he ever fail to be tall and splendid. ·'Oh, he looked so disappointed!' Lottie told me; 'it was the richest fun ever was! I won't let you give it up now; I am just in love with him myself, and if I were in your place I would have him dead in love with me in a week. Now, I've got to go home soon, and before I go I want to see your note written, for it wouldn't do not to write something. Evidently the man is in love with *Miss Vane*, whether Miss Vane means you or somebody else; just as evidently he is not engaged to her, or he would not call her *Miss;* it is also very clear that he is on good terms with her; and if with so much knowledge to start with, you and I do not succeed in making a pretty big romance, we are not of much account.' We got pen, ink, and paper, and after much plotting and planning succeeded in getting up a very non-committal note; we 'did not know how soon Mr. Vane would be on,' were 'sorry to have put him to the trouble of calling twice in vain,' would 'ask him to call that evening, but were going to Wallack's'—Lottie and her brother had already engaged me to go there. That was all, signed with my initials.

"In the middle of the play that night at Wallack's, Lottie pressed my arm; directly opposite us, standing, was a man, the same, Lottie said, as he who had asked for me. Oh! but he was handsome! I would have risked a great deal more than I had risked to have such a man in love with me. Such fire, reserved fire, such quiet spirit, such force, such character in every look and gesture! I can't help liking him a little bit now, as I think of it. He was that kind of a man that if you once got in the way of caring for him, you could not get out of it; he would always sort of hold you, even after you had stopped loving him. I forgot to tell you he sent a most beautiful bouquet to me before it was time to go to the theatre, with a note thanking me for mine, telling me he had to start un- expectedly for Philadelphia, and if it ' would interest me he would like to give me the latest news from that quiet city. I deserve some compensation for my repeat- ed disappointments,' he wrote. This was just what Lottie and I most wanted, and after I came from the theatre I answered his note, and gave him the desired permission. I told him I was very much bored in New York, that I had read all the books I could lay hands on, and written up all my letters, and was very will- ing and glad to be amused. The first answer to my letter was a couple volumes of poems sent from Appletons', beautifully bound; one was '*Idyls of the King*' which had just come out, and the other the most complete volume of Whittier I had ever seen. When he wrote me he spoke of them: 'He hoped,' he wrote, 'I had not already read the *Idyls of the King*, for they would furnish me with dreaming for months to come; and as for Whittier—he knew I would find *his* poems always fresh.' Evidently he knew *her* taste well."

"Evidently," I said, seeing I was expected to say something.

"It isn't to be supposed," she went on, "that I was very enthusiastic about that Quaker fanatic's poems, but his sending it proved to me conclusively that he thought I was not I."

"How could you doubt it ?" I asked.

"I don't know; men do all sorts of things if a pretty face strikes their fancy. Well, to continue, or my story will never be finished. He wrote me often; I wish I had his letters here; I am sure they would interest you; they nearly broke my heart to read and think they were not for me! Such witty letters, so entertaining, so sensible, with a sort of tender tone running all through them! What a woman she must have been to have inspired such a man with such a devotion !"

"How much easier than one less a man," I said, "it was because the man was himself so grand that he loved so grandly; ten times a better woman could not have inspired a lesser man with half such love. But go on."

"In one of his letters he said: 'Hoping it will not be long before I shall see you in your summer home, I cannot wholly regret my disappointment in New York, since it was the cause of your melting in so far as to write me. That little card you sent me at the Everett House was the very first scrap of your writing I had ever seen.' This encouraged me very extensively, you may believe, and after that I wrote more carefully. I was always proud of my writing. I was very careful of the matter of my letters as well, writing nothing of mamma, papa, nor any people I met, but of books, music, amusements, lectures that I read or heard, and considerably of my own feelings and thoughts. He opened his very soul to me."

"Oh, how could you!" I interrupted; "it was a thousand times meaner than stealing or listening behind doors, this appropriating thoughts intended for another, this reading his heart!"

"You were not to blame me, Mrs. Aberthnay; that was in the bond. If you begin to blame me there will be no end to your indignation."

"Then I will not," I said; "but tell me, what did you expect the man to think of you when your—*mistake* was to come to light, as come, of course, it must?"

"Oh, my dear Mrs. Aberthnay, you must be very
10*

innocent! As if there were not fifty ways of getting out of a worse scrape than that! I had no fear but I should come out of it all right as far as his opinion went. My only fear was, what effect I should have upon his affections, for I loved him with all the romance of a first love, and as I could never love any man whom I met in the regular proper manner. Stolen fruit is always the sweetest, and there was never sweeter fruit than that I stole that winter. You must know, during the time I was writing, papa came on and had business in Washington, where he wanted to take a house, but mamma would not listen to such a thing; so it was decided we should remain at the hotel, and papa come on when he could. As mamma generally keeps him in hot water when they are together, I have no doubt he was very much relieved by the decision, except for me; but I was doing very well. Several ladies had taken a fancy to me, and took me around; and as I was young, wore pretty dresses, and reported,—as all Southern girls in the North are reported to be,—an heiress, I had beaux enough; and with pretty dresses and plenty of beaux a girl must be hard to please who cannot contrive to enjoy herself. Very often Mr. Stuart used to write about *Mr. Vane*, and as it was just possible *Mr. Vane* might not be Miss Vane's papa, I always spoke of him as Mr. Vane; but fearing he might be a near relative, I put the Mr. Vane in quotation marks, and all went on unsuspiciously, and we were desperately in love with each other, when I received a hurried note: Mr. Stuart would be at the hotel the next morning. What the warrior feels when he hears the trumpet blast, and so on, felt little I, as the terrible crash was coming. By this time my impatience had grown so great that I had become almost unable to wait, for I felt I *must* have him securely mine beyond a doubt or fear, and the announcement that I was to see him came at the right moment.

"I never before or since studied my toilet more than I did that morning, mamma helping me."

"That reminds me, what did your mamma think of all this proceeding?" I asked.

"Mamma! As if I should tell mamma! Mamma would have a fit at the mere suggestion of my writing to a man. I never even told Lottie Ellis half about it."

"But how contrive to have your mother's assistance?"

"Get mamma on dress and every faculty is absorbed; she would walk quite unconsciously over burning plough-shares, if interested in that matter. I told her I had a fancy for looking pretty that day, and she made me pretty. As Cherubina would say, *I never looked so lovely*, yet my dress was apparently simple enough: a gray cashmere morning dress, quilted with blue, slippers, ribbons, embroidery, all perfectly exquisite. I was hardly dressed mamma, of course, retiring with a sick headache to her room, after the exertion, than his card was brought me. I had determined on nothing; I only trusted to myself, and felt sure of myself that whatever I did it would be the best. I wonder if my heart will ever beat again as it did that morning on the way to the parlor; again quoting Cherubina: *my excitement only enhanced my loveliness.* Shall I tell the rest in detail?"

"Do not lose a word; I am intensely interested."

"Thank you; you are real good. Well, I went to the parlor, in which the servant told me he was; he stood at the door, more royal, more handsome, than the time I saw him before. He started as he saw me,— I know I looked well that day,—and stood back for me to pass. I gave him one clear, full glance, half searching,—for you know I was looking for my visitor,—as I went by him, and it *did* affect him."

"I do not wonder," I said; "I have seen the effect of smaller glances on Dr. Carr. Go on."

"Then I went into the parlor and looked around, and saw in the glass that his impatience for Mademoiselle's appearance did not prevent his turning around to look at me. Ah! how many pillars of salt there would be, if all the world were punished like Lot's wife!"

"They turn inwardly to sticks and stones, which is worse," I said. "Don't moralize; go on."

"I went into the other parlors and came back and

looked at him, and half advanced; he looked at me, and there was some show of intelligence in his face. At last I spoke timidly: 'I beg your pardon; is this, —I am sure it is not,—Mr. Stuart?'

"'That is my name,' he said.

"'Mr. Gilbert Stuart?' I asked; 'and you have just asked for Miss Vane?'

"'Yes!' he said, starting into animation; 'yes! Is she not here?'

"'This is a funny meeting,' I said, very cordially, laughing and holding out my hand, 'for two people who have been spoiling reams of paper for each other's benefit! I hardly suppose I ought to be surprised that you should not recognize me, for four years make a great difference at my age; but what have you done to yourself? You do not look the least in the world like yourself. Come to mamma's parlor.' Without giving him time to answer, I turned into the hall, and rattled all the way. 'I cannot tell you,—of course a lady is not expected to,—the pleasure I have had from your letters. I did not know you would take so much trouble for poor little me, whom you used to tease so dreadfully. Mamma will be so surprised to see you! she has a sick headache, however, as usual, and will not be able to see you; but I shall tell her all about it.' Other things I said more *tenderer*, as the children say, and used my eyes with all my might. It was not hard to look delighted affection and childish happiness up to such a face as his.

"I did not give him opportunity for a word until we were fairly in mamma's parlor, and then his turn came.

"'I do not know what to say,' he began confusedly, 'I must shock and pain you. I am perfectly bewildered myself, for I am fairly in your parlor without having found voice to say you have made a mistake. I am Mr. Stuart, it is true, and you are Miss Vane, I suppose.'

"'Undoubtedly,' I said, with wondering eyes.

"'The Miss Vane I asked for is another Miss Vane.'

"'What do you mean?' I said, 'are you not Gilbert Stuart, who has been writing me from Philadelphia, and sent me word he would be here to-day?'

"'I am that Gilbert Stuart, but you—'

"'Do you really think I am so altered?' I said, laughing heartily. 'Shall I have to wake up mamma to prove my identity? Mamma hasn't changed; she looks as she has done for ten years past, and as she will for ten years to come; and I, little Gertie, about up to your knees the last time you saw me, am her perfect image, people say!'

"'My name is Gilbert Stuart. I have written to a Miss Vane all winter, and sent her word that I should meet her here; she may be in the parlor this very moment: it is a singular coincidence that you, too, should have had a Philadelphia correspondent of the same name.'

"For answer, I took from my writing-desk a package of letters.

"'It is a funny mistake,' I said, 'and a curious coincidence. *My* Mr. Stuart wrote me,'—I took out his last note,—'to expect him this morning; *your* Miss Vane may, as you say, be waiting in the parlor for you. *My* Mr. Stuart will, without doubt, soon be there. I am sorry to have detained you. It is quite a Comedy of Errors. I must say, to explain it as far as I can, that the other Mr. Stuart is a very intimate family friend, whom I have not seen for so many years that I should not be certain of recognizing him; and although my remembrances of him are indistinct, they do not point out a man like you, but I allowed for time and the addition of whiskers!'

"'Naturally,' he answered, 'but nothing could prevent me from seeing that you and Miss Georgie Vane could never be the same.'

"He bowed and was leaving the room, when, as letters will, my package broke the elastic that bound them, and two or three fell to the ground! he picked them up, and oh! but he grew pale!

"'Another coincidence!' he exclaimed. 'I could swear to that's being my writing,' and he pointed to the address. I looked frightened, but answered lightly, 'I wonder if your style is the same also.' I opened a letter and handed it to him.

"'I wrote that letter,' he said, 'and this—and this,' as I showed him others.

"We were both pretty quiet for a while. At last he said, with the air of a man who gives up—

"'All these letters were clearly written by the same person, and that person me. It all comes of my supposition that there could be but one Miss Vane in the world. It all comes from that! I have often thought the style of their answers was not like her character; but I supposed it to be because people often write so differently from the way they talk. They were beautiful letters, it is true. I seem selfish—this is a great disappointment to me.'

"We had been sitting while examining the letters. He rose now, wearily enough; I folded and dropped my hands. I did not need to act much for my heart was really almost breaking. He saw the dejection of my attitude, and was moved with pity.

"'This annoys you,' he began.

"'Annoys me!' I repeated, 'it kills me.'

"He came nearer to me, 'I will myself bring you every line you have ever written me, if you will allow me,' he said; 'it ought not to be necessary for me to *say* I will never speak of this mistake,—this cruel mistake,—to any one. I can never think of those beautiful letters, nor of this morning's meeting, but with the warmest admiration for their writer, and with the bitterest regret that, young as you are, you could not have been spared this mortification.'

"'You are kind,' I answered; 'I do not think of

the mortification. I found a *man*, and have lived
months in the belief that—that there was something
in life worth living for; it *is* hard that, young as I am,
that belief should be taken from me.'

" 'Your friend Mr. Stuart—'

" 'I never cared for him; never even liked him,
until his letters won my whole heart. I often wondered how it could have been in him to write such letters;
I might have known it was not.'

" 'May be it is.'

" 'I know it is not. Good-bye, dear letters! Ah,
Mr. Stuart, if you could have left me in my mistake!
These were so much my own, I thought, these letters,
and all the time they were not mine; I had no share
in them—'

" 'Do not say so,' he answered. 'Your letters
have acted like inspiration to me.'

" 'You are kind,' I said; 'but nothing makes any
difference now.'

" 'We have learned too much of each other,' he
finally remarked, 'for us ever to feel that we are
strangers to each other. You have spoken so kindly
of my letters that I venture to hope I may come sometimes to see you.'

" 'I should be obliged to explain to mamma,' I
answered, 'and she would be very angry. I do feel
that I know you better than those who have free
admittance here; but on mamma's account I would

rather you came introduced. Very likely we have mutual acquaintances here, and if you care for it, I shall be glad.'

"We talked over everybody we knew without any satisfactory result, until the idea struck me of looking over a card-basket. 'Here is an invitation to Mrs. Carter's for Friday,' I said, 'I wish you knew Mrs. Carter.'

" 'I know Mrs. Carter's son,' he answered, 'and I feel pretty certain I see my way clear to a proper introduction. I wish other things were as clear.'

"I do not remember very much of what followed. I said something about returning the books he had sent me, but he begged me to keep them, and I did.

"I met him several times before the Friday of Mrs. Carter's reception came around, but we passed each other without recognition; I was fortunate enough to blush every time, and he was not perfectly self-composed. One day it was in a gallery of paintings; there was never a collection of paintings without containing at least one of *A Young Girl's First Love-letter*. There was one in this gallery, and a pretty picture it was. Mr. Stuart passed me while I was looking at it. I had the grace to color as I said, in so low a voice that I hardly knew if he understood me: 'There ought to be a companion picture called *The Mistake*.' I did not look to see the effect of this speech, but hurried away, and waited and hoped for Friday, with what patience I might.

"Friday night came, and again with all my art, and all my mother's skill, I arrayed myself. It was at the time when we wore the most extensive crinoline, and the most abundant trimming, until women looked like dolls with their entire wardrobe on their backs. I had a silvery kind of dress, with tiny bouquets over it, a train, and a profusion of natural flowers. I did not go until very late; but, late as it was, I was there before Mr. Stuart. I cannot tell you how wide and empty that room looked to me, for my heart was wild with hope and fear, and love and terror, that night. At last he came, and leaning on his arm was a woman, dazzlingly lovely, a novelist would say, mighty pretty, I must own. I raged inwardly, for it was easy enough to guess she was the other Miss Vane. I had hosts of beaux that night; I had saved several dances for him if he should ask, and I did my best to be admired that night. The time did come, although it had seemed as if it never would, when Mrs. Carter came sailing toward me, and with her Mr. Stuart, whom in due and proper form she presented to me. It would be some little time before I could dance with him, but he waited, and entertained himself in the mean time with the lady he had brought, or who, perhaps, had brought him. It was not Miss Vane, he told me, but a Mrs. Somebody who had taken him as escort, and thereby gained him an introduction to Mrs. Carter.

"I cannot tell you how that evening went, nor the next, which we spent at a private exhibition of paintings, to which the Mrs. Somebody insisted upon taking him, and Mrs. Carter me.

"He made me several morning calls, and was introduced to mamma.

"One day he came with my letters, which had never got returned, and also with his adieux; he was going home to Massachusetts that day.

"I said something about Miss Vane, which called forth this reply: 'You are very much mistaken in regard to my relations to Miss Vane. She is beautiful and winning; but her life is so joyous, her position so full of sunshine, that a man would commit a sacrilege almost who could woo her from such a home, and I have never spoken one word of more than ordinary friendship to her.'

"'There was more than ordinary friendship in those letters,' I answered, 'or so it seemed to me when I thought that I——' Have you ever thought, Mrs. Aberthnay, how much more that means which you leave unsaid than any thing you could say?

"I cannot tell you how long we talked, nor at what particular point I covered my face with my hands, and let him guess that I cared for him. Nothing that he could say consoled me, and it was hard for him to leave me, feeling as I did. He talked a long time, kindly, tenderly, as a brother might have done, only a brother would have growled and called you a goose, —and finally rising, took my hand to say good-bye. It is very shocking; but I'm obliged to confess he took my hand, but deferred the good-bye; and before he got to the *good-bye*, I had dried my tears, and with his arms around me saw his grand eyes looking down lovingly into mine. Even then I knew it was more a pitying tenderness than the devoted love he would have given the other that was mine; but I took gladly what I could get, and hoped for more.

"Mamma was quite satisfied, and planned half my trousseau, while he was telling her all that he would try to do for me. He wrote to papa, and papa professed himself satisfied if mamma and I were, and all went merry as a marriage bell."

"This other Miss Vane," I said, "did she care much for him, do you think?"

"I never thought about it, but I was frantically jealous of her. Well, we were engaged, and this is the diamond that sealed the engagement. You may think I was happy, for I loved him almost to madness, but I was not; I did not fill his heart, and, that I did not, hurt and irritated me. After a time he went on home, and we corresponded again. Whether he flirted with Miss Vane, the historian relateth not; but it is very certain that I flirted wildly, any thing to feel I could inspire some affection.   I ran a wild course, and many is the man for whom I cared not the snap of my fingers, who believes to this day that my childish fancy had been beguiled into an engagement irksome to me, and that my heart was his, as my hand would have been, could I have freed myself from my bond.

"One of these men was Mr. Carter, with whom I one night went to a children's party, and came home about half-past nine.   And when I came home there. met me Gilbert; but Gilbert pale, thin, and stern.   I suppose he was jealous; for, after some conversation, rather restrained on both sides, he said: 'Gertrude, do you think we love each other very much?'

"'I don't know about you,' I said; 'I love everybody,—some more than others, though.'

"'And this Mr. Carter,—may I ask his degree?'

"'I love Mr. Carter about as much, we will say, as you love Miss Georgie Vane.'   I like a man to get jealous; you can manage him as easy as breathing, then.

"'And if I should love Miss Georgie Vane with all my heart and soul, in life and in death, her and her only, what would you say?' he exclaimed.

"'That you were a coward and a traitor,' I replied promptly; 'a man whom both ought to scorn, for you have not courage to be true to either.'

"'It is true,' he said.

"'It was my misfortune,' I continued, 'to love you

before I knew you; and when I knew you, you attempted to be generous; you offered me your heart and hand,—I gave you mine, freely; you chose me, at least *asked* me, to be your wife; and you dare come to me, your affianced bride—to me with your ring on my finger, your vows in my ears—and talk of love for some one else! How proud would she be of such a love! How strong it must be, since it triumphs over your duty, your honor, your grand self-sacrifice, and oh! so constant!'

"'Do not you taunt me!' he said. 'She has the right to scorn me, and she is gentleness and kindness itself.'

"'No doubt!' I cried; 'you are to be treated with much gentleness; you ought to be tenderly cared for, and greatly pitied, that you should be bound to one so unworthy as me.'

"'Oh, Gertie, spare me!' he said. 'I know you are a thousand times too lovely and too good for me. Pity me to-night, for my heart is breaking. I have had that to bear lately which I could just bear, and no more.'

"'What is it you wish of me?' I asked. 'To free you? To give you liberty to marry the other Miss Vane?'

"'It is not possible,' he answered; 'but it is possible that you and I, who are to hold the dearest relations of earth to each other, should try to see each other at the best, and to be kind and forbearing to each other. I know you have too much reason to doubt me; but I hope to show you yet that I can be strong and firm.'

"A great deal more he said; I cried, and he who came, I am convinced, to make one desperate effort for his freedom, went away more firmly bound than ever."

"How could you take love merely as duty, or consent to be second where you should be first?" I asked.

"Because," said Gertrude, "I loved him, as I have told you, almost to madness, and I always thought he would end by loving me as I wished. Then, again, I hated Miss Georgie Vane, and was determined to hold him until, come what would, she should not have him; again, if there's any jilting to be done, it is the lady's privilege to make the first move; and although I should not have married him on his half-love, I liked his attentions, and I was resolved some day he *should* love me, and suffer for me.

"In due course of time Miss Georgie Vane took unto herself a husband, Gilbert himself told me; and not long after that event my father and Gilbert had a quarrel on politics, which furnished me with another excuse for delaying our marriage, which I meant should be delayed until he fully loved me. Then came the war."

"Does he love you satisfactorily now?" I asked.

"I neither know nor care. I would not marry him now for all the world.

" Why not?"

" He is a Yankee; you don't suppose I would marry a Yankee, do you?"

" You would if you loved him."

" If I married all the men I have been in love with I should have a pretty string of wedding-rings. I never saw that man yet that I was fully willing to marry,—if I could get any one else. I don't want to be an old maid; nobody does. I like them all for a while; but it is a little while. The man that finally gets me must court and marry me in a short space of time."

" I will tell your next admirer of that little eccentricity of yours. What did this Mr. Stuart say when you announced your final intention?"

"I have never announced it. He will find it out sooner or later. I scorn any communication with a vile Yankee!"

" Even so much as to return a Yankee's diamonds?"

"I suppose you are right. If I know any one going North I will send him back his things. He can give this ring to Miss Vane."

" Tell him you send it to her."

" She is married."

" *N'importe.* It will be optional with him."

"I will," she said; and so ended Gertrude's story.
11

CHAPTER XXI.

Not two weeks after, Gertrude had another story
to tell. Dr. Carr's assiduous attentions had not been
without their natural effect upon that young lady's
impressible heart. She loved him, she said, as woman
never loved before; and more to the same effect.

"Before there was war," Gertrude informed me,
"I always declared I would marry a doctor, for his is
the noblest of professions. A man cannot be a good
doctor without he loves his profession, and he cannot
love his profession without loving and honoring human nature—"

"Hear! hear!" I interrupted; "Miss Gertie Vane
on doctors."

"'It is true," she returned; "I said so before I ever
knew Dr. Carr. A good doctor is always a good husband; he appreciates us women, and our patience,
energy, and resignation. That was before the war;
since the war, it is, of course, every girl's ambition to
marry a soldier. How mean will look the house,
twenty years from now, in which there is neither flag,

sword, nor musket! Few are so happy as I that I can unite my two ambitions, and marry a soldier doctor. But, Mrs. Aberthnay, dear Mrs. Aberthnay, what *have* I said?"

For my face was burning, and for the first time since Carl's death tears came to my eyes. Oh! Tennyson knew well the true life of this world when he summed up its miseries in that one sentence:

"Lost to use, and name, and fame."

Carl would not yet have been thirty years old and I was nearly five years younger, and what was there left of or for either of us? His enemies held his sword, and he could never fight it back. On the walls of my house, twenty years from now, there would be neither flag, sword, nor musket. The rightful doom of a traitor, you say. Oh! I implore you not; I go on my knees to you,—say not that black word over my noble husband. Were he even that, you could wish him no worse doom than was already his— "lost to use, and name, and fame." Put the harshest judgment on my actions, and give them their sternest sentence, and it would be a sentence no harder than that I was already bearing. All the labor without the fruit, all the battle without the victory, all the suffering without the crown! "How mean," said Gertrude, " will look the house twenty years from now, in which there is neither flag, nor sword, nor musket." And

that was to be the end of our house, his house and
mine,—two noble names bound together,—and only
shame their fruit, two weary, suffering lives, and their
misery barren !

Would it have been better had he lived ? I say
yes. Yes, I would rather point out to another generation the flag, battle stained and conquered, that
borne by a heart that, though erring, thought itself
right, had faced death though in a wrong cause, than
the rarest frescoed walls free of any battle sign or
trophy. For him who can live in the midst of heroic
deeds, and not even think a courageous thought; for
him who can live surrounded by brave lives, and have
no desire to emulate them; for him without the patriotism, the honor, or the manliness to decide and decid-
ing to act, there is a contempt such as no mortal can
ever feel for a brave man, though brave for the wrong
side.

I did not tell Gertrude why I bent my head, and,
startled by the suddenness of her remark, gave way
to my sad thoughts, my life long desolation.

When I again saw Dr. Carr I gave him a hint of
Gertrude's little eccentricity; he took it very well,
"Gertrude is a good girl," he said, "but as fickle as a
May morning; but a firm hand and a kind rule will
make all things right. I have seen just such girls,
after breaking hearts by the score, settle down into
the very cosiest and nicest of wives. Besides, Gertie is

so handsome, a man would risk considerable for her."

"She is very lovely," I answered, "and most affectionate."

"I have set you an excellent example," Dr. Carr said, "and been most obedient to all your hints and instructions. May I presume to interfere a little in your affairs? You are reputed a most loyal woman, and considered a model of patriotism; no one knowing your character at all could, for a moment, doubt that you would be both loyal and devoted to any government were it that of Tippoo Sahib, or any other savage or tyrant known to the world. I do not think you change your convictions easily, I even think the force of habit is stronger with you than with almost any one I have ever met. Once your thoughts get in a groove they will not be easily moved; that switch is not invented that will run you off the track. With this view of your character it is not strange, is it? that I should sometimes think your loyalty and your patriotism are just where they were when you lived in the shadow of Bunker Hill, and the Yankee Cradle of Liberty, Somebody's Hall."

"Well?" I said.

"If it were not so, it must, for many other reasons, be lonely for you here in a country where you are almost a stranger, and entirely without relatives. My little Gertie and I have talked it over often, and since

Col. Vane's promotion, we think it would be quite easy for you to go back to the North, if you should desire it."

"Dr. Carr," I answered, "with all my heart and soul and mind and strength, I love, honor, and believe in the United States, and with all the strength of my soul I yearn to be there, but I doubt my right. I can do good here; I do not know that I can there. I do not deserve that I should be given that dearest wish of my heart. I refused the protection of the North when it was freely offered to me; have I a right to take it now?"

"If you talk of right and duty, and that sort of thing, why, I am vanquished at once. I have here a safe pass to Gen. Vane's headquarters; you may take it and use it if you will; if not, I will repeat the words you have just spoken. Gertie will swear to any thing I tell her, and you will be tried, convicted, and punished as a traitor. You may choose."

"You are peremptory; a woman scorns to oppose force. I will go."

I had a call from Mrs. Vane, the first time I had ever met that interesting lady.

She was in a state of perpetual flutter: "You have taken so much interest in Gertrude," she said, "and have been so very kind to her, that I quite feel as if you belonged to the family, and as if I could speak freely before you. I am quite opposed to Gertie's marrying the doctor. We have suffered a great deal from the war. All Mr. Vane's property is at the North, and would scarcely be available even if there were no war, for there was a disagreement between Mr. Vane and his relatives. Indeed I might as well be frank with you. Mr. Vane was a widower when I married him. His former wife must have been a very peculiar woman; at any rate, she was the cause of unpleasant feeling between Mr. Vane and his brother, and they have never been on good terms since, and none of his relatives will ever do any thing for Gertie, I feel convinced. Before the war Gertie was engaged to a very exemplary young man by the name of Stuart; he was very fond of her, and I am quite convinced will wait for her, and claim her when the war is over. I do entreat you to use your influence with Gertie,—she will do any thing for you,—to induce her to postpone her marriage, if she will not break it off altogether; the doctor has nothing to live on, nor Gertie either, and every thing is so dear. I don't know how I can ever get her a proper trousseau. It will take nearly a year's pay to marry her as a daughter of mine should be married. It is no use for me to say this to Gertie, she is so headstrong; she thinks she knows more than any one else. Mr. Stuart was rich, and, I suppose, still is wealthy, and is in every respect a better match for her."

"But Gertie is so very Southern, I do not think she would be willing to marry a Union man."

"Fiddle-de-dee! Gertie talks very large but she does not care the worth of a pin. Her father means she shall go North very soon; she will probably meet Mr. Stuart again, and every thing be settled. He always liked Gertie more than she thought, but she plagued him terribly; they will both love each other better for the long separation."

"And Dr. Carr?"

"It is very easy for a woman of the world to see Dr. Carr is only attracted by Gertie's pretty face, and in six months they will be as indifferent to each other as if they had never met. I am so used to Gertie's ways. The only man who could ever make any thing of her is Mr. Stuart, and I am persuaded that if they could meet again they would become very much attached to each other. Do persuade Gertie to wait a little. Oh! if she would only go North with you!"

Mrs. Vane little knew what she asked of me! Just as every thing seemed clear between Gilbert and myself, there came this new complication.

"I will certainly speak to Gertie," I answered, "and if she can be induced to go to New York, or North anywhere, I will take every care of her; my house shall be her home, and I think myself that if she again meets Mr. Stuart their engagement will be renewed. I decidedly approve of its being broken first, and if renewed let it be at his urgent solicitations. Let us not interfere, he will like her all the better, thinking he has lost her."

One thing, however, I did intend; to make no foolish self-sacrifice for her sake. It should be a fair field, and no quarter between us.

I found Gertie very willing to postpone her marriage. Nothing was said about her going North, but it was considered possible I might be able to send her a few things for her bridal toilette. She would wait a year for the possibility.

Dr. Carr bore it better than I expected: "There is some thought of her being sent North," I said; "I cannot promise you to keep her constant."

"Do not try it, my dear Mrs. Aberthnay; I am already over the first heat of my love, for I am as inconstant as Gertie. *If it is to be, it will be,*—if not, no fretting will make it better."

"Will you take his letters back?" Gertie said to me. "I have addressed them; you can put them in the express at New York."

"If it were not for Dr. Carr, I suppose you would come with me?"

"I don't know; are they stupid there, do you suppose? I *would* like a little excitement."

"I will keep a room ready for you," I answered, "any time you feel inclined to take a run up North I shall be overjoyed to see you."

And so we separated.

11*

CHAPTER XXII.

I was received with great kindness by Gen. Vane, to whom Gertrude had written so much of me, he said, that he quite felt as if he knew me.

"I am very much obliged to you for your kindness to my little girl. There is a world of good in that light heart of hers if one only gets at it. Her mother, who has not half her character, is always in a fret about her. One of those unfortunate cases of a complete misunderstanding between mother and daughter; another result of the abominable system of education which we admire so much in this country. I don't in the least doubt that there is a natural virtue called filial affection. It is equally undeniable that that affection, like all other affections, is keen-sighted and very jealous. It will not have its object less loved, less honored than others; and if that object fails to win the honor and love of others, or show itself worthy to gain that honor, it is very clear it will lose that which came to it naturally. Mrs. Vane was a brilliant woman when I married her. If Gertie had known her then, she would have bent to her with perfect docility, but, like all American women,—no, I will make a few exceptions,—she allowed marriage to be the end of her life, when it is really the beginning of a woman's existence; all that goes before is but a preparation for this. When Gertie was old enough to find companionship with her mother,—when her mind was fresh, undisciplined, incomplete, but still a mind, what had her mother to offer? She had forgotten her French, she had given up her music, she only read a few novels and the cookery-book, she had given up society and society graces, she had ceased taking interest in people; and what was Gertie to do? She snubbed her mother in a way at which I had to blush. She made no allowances; what child ever did? She went her own way, and found companionship where she could; and, disappointed in her mother's society, judged her deficient in every thing."

"It is the story of a thousand others," I said.

"I ought to make one exception," he added, "since you have seen so much of my family to make candor a necessity. Gertie bows down to her mother in one respect; in one thing she trusts her judgment implicitly, that great and mighty theme of *dress!*"

"It proves what could have been done if her respect could have been excited by other things. It is an old story, that no two people can meet a dozen times without discussing. I have great hopes that this war will make a change in this respect; there will be made so many sudden fortunes by the 'people,' that rank and position will cease to depend, as it has hitherto, on wealth. Mind, character, and education will define station; men and women are learning now on how very little they can live comfortably, and the cares of luxury will no longer take precedence of every attainment; and women, relieved from the charge of large establishments, will have more time and strength to be accomplished, intelligent, and good-tempered."

"A dream of Utopia, my dear Madam. You have seen yourself that the love of display is as strong in the Southern cities as it ever has been, and the only result of the much-vaunted economy of our women will be to show them how much more they can do than they thought they could; and when the old order comes back, there will be this new order to double their burden. In the North, we hear, extravagance is running riot."

"But it will soon run its course," I said; "and I doubt not, women South and North will learn to blush to go feasting in purple and fine linen, while every day new hearts are sitting desolate in their mourning. Mrs. Vane tells me there is some prospect that Gertie will go to New York. I shall be most happy to receive her if you will let her come to me, and perhaps we two may do each other good."

"You go back to your parents, I suppose?"

"I have none; my mother died before I can remember, and of my father I know only that he seems to have forgotten my existence. My uncle, who took me as his own child when my mother died, has ever been tenderness and generosity itself in my regard."

"If, instead of that black dress, and wearing your hair tight under that widow's cap, you were dressed in brilliant colors, with your hair arranged as it was worn twenty-five years ago, you would be a living portrait of some one I once knew."

"I shall never have the heart to wear brilliant colors again, for the reasons that I have left my girlhood and my wealth behind me; still if, after the war is over, you will allow me to thank you in my own home for enabling me to reach it, and if it would be a pleasant picture, I should be glad to array myself to please you."

"It would not be a pleasant picture," he answered abruptly. "May I ask your maiden name?"

"Georgie Vane."

"I supposed so. If you have not had your suspicions, you must be slower of perception than I think you; but, taught as you must have been to hate me, I wonder your mother's daughter would stoop to accept any thing from her husband's hands."

"I have never been taught to hate you," I answered; "and in accepting my safety from your hands, I believe I take only what it is your right and pleasure to give. I have never sat in judgment upon you. It is twenty-five years since those things happened; and I doubt not you are painfully wiser now than you were then. If I am like my mother, or rather, if she were like me, there can be not a wish or thought of revenge in her heart. Yet, as there is a certain poetic justice sometimes occurring in this world, permit me to say that I consider it has been fully meted out to you, insomuch that, having once known and loved, and been loved by a woman such as my mother was, you have bound yourself to life-long companionship to a woman such as her successor is."

"Those words are bitter enough to cancel half of those I said to your mother; but I like them better than milder ones, for they show me at least you do not despise the reputed character of your father so much that you will not honor him with your sarcasms. You have grown a daughter to be proud of."

"And you, sir, were we to meet as simply friends, would soon win my admiration. I make no claims to any especial tenderness for you; if I judge you ever, I judge you as a man, not as my father, or my mother's unappreciative husband."

"You are very kind! Perhaps we may meet some time again, for I do claim especial tenderness for you; I do claim the warmest feeling of my life for you; and as I never longed for love even from my first love, your mother, I do yearn for a kinder feeling from you."

"You must win it, then, sir; for it is absolutely not in my power to give it otherwise. Filial affection, you said not an hour ago, was a natural virtue; it is dead in my heart; but there is room above its grave for the growth of a vigorous affection, I assure you."

"If there is any thing left of me, body or soul, when this war is over, I shall try to plant something there."

"Yet coldly as I have spoken, sir, do not think it is nothing to me that I have found a father. I thought my life was dead since it had lived in vain. My husband, as you know, died a prisoner; my uncle is old and not married, and is lately rendèred quite infirm by a fall from a horse, from which he can never fully recover; there is no one to lay up honor for my name when this war has passed; there is no name, a name of use and fame, to which I can point, and say I was something to him."

"I understand you. But you are yet only a girl; your beauty is not yet at its height; you can and I hope will marry again, and this time let it be to some soldier who will hang the Federal flag over the black stain of a rebellious husband and a traitor father."

I flushed a little; but I only answered by speaking of Gertie. "If she comes North she will come to me?"

"I thank you," he said stiffly; "I prefer she should go to her mother's relatives. It is now time for me to leave you; I think you understand precisely every thing that you have to do. I do not believe you will have any difficulties of moment; I will attend to Major Aberthnay's property, and hope I shall be able to preserve it for you." He paused a moment, then took out his watch, a magnificent one. "It is scarcely fit for a lady's use," he continued; "but I doubt not your uncle, who seems to have transferred,—I will not make you angry, so no matter,—I am poor in mementoes now, but I pray you accept this as a pledge of remembrance, or as any thing you choose. I presume it would be asking too much grace to request a line some time to assure me of your safe arrival?"

"Should I find an opportunity to send you I will write with pleasure."

Then David and I turned our backs on the land of the South, and with our faces Northward hurried on our way.

CHAPTER XXIII.

I could not pass further on until I had seen my husband's grave. It delayed me some weeks, but the force of a strong will is invincible. I went at evening, during a September storm, for there was such confusion and fear on every hand that I did not dare risk an hour in going. Evening settled into darkness and night, while David and a guide we had with great difficulty procured, searched, and at last found it. By the light of their lanterns I read the rough inscription on the wooden slab:

"———— Aberthnay, C. S. A.

Died ———— 1862."

I sent the men back to a house near at hand, while I stayed and kept one night's watch over that lonely, almost nameless and never honored grave, over which had passed and repassed the trampling feet of broken and routed armies.

CHAPTER XXIV.

At New York I sent the parcel of Gilbert Stuart's letters which Gertrude had confided to my care, her engagement ring, and his presents, back to him according to her instructions, and in such a manner that he would not be likely to connect the sending of them with my return.

I say nothing of the feelings with which I took the cars for home, for glorious old Massachusetts's truly sacred soil. I dared not think what changes had come to that home. Yet there seemed little change around. Broadway was as crowded, its windows as richly filled as when I drove down in the carriage with half-closed curtains with Carl.

Here and there I had met a soldier, and was reminded that there was really war in the land. Officers I saw in abundance, in fresh new uniforms, as if out for a holiday, and with them often stylishly dressed ladies looking proud and happy.

It was a glorious day in early autumn, and a brilliant October sun gilded the old familiar words,

which I think I shall never see without a heart-bound:
"*New York and Boston Express Line.*"   October has
always been called my month, typical of me in my old
days of joy and happiness, and I hailed it as a good
omen that its beautifully blue skies guided me
home.

Do we really *think* on days like this I am chron-
icling,—days when all our days seem to have culmi-
nated in one, and all our lives pass in review before us?
Back came the days when Carl and Uncle Tom would
put me in the cars or meet me coming, when Carl's
face would flush, and his eager eyes single me from
the crowd, and joyously look down their greeting;
over again I lived the alternate joy and pain of our
intercourse, my own hardness and his wistful pleading,
and now love or coldness availed him nothing.

Nearer, nearer flew the train, and at last the
blessed Massachusetts breeze, the loyal Massachusetts
breeze that no traitor-breath had ever tainted, blew
glad welcome in my face.   I forgot the widow's cap,
and with all the buoyancy of youth and happiness
bent forward to answer its greeting.   If the calm,
stolid travellers around me were astonished to see the
stern-seeming widow flush up into animation and excitement, it mattered little to me.   Ah! how truly I
felt in the words of one of my favorite poets, Adrien
Rouquette:

> "*L'air de notre patrie est le seul air vital.*"

And now the "iron horse" hurried on, rattling over the well-known bridge, crossing the narrow river where I had so often been boating for pond lilies; running on with its joyous tidings to the grand old forests with their fullest splendor of purple and gold, and brown and scarlet; screaming through the little towns, nests of cottages shining now in sunset beauty; winding around the soft green hills, lighted by flaming autumn berries; dashing through fields thick with heavily-laden trees of fruit; out again into the sunlit town, and now slower and slower, for the end is near.

There was no carriage with its prancing horses, no Uncle Tom with his bluff "Well, old lady!" to meet me as I sprang from the train, and burning with impatience turned into the grassy lane, where silence and solitude walked with me. Silence and solitude followed me into the narrow street, through the old brown gate, under the arching elms, up to the vine-wreathed porch, past the half-open door into the diamond-floored hall.

Like pilgrim at the shrine I could have kissed the cold marble; but my joy and impatience hurried me on to surprise those who counted me as almost of the dead. A long loose circular of my favorite scarlet hung in the hall; I wrapped it around me to cover the black dress, and laid my own sombre wrappings, even my widow's cap, aside.

CHAPTER XXV.

I KNEW it was probably their hour for tea, and I hurried into the library separated by glass doors from the dining-room. At the table, as I could see through these doors, were seated three persons. Facing me sat my Uncle Tom,—my Uncle Tom, with eye-glasses on before folk! Opposite him was a lady, whom I easily conjectured to be Kate; between them a young man in an officer's uniform.

Uncle Tom looked up suddenly; "Kate," he said, "there is some one in the library."

I sprang into a corner.

"I guess not," answered Kate, turning round.

"I tell you there is, or was," he persisted; "I saw something red by the doors."

"Probably the light through the curtains," Kate answered; "we are having gorgeous sunsets now."

"I move we make a search after tea," the officer remarked.

"Kate," my uncle said, "what do you do to the

tea; it does not taste like tea. I have not had a decent cup of tea since poor Georgie went away."

The glass 'doors slid back at a touch: "Let me, uncle," I said, as quietly as if I had not been away a week.

My uncle sat as if paralyzed, his eyes dilating as he stared at me.

Kate, more practical, rushed to me. "Why, Georgie Vane," she exclaimed, "what a way to surprise people! I feel as if I had seen a ghost, and in my cloak, too! *Are* you real?"

"Georgie!" my uncle said, faintly, in a tone between an exclamation and an interrogation, "My Georgie?"

"Yes, uncle," kissing him.

"My own, own Georgie?—my pet, my darling, my old lady really?"

"Yes, uncle."

"I can hardly believe it," interposed Kate; "I am sure I am as white as a sheet. There never was such a surprise! How *did* you get here? If you had sent us word so we could have had the carriage."

"I could not have kept quiet in a carriage!" I answered.

"It is really you, Georgie?" again asked my uncle.

"As sure as can be," I answered.

"Well, go there and make me a cup of tea," he ordered.

" Before I abdicate," said Kate, "let me introduce Captain Lewis; my cousin, Mrs. Aberthnay, just from the land of secesh."

Captain Lewis arose and bowed, but he could not let down his eyelids.

I made my uncle's tea under a rattling fire of questions from Kate.

My uncle tasted his tea. " It is Georgie," he said, and rising, rang the bell violently.

"Here, all you people!" he cried, as every one in the house rushed to see what was the matter; "here, all you people! rejoice and make merry, and kill the fatted calf, for she that was lost is found."

Every one who had ever seen or heard of "Miss Georgie," headed by Mrs. Glynn, now gathered around me, for in five minutes' time I had succeeded in setting my uncle's usually quiet mansion into a terrific uproar. Some hurried me up-stairs and pushed me on a lounge; one unlaced my boots, one pulled down my hair, another disencumbered me of my heavy dress, while another stood ready to envelop me in one of my old wrappers that Mrs Glynn kept as sacredly as relics. They washed my face and combed my hair as if I had just been brought in from the dirt, and with a zeal not complimentary to Secessia.

As soon as I was considered clean enough I was permitted to descend to the dining-room, where there was a scene I shall never remember without laughing and crying together. While the women were employed with me, Uncle Tom had not been idle. I had told David to wait half an hour at the station, and then find his way to the "big brown house with the cupola," which we could see from the railroad depot; for I wished to make my entrance unattended. His half hour had been a short one, or he had taken a "short cut," for very soon my uncle's quick ears had caught the sound of boots on the gravelled pathway, and David was at once hailed and pressed into my uncle's service, as the young officer had been. In order to enlarge the table they had taken off the tea-things, and, manlike, piled them in a corner. With another leaf in the table the cloth proved too short, but they had concealed, as they supposed, the discrepancy by the tea-tray; they had piled upon the table every article of food to be found in garret, cellar, kitchen, or orchard, and, with a consideration natural to him, my uncle had given David to eat of the leg of a chicken, but not the usual facilities for disposing of the luxurious drumstick.

The picture that presented itself to my view as I reached the door of the dining-room, was a ludicrous one. My uncle, with his face very red, was pulling very hard at a stubborn cork in a bottle of his rarest wine. Captain Lewis, with coat-sleeves daintily rolled back, and looking very much disgusted, was trying to find place for a dish of jelly; and David, on a broad grin, with teeth and one hand kept tight hold of the drum-stick, while with the other hand and one knee he was upholding a dish of meat, apparently waiting for the Captain to find room for it.

One would have imagined all Secessia was in a starving condition, and I, as their representative, was expected to eat enough for all.

"But, bless his heart!" as Mrs. Glynn privately informed me, "he'd die, master would, if he couldn't do something for you."

And so I sat down, and was waited on. I refused not to "make an effort" at every thing he piled upon my plate.

Kate and the captain sat side by side, and made low-toned comments; and when, at last, I was considered to have eaten enough, and we had adjourned to the parlor for a good talk, Captain Lewis opened his mouth and spake:

"What do you think of our prosperity, Mrs Aberthnay? Does it not greatly surprise you? I wish you could tell your rebel friends of our abundance. A large number of us are in favor of starving them out. I presume you have seen terrible destitution there?"

And I answered, "You of the North and they of the South seem to know about as much of each other as you do of the Kamtschatkans."

"Do you mean they are not on the verge of starvation?" said he.

12

"I do," said I; "and I mean more. You must fight them in earnest, in fair and open fight, if you wish to conquer them."

This was all I ever told of my experience in the South.

When David had been feasted and lionized in the kitchen, I saw him to give him some orders.

"Dis berry grand place," he volunteered; "dey's berry proud to hab you, Missus. Wish Massa Carl could see how berry glad dey is!"

CHAPTER XXVI.

AND so I was home again,—home in all the dear old places, and scarcely able to realize such tempests of sorrow had swept over me, except, perhaps, by the calm they had left.

Nearly all our young gentlemen friends with whom we had been boating, riding, picnicing, and dancing, were off to the war; many had been killed, some were maimed for life; scarcely a dwelling in the land that had not been under the shadow of death. Not a dwelling in the land, thought I, but has hopes to have a flag, or sword, or musket to show when this war shall be a page in history.

Gilbert Stuart, Kate said, had been among the first to leave. He had gone first as a private in the old Sixth,—the immortal Sixth, whose blood stands recorded against the city of Baltimore,—a record which tears and blood such as no city has yet shed, can ever wholly wipe away. Gilbert was an officer now, Kate thought, though she knew but little of him lately. Others, mere boys when I was married, were distin-

guished officers now; and young girls then, like me,
were widows now.

Crowds besieged me, for I was a wonder. I had
come from Richmond; I knew all about the rebel
army and all about the rebel politics. I was pestered
with questions, but I told nothing. What right had
I to tell? The South had trusted me; and I could
not betray the trust. They hinted that I seemed half
secessionist, but in time they found that I was stronger
Union than many of them.

Many weeks passed and stretched away into
months. I had become quietly domesticated at home
again, wondering sometimes what had become of Mr.
Stuart. Had he died in the prison hospital, or escaped
death that time to meet it on some battle-field? Who
could tell me? I had thought I should hear from
him after his reception of his letters, for Gertrude had
requested him to give the ring to me, if not from himself as from her; and, if alive, he had ample time to
have heard of my return from the South, for it had
been talked of far and wide.

Perhaps he did not think me worthy of the ring
now. Something of the same spirit which had moved
Gertrude, when she said, " I meant he should love me
and suffer for me some time," arose in my heart.

One night a gentleman did call to see me, and in
the self-same room where I had so often dressed to
meet him I read his card.

The Captain's uniform to which he had now risen, became him well; manly, and stately, and stern he was now,—a man whose voice might make regiments start and tremble, if raised in command, and, if lowered to tones of sweet persuasion, might win the hardest heart.

Haughty, stern, and impatient now, where he had before been easy tempered and too patient, I wondered had Gertrude or I, or neither of us, the most to do with this change.

"I learned only a few days ago that you were here," he said, in rich but rather ceremonious tones. "I have been home on sick leave; home now means New York; my parents are there, but my sister is married and living here. I am glad to see you safely in your old home. It will be to remain until the war is over, I trust?"

"I expect it to be my home for the rest of my life," I answered; "I have left many pleasant friends behind; but I do believe the time is not far distant when there will be as free communication between us as there was formerly."

"I, too, found friends in the South, and in the day of my sorest need. I was wounded and taken prisoner; but either through a mistake, or the charity of a Southern lady, was taken to her house and cared for as if I had been the favorite son of the house. If I live until this war is over, I shall endeavor to find and thank her for her hospitality, her more than hospitality."

"Was that in Richmond?" I asked, restrained by his distant manner from saying more.

"Yes, and at the very time when Richmond was in its greatest panic. It was a fortunate thing for me; for Union prisoners, men of health and vigor, are constantly dying under the iron hand of their captors, and I could not have hoped for any care in the prison."

"Yet they try to give it?"

"Officers do,—for gentlemen are gentlemen all the world over,—and a being with a spark of manhood, courtesy, or of courage, would scorn to taunt a captive, and would always be tender to a wounded soldier. I cannot say as much for the ladies."

"These things must be hard to bear?"

"They are terrible. To hear their taunts and sneers, and feel your blood boiling, and not be able to strike or answer one word, because they are women!"

"Don't speak of it," I said; "I cannot forgive them, but I would like to forget it."

"I very seldom speak of it," he returned; "for the sake of that one noble woman who acted the Good Samaritan to me, I have been, as far as regard for truth would permit, their champion."

"Gallantry and gratitude must have a hard task to raise you to that point," I answered.

Our constrained conversation now gave place to an embarrassed silence, and to relieve it he asked me if I still sang.

"More than ever," I said; "music is my only expression; sometimes, if we have not expression, we must die."

"I have not attempted," he replied; "I feel how useless the attempt to say to you how much I sympathize—"

"Do not," I answered. "Nothing can be said. What would you wish me to sing for you?"

"One of your own songs. You know I always liked them the best."

"Did you? I had forgotten."

And that was the time I told a lie.

"I have about given up song-making," I added; "I wish I had a stirring war-song for you, but I have not; and as I cannot improvise I must give you something else. This is my latest; written when Yankee indifference one day roused my ire," and I sang:

> "Where, oh where, are the brave knights gone—
>   The loyal and the grand—
>   Who drove the cowards, Guilt and Wrong,
>   Through all their storied land?
>   Where, oh where, are the brave knights fled—
>   The loyal and the true—
>   Whose shafts, by Mars or Cupid sped,
>   Ne'er falsely aimed or flew?

> " Where, oh where, are the brave knights now,
>   With their fond love of right,
> Who never failed the needed blow
>   To punish wicked might?
> Where, oh where, do the young knights rest!
>   Who galloped far and wide,
> With flashing eyes and dauntless breast,
>   To fight at Honor's side?"

"There's more of it, an interminable string of verses. Do you want more?"

"Oh, decidedly! I am curious to know how you get along without your knights, if only echo answers *where*, and what you will do with them if found."

"You shall hear:

> "Now here we see the open lists,
>   And Treason talks aloud,
> And strikes with lance and clenched fists
>   The shield of Truth so proud.
> And Liberty, with pale, thin hands
>   Chained o'er her aching breast,
> All helpless at his mercy stands,
>   Claimed as his slave and jest!"

"I trust," he said very gravely, "your last word is not intended as a disrespectful allusion to the very witty Father of his Country?"

"I assure you not," I replied. "It was for the rhyme."

"I am doubtful yet," he said; "but perhaps your next verses will redeem the unlucky word."

"But what," I asked, "will redeem the fact?"

"That is disrespectful to my commander-in-chief. Is not this a free country, and shall he not have his little jokes?"

"I submit," I answered; "but that is quite enough of my song."

"Not by any means," he answered; "it does not give it a finish."

"Oh well, one more; *one of many:*

> "Oh! that as in days past and gone,
> Pressing full deep the spur,
> Gallantly would come dashing on
> Some knight to rescue her.
> But give us blood and grief and tears,
> Through our slumbering land,
> Till we have roused from other years
> The brave old knightly band."

"You will join it, won't you, Mr. Stuart?"

"The 'brave old knightly band,' I wish I could."

"No knight ever fought in a better cause," I answered; "for the cause of country, government, and humanity, is the cause of God."

"God help it!" he answered; "it seems a hard fight, sometimes."

"You go back to it soon?"

"In a day or two; perhaps to-morrow. I can hardly hope to see you again, yet I am loth to say good-bye."

12*

" And I,—it is hard to see the sturdiest private in the street, trudging off to the war with his knapsack on his back, and somebody's good-bye in his ears."

"I suppose you pray for our soldiers?"

" I do, indeed; what woman does not?"

" Then you will pray for me?   Good-bye."

He held my hand an instant, and looked down into my eyes.

I felt myself coloring, but I drew away my hand instantly.

He said nothing of Gertrude's ring, but every tone of his voice, constrained though it was, told me he knew he was free.

CHAPTER XXVII.

My life was a weary one; but I need not tell you that. You see yourself it had been shattered, and had not an interest to bind it again together. I could not settle down to quiet charities, to little patriotic sacrifices; I could not busy myself reading or studying, for to what end should I study? My life had, indeed, been "broken at the fountain," broken when it was so young, so hopeful, it seemed to itself hardly to have sprung into being.

Kate, on the contrary, was full of animation; she was president of half a dozen benevolent institutions, and yet had always time to spare for amusement. Captain Lewis was now resting under the shadow of her wings; and his very evident fear of her struck me very comically. It made one little change in my sad life, watching the progress of this little comedy, pretty sure to end, as comedies should, in speedy marriage.

"Do you know that Captain Lewis, the odious man, is positively going off to-morrow?" Kate said to me the evening after Gilbert's visit. "It is just too aggravating for any thing in this world, just as we were getting on so nicely! I am going to Mrs. Wilcox's to-night, a sort of God-speed party to the officers here,—that is, if I ever get dressed. Mrs. Martin has been holding me, after the manner of the Ancient Mariner, until my patience is quite exhausted. Will you help me?—*do* dress my hair for me; I look like a different person after I have been through your hands. Will you?—that is a darling. Here!" She threw me a wrapper. "Hurry now, and do me up pretty."

"Captain Lewis is not half good enough for you," I said, taking down her hair.

"I don't suppose he is," she answered; "we are not expected to marry men half good enough for us. I expect to marry because I don't want to be an old maid, and because I want a home of my own. I shall be quite contented if my husband hasn't any very serious faults, and for the rest I mean to educate him up to me."

"But you know, Kate, this home is as much yours as mine; more yours, for my lamp of life has gone out, and I want only a dark corner; the rest is all yours."

"Oh! I know you and Uncle Vane are kindness itself, but no woman likes to sit at the *side* of any man's table. How natural you look in that cashmere. I never saw any woman but you who looked well in bright colors. I expect to have a lovely time to-night. I am just as fond of good times as I was ten years ago. What times we used to have! Do you remember Emma Lewis, Mary Allen, Florence Graham, and the rest? Do you remember the summer they were here, just before Mr. Aberthnay went away? I think that was about the most delightful summer we ever had. I did like Mr. Aberthnay so much! I had a splendid talk with him once. Shall I tell you about it?"

"Yes, do."

"It was just before he went away. Florence, you know, was just wild about him, and, it seems, she told him you had told her you were engaged to Mr. Stuart Gilbert, you know,—or what amounted to the same thing. He let it out to me, or, at least, I drew it out of him, for I knew he was loving you beyond all bounds. I did think then that you liked him, and I was, myself, half in love with Gilbert Stuart,—just a girl's fancy, you know; and so I up and down denied it, and just let him see what Florence was up to; then we talked about you. He said he knew you were not happy, and he asked me to be especially kind to you; and if any thing happened to you, to write and let him know, without your knowledge; he did care so much for you!"

"Did you ever write him?"

"No, of course not, what need?"

"Sure enough, what need?"

"I think I was never so happy in my life when I heard you were engaged to him. I don't think any man ever loved a woman as much as he did you, even then. Do you know, he actually made me promise not to tell you; he was sure you did not care for him, and said it would only be additional pain to you to know about it."

"Poor Carl!"

"There was never a man like him. No one can wonder, Georgie, that your life seems broken. But do not let us talk about it. I like to look up in the glass and see you look like old times; and now that your hair is tumbling down you are my Georgie of ten years ago. Do you know, Uncle Tom has never got over that surprise yet. Every little while he says to me, 'Wasn't it a surprise, Kate?—just as if she hadn't been a week away! But I'll be even with her,—I'll be even with her.'"

"Uncle ought to be home soon." He was in New York. "We two women are not much of a household."

"Not much. Do you know about David?"

"No; what?"

"He is going down to the army as officer's servant, if you will let him; he expects to send you his wages! You can't beat freedom into that *that* 'child's' head. But you will have to braid faster than that if you expect to get through to-night. It looks well, doesn't it? I wish I had some flowers."

"My camelia is in bloom; you are a good girl and you shall have it. What is its motto?"

"I don't know; why?"

"I suppose it will end in Captain Lewis's button-hole."

"Ar'n't you mean!"

"I will go down and see what I can find in the conservatory," I said; "I suppose I shall not meet any one." .

I pushed my hair out of the way, and the old habit sent it back from my face as I used to wear it. It startled me to see it rippling so naturally into its old folds, and sparkling all over with smiles at its release. I wound it in a hasty coil, and hurried down stairs to get the flowers in the little conservatory beyond the parlor. Something,—the change of dress, perhaps, or the backward rolls of my hair,—reminded me of that other flight down the same long staircase; something,—the same angels that attended me then, perhaps,—seemed to promise better days to come, peace and that soul-comfort and calm which is the crown sooner or later given of all grief.

I pushed open the parlor door, and there, leaning against my piano, stood Gilbert Stuart awaiting me.

"I am losing my senses," I said to myself; "or is all this a dream? and am I Georgie Vane, just called from the dressing-room? and are the girls still there? for surely he is here."

I held out my hands; I hardly know if in welcome or to push away that figure. They were closely grasped, and a voice cried, "Georgie! Georgie!"— that voice that could inspire or terrify whole regiments, and would melt the hardest heart.

"Georgie! Georgie!"

"Is this real?" I asked, like one in a maze; "is to-night that other night when I met you here?"

"It is not that other night," he answered; "that was a night that I have expiated by long, long years of bitter pain. I fell once from my strength, and faith, and honor."

"Yes, I know," I said, drawing back a little; "she told me."

"She told you, too, that I was free?"

"She told me."

"Oh! if she could have told you how I fought against her influence,—how bitterly I have repented the folly that bound me to her, and put that gulf between us, between you and me, Georgie. I cannot tell you that I love you; I have told her that; and words that any other woman has heard, are not words to say to you. You know what I would say to you; what burned on my lips last night, but which your constrained manner and sombre dress forbade me to say. Georgie, give me the words I lack; tell me in what manner I may speak to you of the love that has been my life, my joy, and my agony for years, and years, and years."

"Yes, I know," I said.

"You know; it is only a heart like yours that can know."

"Let me think," I said.

"No, no, do not think; I have waited for this day, —waited when there was no hope that it would ever come. Once I came here to implore you, on my knees, to forgive me,—to wait, to let me explain, to give me a word that would make me strong enough to burst my bonds, were they ten times as binding. I have waited; I can wait no longer; you risked your life for me in Charleston; you risked still more for me in Richmond. Yes, I know; Kate told me where you lived there: it was easy guessing then; but I want more. Georgie, I must hear those words, those blessed words: will you not speak? Oh! I deserve forgive- ness since I alone have suffered."

"You—alone—suffered?"

"I alone,—mine the fault, mine the expiation. Have I not expiated it? Oh! that for one hour it were given to me to speak as I would speak,—for one hour that I could find words to tell what thoughts have been mine when death was on every side, and cut down men like grass, and shunned my prayers, laugh- ed at my entreaties, and passed me by, when I so longed for him!—but for one hour that I could find expression for that self-reproach, greater than any rage, which has had triple revenge on me for my sin! Georgie, speak one word to me, and I shall forget all my past misery."

"I do not know what I ought to say."

"Do not mar this blessed day with doubts and fears. You have had your sorrows,—mine no words can tell. Let us join hands to-night, and sorrow will be forgotten forevermore. I dare not say what I will strive to be to you. I fear not to promise any thing, for whatever you would wish me to be, that your wish will make me. If you will but say the word, Georgie, you stretch before my feet a life of joy, and good, and glory; there is no path I could not tread if that path led to you. There is nothing I might not be, if you willed me so to be. Will you throw away my life? Will you throw away my future, and trample upon my past? I hold all that I am, or hope to be, or aspire to do, in my hand; one word decides it."

"I implore you, spare me."

"I will not spare you. This thing shall be. Is my life nothing?—is my soul nothing, my will not to be counted? I will never let you rest. I will follow you night and day. I will love you till love becomes madness; and while there is breath within me I will breathe for you, and raise my voice in supplications. You are drawing farther away? I frighten you?

Darling, darling Georgie, whom I love with such love
as man never gave before, speak to me as I would
have you speak, and you shall never again hear my
voice,but in tenderest tones,—never hear a word from
me but of unalterable devotion; but, Georgie, you
must speak that word. What would you say if I
gave way at the first fire of the enemy? Shall I give
up now, when I fight for more than life, or land, or
government?—when I fight for heaven here and
heaven hereafter. *Will* you speak, Georgie?"

. "I loved you once, I know, with a love strong as
your own. You threw aside that love."

"I did, I did; for one hour I was another man. I
threw away a pearl beyond price; but myself again,
I will have back that pearl. I will seek it early and
late; nor will I rest until it is mine. No, Georgie, I
will yield,—I will go out into pain and utter desolation, if you say so. I have pained you enough.
If I can control myself I will plead no longer; just as
we stand fronting the battle-line, waiting victory or
death, I will try to stand."

He folded his arms and stood still; he was pale as
death itself, and it seemed as if every nerve was
strained to preserve the silence and outward calm he
had promised. At my feet lay the love I had worn
out half my soul longing for; yet, now that it was
mine, I was slow to take it. I knew not what answer
to make; my soul was stirred and surged tumultuously

within me. "Pray God give me a sign," was my only distinct thought. I looked to him, wondering if I would dare lay my hand on the great waves of his heart, and say "Be still!" He watched me; and seeing that my lips stammered, he was satisfied. With one long breath of relief, he came slowly toward me.

"My God! this is joy!" he said, and would have put on my hand Gertrude's ring, and bent as if to kiss me. God had given me the sign,—all was clear enough then. "No," I said, "I am married. I am Carlton Aberthnay's wife in life and in death. Dare not touch me. I see it now. The grave does not break the marriage vow. I would not dare meet him in heaven if I listened to one word more from you. Do you hear? You speak, if you speak at all, to a married woman,—no more to Georgie Vane."

He staggered back.

"Many sins have I committed," I said; "but I shall not add this one. From my heart I pity you. God may perhaps forgive me that I let it come to this. Carl may pardon that I have heard words his wife should not hear. Will you forgive me for the pain to you?"

"I will not," he repeated; "I will never forgive you."

"You shall forgive me, Gilbert Stuart; you shall pray me for forgiveness! Do you remember for how many years you followed my every step, and wound yourself into my every thought? Do you remember how freely, how trustfully, how unaskingly I poured out my love for you, and you took it? Do you remember when I flew down those stairs to meet you, with my heart and soul all yours, that you took me by the hand, and in cold blood stabbed me to the heart? Do you remember how you followed me, wounded, bleeding as I was, and widened and deepened my wounds? Do you remember that you plunged the iron into my soul to grind down my life and his— my noble husband's? Do you think these things weigh with me? Their bitterness has passed. In one moment I see the folly and wrong of a life that owes you nothing now. That one moment's revelation is worth all that you have made me suffer.

> 'The flash that lighteth up a valley amid the dark midnight of a
> storm,
> Coineth the mind with that scene sharper than fifty summers.'

I thank you for that flash, Gilbert Stuart, for it gives me back my husband's love; it gives mine to him; it gives me his memory, and the hope that one day I may be worthy to meet him in perfect love and perfect understanding."

"I only bide my time," he said, turning to the door.

"You will never speak of love to me again," I said. "You dare not. And now, good-night."

"I believe that you love me," he said; "and this farewell is not final."

"Final or not matters little to me," I answered. "But this does matter, that you should know that I do not love you. It is true that the belief that I loved you grew with my growth, and became almost a part of me. The force of habit is great with all; it was like iron chains on me; when I met you at intervals, you pieced and strengthened the links that were wearing away. That I thought I loved you was a burden upon me under which another, a better and higher love, I can see now, was living and struggling to the light. I thank God that to-night that burden is thrown aside, and that love is free, and I am free. I thank God that the memory of my husband's virtue, and the hope that he may claim me in heaven, are stronger and dearer than any love, pride, or fame this world can offer. I thank him that my storm-tossed life is at last at anchor. My heart, with all its joy, aches for you; but I believe you will live to smile a painless smile upon to-night and on me."

"There is no anchor for me," he replied bitterly, turning to go; "for the rest of my life I drift."

CHAPTER XXVII.

As Gilbert reached the door my Uncle Tom met and arrested him.

"No one here?" exclaimed my uncle. "This is polite treatment. Oh, there is Georgie. Well, young lady, what has happened now? Looks quite like herself, doesn't she, Stuart? Come back, come back, my dear fellow; no running off like that. I have just this moment made my appearance after a week's absence. I deserve a warmer welcome. Mrs. Glynn's eyes promised something better. Come in, Stuart. How well you look, Madam! Just stay that way, if you please. All the paraphernalia of mourning shuts you up from me, so that I hardly know my Georgie. We shall have her blithe as a lark, now she is home again, shan't we, Stuart? And then, if Major Aberthnay turns out alive and commander-in-chief, he will still find a beauty for his wife."

"How can you jest on that, uncle?" I said. Before he could answer, there was a terrific rustle of silk,

and Kate and Captain Lewis appeared at the door
through which Mr. Stuart was trying to escape.

"You are a great flower-girl," Kate exclaimed,
standing in the doorway.

"It is too bad," I answered, "but not too late."

"Thank you," she returned; "I have plenty now.
How do you do, Uncle Vane?"

"I am very well I thank you, *Aunt* Kate. Where
are you going without my mighty permission? You
will just please to wait for supper, you and Captain
Lewis. I am going to have something good for supper."

"Can you wait?" Kate asked the captain.

"Can he wait!" echoed Uncle Tom. "*Will you
wait for supper?* Oh, what a question to ask an army
officer!"

Kate made a comical face, which, however, did not
suit her as well as the same contortions did when she
was a few years younger. Kate had grown very fair and
stately in the few years past. The dresses that looked
cumbrous upon her at eighteen, now swept gracefully
around her, and suited her face that had grown womanly, resolute, and self-confident. You may imagine
her standing in the doorway, in her favorite russet-
brown silk, rich and heavy; her long, sweeping white
cloak; flowers that Captain Lewis had brought, in
her hair and in her dress, and a magnificent bouquet
in her hand. I don't know that Gilbert was struck

with her beauty, but I think he noticed the amplitude of her skirts that effectually cut off his retreat, as she stood there with Captain Lewis, not over-pleased at the detention.

"I give you ten minutes to dress," Uncle Tom said to me. "*Don't* change that dress."

I left the parlor by a door that led into our sitting-room. Some one spoke; there was a figure there; Carl's, or his spirit.

"I do not think," I said, as soon as I could command my voice, "that any evil thing would be permitted to take your form, my husband. It seems a fit ending to the tumult of to-night that your spirit should come, not to reproach me, surely, but to let me say that, at last, I am yours,—all, all yours,—and that I live to meet you in heaven."

"Do not be afraid, Georgie," the figure said, approaching me. "I am not a spirit; I am your real, living husband, if you will own me. These are no spirit arms that hold you, darling."

"My Carl! I am surely dreaming, or my senses have given way; but it is a delirium so sweet I would never be sane again! Yes, darling Carl, hold me tighter!—speak fast, faster, that I may know. Do not speak, for fear it may not be you. This is too much joy for reality. I loved you all that time, but I was not sure I did. I love you now so much that if I awake from this dream I shall die."

13

"You shall not awake, Georgie, darling, pet Georgie. It is reality at last. You know how often these false reports of death in battle come. I did nothing to contradict that of mine, as I shall tell you by and by. Do you question still, my own, own wife? To think this joy was waiting for me! This love ready for me! It is I who seem to dream!"

"Keep talking, Carl, for then it seems as if it might be. Worse than any death or desolation it would be if you should slip from my arms now. Oh! a thousand times I have clung to you as now; a thousand times your kisses have rained on me as now; and in stronger words than I can speak I have told you of the bitter mistake I made, implored your forgiveness, and felt myself forgiven as you forgive me now, darling; and with your words yet in my ears, I have opened my eyes, and you were not there. Can it be so now?"

"No, pet,—no, no; this is no dream for either of us! Joy, joy, life, reality, are with us as they never were before! Exultation and joy, for I live and you love me!"

"And you—I have not lost your—"

"Hush! hush! Never, darling, waking or dreaming, my Georgie, dare to question the love that is yours; that the grave cannot take away, that all life lives to prove and to increase! Are you satisfied yet that I am I?"

"I am satisfied that if this is a dream that I shall not live if I awake; and so I believe."

"The strangest thing," I said, when, long afterwards, I found more rational thoughts, "is that the first surprise over, it does not seem strange to have you here. How often have I caught myself starting at the sound of a voice, or even the ringing of the door-bell! How often has my heart bounded at a face or figure in a crowd or in the street, and then sunk back in sickening knowledge that you were counted dead. I would tell myself of that, and yet,—Tennyson has the same thought in one of the most beautiful parts of his *In Memoriam*. I used to think I should not be surprised to meet you anywhere, and, as Tennyson says:

> "'And if along with these should come
>   The man I held as half divine;
>   Should strike a sudden hand in mine
> And ask a thousand things of home;

> "'And I should tell him all my pain,
>   And how my life had drooped of late,
>   And he would sorrow o'er my state,
> And marvel what possessed my brain;

> "'And I perceive no touch of change,
>   No hint of death in all his frame,
>   But found him all in all the same,
> I should not feel it to be strange,'"

"And yet, my darling Georgie, the struggle be-tween your soul's recognition of the truth and your fears to trust its voice, not an hour ago, almost fright-ened me, and I trembled lest at the very moment I had found not only my Georgie but my Georgie's heart, I had lost both. I was greatly against the surprise; but Mr. Vane had set his heart on doing it just so, and was inxorable. I cannot tell you how I suffered as, absolutely forbidden to seek you, I waited for you to come. I listened, I heard all their voices, I waited, I strained my ears, I ached to hear yours, but you did not—I know you did not—speak, I could not have lost the faintest sound of your voice, until after your uncle spoke of me. Then, when I did hear it, I seemed paralyzed with mingled emotions. Had you been one moment later I should have recovered, and, unable longer to wait, gone to you. You looked like a spirit as you came in, Georgie."

"Well I might, for I had come from the crowning battle of a ten years' war,—a crowning battle that was a victory. It was the battle of mind over matter, and mind won the victory."

"What was the war?"

"Not now; do not ask me now. Some day I shall have a story to tell you of an old habit that I clung to perversely, that I conquered not two hours ago. There is nothing now, my Carl, to come between us. Oh! that I could bring back the days in which you plead so hard, that I might give them undying love, as I do these!"

"No, we will not call them back; they were dear, blessed days, because they prepared the way for this. Do you know, Georgie, that for all the years your face was set against me, for all the grief I have had that it was so; for all my passionate pleadings, and for all my pain, it seems as if I had always seen you and held you as I do now, my own loving wife?"

"Yes, Carl; for I think my heart was yours all that time. It should have been. I know it was. I was like a lost spirit when you were gone; there was no rest, no peace, no anchor for me. I tried to think other things were the cause of my unrest, but they were not. Oh! I have a long story to tell you of my life after you left. And you,—when will you tell me of yours, and of your coming here?"

"It is a long story, and must be heard and told at our leisure. Who are in there?"

"Uncle Tom, Kate, Captain Lewis, and Captain Stuart."

"Our old friend Gilbert? I suppose we must go to them."

"I have to dress. Uncle Tom gave me ten minutes to dress. Kate is going to a party after supper, I suppose she is inwardly fretting at this delay. I ran down to the parlor to get her some flowers and was caught, and have not had time to dress since. My hair is in a great state."

"You don't go out of my sight for anybody or any thing. Roll up your hair and come. Rebellious already? I will be your hair-dresser. It is a long time since I have seen these bright rolls, Georgie."

"What will you do when they are thin and gray?"

"You know. Wicked Georgie for asking such a question! Now, come; Uncle Tom has told them all, I suppose?"

"What do you call 'all'?"

"The little fact of my existence, which is about the smallest part of all."

"Perhaps!"

It was evident Uncle Tom had contrived to interest them in a long story of the great event, for he was still talking when we entered the room. Kate sprang forward to meet us, and Gilbert Stuart took advantage of her movement to make good his escape.

"This," I heard Captain Lewis say to Kate on the way to supper, "this beats all the houses I ever saw for surprises. It will be our turn next."

"I owed you one, eh Georgie, didn't I, old lady?" said Uncle Tom, rubbing his hands. "I am even with you."

"Ahead of me, uncle; I shall never dispute your success."

"You're welcome home, sir," said Mrs. Glynn, as we entered the supper-room.

At which we all saluted Carl with a laugh. I think my Uncle Tom put her up to it.

CHAPTER XXVIII.

"Now," I said, when Kate and the captain had eaten their supper and gone, "I want your story from title-page to finis. I suppose we have dragged out the greater part of it by our questions during the last half hour, but I want it altogether."

"It isn't possible," cried my Uncle Tom, "that you are going to tell that story again? It is no less than fifteen and a half times I have heard it already! He was button-holed, Georgie, at every step in New York, and in the cars coming on it was just fearful. How is it there are always some people everywhere ever ready with information about everybody, who never fail to find you out under fifty disguises? Nobody could question for an instant that our young man there was an officer; that knowledge of itself is about as much as most men need to start examinations and cross-examinations."

"Once it was my own fault," said Carl.

"How was that," I asked.

"A young sprig in a new uniform," answered my

uncle, "who had evidently yet to hear the first sound
of an enemy's gun, was giving forth his mighty opinions
about the great contest. 'The South couldn't keep it
up much longer,' he said; 'they were a half-starved
set of poor devils at the best; it wasn't any thing to
whip *them*. As for their leaders, there wasn't an
officer fit to command a regiment of our men among
them.' Our young *Napoleon*, I was going to say, but
the name is already appropriated, so I will call our
young sprig only a hero, was as hard upon the abolitionists as upon the secessionists, didn't think the
negroes had any thing to do with the war,—and, you
can guess, the usual rigmarole. I saw that Carl was
blazing; I was only very much amused, and quite
undisturbed by the sledge-hammer of criticism with
which our hero came down upon everybody and
every thing,—Generals, Congressmen, West Point,
and I cannot tell what all. Poor fellow! six months
later how he would blush for his arrogance! 'You
are in the army, I should judge,' a gentleman said,
turning around to Carl, 'how do these things please
the soldiers?' Carl had his text, and he came down
with a whole charge."

"I was very sorry for it afterwards," said Carl,
"for the little fellow liked his brief hour of lionizing,
and it was too bad to interrupt it; but I came North
expecting to find but one mind, one thought, one view
of the rebellion, and my enthusiasm surprises people

as much as the rustic's unrestrained laughter at old stage-jokes. I am still on the invalid corps, so excuse my story, Georgie, if it lacks hair-breadth escapes and thrilling scenes. I cannot go through the story of the past six months, although in the simplest words and merely in outline, without feeling intensely the old struggles. I am not much at telling stories."

"People generally make the preface after the tale is told," I suggested.

"You must know then," Carl continued, "that I went into the secession movement with the best intentions in the world, and with a romantic idea of liberty, tyrants, and 'down with the fierce oppressor.' As the movement grew more serious, and men discussed not only its expediency but its right, I found myself several times knocked in the head by arguments that left their mark. I was, however, heart and soul in the cause; with all my heart and soul believed it right, or, perhaps, as we are all human, I should not have so readily promised Georgie, who, you know, Mr. Vane, was stout for the Union, that if I ever doubted the right of the Southern cause that I would give it up. I am not going to tell you of my battles and heroic achievements at present; I was asked how I came here, and it is of inward struggles I have now to speak. I went off to the war, strong and unshaken; I shut my eyes, as every soldier should, to every thing but the right of the cause which

13*

no bad leadership however much it may injure can ever make less right. But as I was thrown among our officers and soldiers, I was forced to see, and to see with disgust, to how many low and base motives appeals were made, and how few, how very few were moved by sterling principle. But there were other men, earnest like myself, men whose souls had panted for action through many idle years, and we helped each other's doubting faith. I do not believe because others scorned to own to any lack of faith that they did not also doubt. After awhile it became my place to be much among the prisoners,—prisoners of both sides. I met among the Union prisoners, officers and privates, men of intelligence, culture, understanding, and of thorough worth; men who fully and clearly saw and knew for what they were fighting. They spoke of us with decision in regard to our political sins,—they never minced matters about these,—but I scarcely ever heard one betray any vindictiveness, bitterness, or any personal animosity. Considering they fought well, believed in the war, and intended to carry it through, and were influenced in their opinions by no desire for our good will, nor fear of us, I liked their mildness. One officer, I remember, one day said to me: 'I have been over many battle-fields, and have everywhere been struck by the truly noble physique of your dead; it is hard such fine fellows must go down like so much grass, but the cause of the nation demands it, and you know we fight you just as hard as though we had not a thousand times rather welcome you to our tables in thorough good fellowship. Are you brothers or barbarians we must fight you just the same, so long as you rebel against our government and yours. But we fight ourselves, almost, in fighting you; we have an older brother sort of feeling toward you; we can't judge you quite as severely as if you were not a wayward younger brother. You will never believe how much of affection there is in our feelings toward you. Men like you, Major, can understand it, others may call it cowardice, servility, or some other unworthy name; the fact remains unaltered.' Our own soldiers always came back from the North subdued by their visits to the strongholds of the nation; no sneers, no contemptuous remarks, no insulting names for them as they went sullen and sulky to their prisons. I have known of very many acts of real kindness and consideration from the Union guards to their prisoners; sometimes when these latter have been tired, worn, sick or wounded, perhaps, the others have dismounted from their horses and let their prisoners take their place, they trudging by on foot. But mark this—their food, their horses, their blankets, they might share, or give, but never liberty, or an acknowledgment that they were not 'rebels,' and as 'rebels' fought and conquered. This is the spirit I like; no appeals to selfish motives or ignoble passions to fire your Northern heart, but the pure love of principle; no weak and mistaken mercy, but Roman-like justice. These things I saw, and each in its own way helped on the work of my conversion.

"I was slightly wounded during the winter,—I never wrote you of that, Georgie; it was not worth while to worry you about so small an affair. I fell into the hands of the Sisters of Charity, even under the care of your old friend Emma Lewis; who had also, she told me, taken care of Captain Belton, who regards himself as one of your converts. He proved himself a valuable acquisition to the Union army."

"He was killed, poor fellow! on the Peninsula."

"Don't say *poor fellow*, his death completed a noble, martyr-like career. Sister Louisa was very reticent and demure; I teased and tormented her in every way I could devise to make her talk about the war, but she was on her guard—it was not for a Sister of Charity to speak. One day, at last, I roused her. I talked against the Government; made fun of its officers until grace could stand no more; Sister Louisa colored and said: 'All the ridicule in the world, all the satire of Junius, cannot make our Government less a Government nor your rebellion less a rebellion.' It was a great deal to have drawn from a Sister of Charity, but the old Adam was strong in Emma even then. The ice once broken I got her to talk seriously with me; I risked nothing in opening my heart to a recluse. She is a tough little Union woman, and gave her reasons for her faith with a will, and with never a waver in her voice. She has grown a splendid woman, Emma has, and I owe her more than I can say. After a time I left the hospital and tossed about in various ways, and worked hard to keep thoughts out of my head, and to show myself really a soldier. I kept from thinking moderately well until I was again wounded in the summer. I did hope I might die then, and be spared the pain of decision, which is *the* pain always; to *act* is nothing. I found it hard to decide; I could not fight against my convictions and my promise to Georgie, and it was hard to desert the cause I had been one of the first to embrace. But my convictions and my health would not give way, but struggled on to strength. I could not die; I was forced to decide. I could not stay longer in the house of the kind Southern people, who, proud to have a Southern officer in the house with them, exerted themselves to the utmost to take care of me, and were, indeed, mothers and sisters to me; and I got away from them as soon as I could, resolved if I had to live to make my way to headquarters, resign, and then who could tell what? I had hardly clearly made up my mind in this respect, than I was taken prisoner. You can imagine my rage and chagrin. To declare myself an unbeliever in secession, to give up my commission after having been a prisoner, admitted of too many suggestions against my honor for me to think of it. In this painful state of mind I was taken into the Union lines, and into the hands of some officers who treated me with every attention, care, and kindness. I was very much exhausted, so much so that they soon expressed their fears that I was past recovery. I did nothing to undeceive them. They forced me to take a little wine. Every thing seemed in confusion, but I lay quietly and without motion, while orderlies came and went, or gathered around the tent door. I gathered scraps of their conversation; fortunately it was a kind that did me good. The tents were near together, and as the evening grew quieter I could hear, was forced to hear the conversation in the next tent to the one to which I had been taken. I wish I could repeat to you kind words, high-toned sentiments, brave energetic thoughts which were thrown in my way that night.

"For some reason I was carried farther on, or in a different direction, and, I think, they broke up camp, or there was danger of an attack, for two men were left in charge of me, and there was complete silence around me. A thunder-storm came up, a violent one, and at every burst of thunder my guard started, and muttered something meant, perhaps, for a prayer. They did their duty by occasionally pouring down my throat a few drops of some liquor which had been left for me, and pouring down their own large quantities of the same, until, as will sometimes happen, the bottle showed itself to be empty. One of the men expressed his convictions that he could find more if he looked in the right place, and with his bottle under his overcoat started on the quest, leaving his companion alone with me. This man, evidently, did not relish a lonely watch, a dark night, a thunder-storm, a dying rebel, and no whiskey, and soon moved after his partner. ' Are ye alive?" he said to me before leaving; ' poor fellow! I'm loth to lave ye, but I'm afeard somewhat's happened to Mike, and it's our duty to stand by each other; but I'll not be long gone.'

"I made no answer, of course, and off he went. The rascal left his overcoat, into which I put myself, and, forcing my strength back, I got out of the tent. I found myself unable to go far, but found a hiding-place so near at hand that, to speak after the manner of the Hibernians, it was beyond suspicion. The men after awhile returned, very angry, very tipsy, and very much scared. 'I knew the divil would have the —— rebel,' said one, as they went around looking for me. 'But what would the divil want of me overcoat?' asked the other. 'Maybe the ould gintleman don't like the climate,' suggested the first. ' Or is afeard of the draft, maybe,' added the second. Talking in this way they passed me, and aided, perhaps, by a quantity of bills I had forgotten purposely, they decided to give up the search, and from them came the testimony, I suppose, of my death. I am sorry to have such things to record of Union patriots; but human nature is human nature, you know.

"I got to a small hut in the wood, was taken in, gave the owners some money, laid down on the floor, and had a raging fever. They took such care as they could of me, and as I was not destined to die, I lived. When I was able to stir I got back to the South. No one wondered that I resigned, for I was completely smashed up. I worked along slowly, very slowly indeed. You were gone to the North I supposed. I made no inquiries lest I should interfere with your plans. I made arrangements to follow you; slow arrangements, for I was laid up every few days. I got through the lines of both armies; it would be imprudent, as the newspapers say, to give the details.

"Resting at New York I was recognized in my olden capacity as a Southern officer, a muss was made, and I was arrested. No one would listen to me; time and my money were wearing away; but believing every day must be the last, I forbore any steps for my release or assistance. However, I couldn't expect any thing better, and tried to wait with resignation. Georgie knows why I did not send word to her, and was even half doubtful, sometimes, of how she would receive me. In due time I was released, without any questions on either side, and then was I mad! If I were not a spy they had no right to arrest me; if I were a spy they had no right to free me; and they knew no more of me on the day they opened my prison doors than on the day they first closed them between me and liberty. I went to Washington; I lost time, strength, money, and temper, but gained no satisfaction nor notice, except that a scamp of an editor got hold of my name, and made a paragraph about me. Said paragraph came to the notice of somebody who knew Mr. Vane; who, meeting Mr. Vane one day, questioned him of me. Exclamations and explanations followed. Mr. Vane took his cane and started after me. He came in good time; he owed you a surprise, he said. I make no attempt to tell you all he did for me; but we journeyed together, and here I am. These are but the hurried outlines of my history; if I live I shall give you incidents enough to fill them up to a three-volumed novel. But this must do for to-night. You know, Goergie, I have a story to hear."

"Yes, Carl, and you shall hear it, although I have told you nearly all. I told you before that I visited a 'grave supposed to be yours. Oh, what a night it was! You must have that name changed."

"No, I mean to leave it. They carried it rather far, but it is true in one sense. *Blank Aberthnay*, C. S. A., *is* dead and buried. There is poetic and proper justice in that inscription. A leader, as he was proud to be in this great contest; one of those who set this terrible ball of battle rolling, he owed his grave to his enemies, and of him remains only a mutilated name, and three letters that tell the history of his life and his death, his sin and his shame. How like the prophetic wish of your favorite poet:

> ' *Amérique, ô patrie! Amérique, ô ma mère!*
> *S'il est un de tes fils assez lâche et vulgaire,*
> *Pour t'entendre offenser et pour te renier,*
> *Seul, sans pleurs, sans regrets, qu'il meure tout entier!*
> *Que son nom, effacé des pages de l'histoire,*
> *Effacé de tout cœur et de toute mémoire,*
> *Entouré du linceul d'un éternel oubli,*
> *Dans la nuit du tombeau descende enseveli.'* "

ADRIEN ROUQUETTE.

"And now," said my Uncle Tom, "what is to be the next move?"

"As soon as I am strong enough I am going into your army, and repair as well as I can some of the injury I have done the country."

"And it shall be my part," added my uncle, "to get your commission. Don't give yourself a moment's thought on the subject. I will attend to it."

"Commission me no commissions," Carl said; "I have always had great regard for the good son who stayed quietly at home, and for whom the fatted calf was never killed. I have no right to any of the honors of the land, and yet it is an honor to wear the uniform of the United States in any capacity. I shall be grateful if I can be allowed to wear it in its humblest manner, and shall be glad if I am permitted to take my chances at the eleventh hour with those who have borne the heat and burden of the day. Don't cry, Georgie; I haven't gone yet."

"Half my tears are tears of pride. No king ever laid down his crown, and took up the cowl of a monk with purer charity, and higher courage than you have changed the livery of secession for that of government. I am proud of you, dear Carl, for I know, darling, what it has cost you to do it. God knows, too."

"It costs much, and yet less than you think. It is the only thing that I could do. It is not a matter that admits of question or doubt; it is, indeed, a luxury to do a work that is so clearly chalked out. I think the pains of doubt and indecision are very nearly the severest pains, and the most difficult to bear of any in this world."

"I think so too, Carl," I said, "and I think as well it is a luxury to do a work that is so clearly marked out as mine."

"Yours!" echoed Uncle Tom, "a woman's work! What might be the labor of *your* life?"

"Woman's work has generally no name, but it is none the less a work, even though it is nameless, or well loved."

"I never knew her to do any thing in her life," my Uncle Tom said to Carl; "she isn't even president of a single benevolent association."

"I have something to do, nevertheless," I answered.

"What can it be?" he asked.

"To love Carl," I answered, and I have been doing it ever since.

CHAPTER XXIX.

WHAT more can I tell you, ye patient friends, who have followed me through all my faults and follies safe to my anchorage ? As the painter who represented a father's grief by a face covered with a mantle, signifying it could not be expressed, would I paint my exceedingly great happiness for you; only the mantle should be of golden texture, and of dazzling loveliness.

My husband grew stronger and nobler even than of old, and as soon he could he fulfilled his intention of going down as a private. How few who read these lines will need to be told what days of agonizing suspense and racking terror followed his departure.

Days came and went, and those who loved me kept up the courage that would sometimes fail, by assuring me the days could not be long before the war would be over, and so they have gone on telling me. But the day came when my personal terror and dread were to have their end.

One day I read my husband's name in the paper, a few more and I was with him.

"My fighting days are over, " he said, mournfully, "I shall never be fit for service again. It is too soon; I did hope you would have had a soldier's sword to show to our children, but a sergeant's uniform and a musket are all there is to cover the stain of rebellion."

"It is all wiped out," I said; "there is no stain left. And now I have back your honor, and I have you, my darling, never to lose you again, to be hands for you evermore, my darling Carl. Hush! not a word, I am your tyrant henceforth, and oh! what a tyrant I shall be!"

A few days ago he called me to him. "In your duty to the country, do not forget your duty to society, Georgie pet. Read this," he said.

And I read, under the head of "Marriages," in the *Herald :*

"*Stuart—Vane.*—On Thursday, at the residence of L. C. Carter, Esq., Gilbert Stuart, Captain —— Mass. Vols., to Miss Gertrude Vane, eldest daughter of G. W. Vane, Brig.-Gen. C. S. A. Richmond papers please copy."

"It's *Stuart* and *Vane*, notwithstanding," my husband said.

"Yes," I answered, "but he has taken a different manner of vanity."

"Well," added my husband, "I am glad friend

Stuart is *At Anchor* at last. There is anchorage for all of us if we are only patient and faithfully follow the light that is within us. Which sentiment, by the way, being very true, suggestive, and exceedingly well expressed, will do for the moral of your book."

"I wouldn't end up with a moral," I replied, "for any thing in this world. If you and I haven't lived long enough to prove a warning or an assistance we had better give up."

"I haven't an idea of such a thing as giving up," said Carl, "we are only just beginning to live. I feel that you and I have not battled so long for nothing, but that through all we have been preserved and strengthened for some thoroughly good work even in this world. There is nothing we cannot do if we work together. I have seen, at the seashore, boats rocking idly on the waves, day after day, when suddenly I would see them, sails spread, flags flying, and all hands busy, dashing bravely off to sea. Perhaps they had been hauled up for repairs, as we are; at any rate, they sailed none the less swiftly, and were none the less strong and secure for having lain *At Anchor*, at the Master's will. There's a moral in spite of you, Georgie."

THE END.